Rising Tide

By Hyden Wood

Prologue

One of the librarian's twelve assistants sat, solitary, opposite him.

"You understand what is required of you?"

"I do."

"You understand that you do this alone, that you cannot return here?"

"I understand".

"Your colleagues will try to stop you, when they find out."

"I would expect no less."

"And you do this freely?

"I do."

"Good. They must be given a choice."

Rising Tide

one

Elisabeth sat sprawled on the concrete grid of pavement, oblivious to the mechanised routine of the city around her, staring forward at the unyielding wall of glass. Her reflection flat, tears running down the familiar creases of her cheeks before falling, salt-less to the street below. Further, through the window, a screen of flickering plasma light, a triumph of colour, of blues and almost-blues, off-whites and red. An image of a polar bear sitting also; its personal island of ice permitted no more.

It was an old film, one she had seen many times before. The last of its kind, floating towards the mythical. She knew what came next; knew the heartbreak and the horror, the meta-dislocation as the world she knew emerged.

In the city-state, trams continued to score their routes through the streets behind her as Elisabeth sobbed, overcome. Alive in the pictures the bear had not yet died, but she would, and ahead of her time. Her landscape of glacier and snowbound plain was no more, had been stolen from beneath, rinsed from above, ebbed away.

She stood, wrapping her course-knit shawl around against the London winter, and walked to the bridge.

In the middle stood a man in a wax jacket, his collar turned up against the chill. He looked down past the balustrades to the running waters of the Thames below, as the shafts of a weak February sun reflected off the glassy surface like paper cuts, slicing their way towards the cathedrals of finance proudly parading on the northern bank. He seemed lost in thought, watching the small eddies appear and disappear as the water-born buccaneers fought their own game of survival.

For her, something familiar; something knownabout the gait, the rueful yet solid stare; something remembered, of the hands grasping the iron railings as if they held an answer; something experienced, in another time.

She didn't hesitate; continuing to approach the man she knew was Daniel, rubbing her eyes dry in the wool as she climbed the slope. He continued to stare, transfixed with the river, lost in thought.

"A long time".

He turned, distracted, his concentration broken by something in the voice that gently knocked.

For a moment he saw only the bedraggled hair, the ramshackle hemp bag and fraying woollen wrap; but then he looked at the face, and the tired, glistening eyes, and saw Elisabeth; older, sadder certainly, but her.

"Beth" he began, startled.

"You look well, Daniel."

 "Is something wrong?"

"There's always something; didn't you used to say that? Or was it someone else?" she mused.

"Your tears?" he asked, uncomfortably.

"I was watching the screens, Dan. The old pictures from the far north."

"Ah. Yes". He paused, his full attention now with the woman in front of him, the girl of a decade past. "I know what you mean."

"You do?" Elisabeth asked questioningly, but her eyes began to betray the glimpses of a wry smile. "Maybe you do. Maybe you still have it in you", she said, reaching for his arm and holding it in hers.

Daniel shrugged off the implied reproach; he knew where it came from, knew it wasn't true. He took her hand in his, remembering how her skin felt to the touch, remembering more. "Beth. How long has it been?"

"Some time Daniel. Some little time I think"

He grinned at this. "I think over ten years. I thought I'd see you at the reunion"

"I meant to come."

"I'm sure you did."

She left it unanswered, looking away east to the estuary, watching the gulls diving and skirting the banks, their heads wrapped in the grey-flecked winter hoods that would turn white again as the warmer times returned.

"I hoped I'd be seeing you soon. Next month".

Daniel knew what she meant. He had thought the same when the invitation arrived. Surprised to receive it; wondering if Elisabeth had too, whether they would all meet again and remember their past lives in the cloistered stone passages and islets of close-cropped green.

"I hoped so too."

He'd often wondered if he could have found her, but Elisabeth had always been so uncomfortable with the net, with the personal becoming public. He wasn't sure if Isabella had kept in touch, she had never mentioned doing so; but he suspected the women would know how to find each other. He hoped he could too, if he had tried; somehow he never had. Not since they had left the University behind them, and started out in the world.

"I'm sure. And your wife?"

"Yes. She'll be excited about meeting you, finally"

"Really, Daniel? I'm surprised you've mentioned me"

"Beth, of course I have."

She considered him quizzically, surprised by the answer, and then looked away as the birds started to circle higher and higher, leaving this stretch of river for some new hunting ground. They stood together, silently watching.

She squeezed his hand. "It really is good to see you. Different to how I thought it might be. Better I think".

Daniel laughed, softly, and Elisabeth joined in. "I'm glad."

"Yes. So am I"

"Are you sure you're okay?"

"I'll be fine. The old films get to me."

"And you can't avoid the screens" Daniel said, remembering Elisabeth's old slogan.

"Now as then Dan; at least in the cities."

In those days, when the ideas were new and exciting, when exploring the nuances of position and counter-position helped them explore themselves, when no view was firm and nothing really mattered because nothing was really final, Daniel would argue with Beth for hours whilst Isabella would try to find some middle ground, trying in vain to break down their incommensurable views. The three of them would lie in the meadows and joust with arguments until the sun sank deep beneath the willow boughs and the jug ran dry; and they'd wander back up the river dykes talking as though it were song and they the different parts of the chorus, their conflicting melodies somehow merging to rival the stolen songs of the starlings' roost.

The arguments seemed to matter more, when they mattered least.

Elisabeth let her gaze drift across the eastward bridges, each spanning the river in its own unique collage of rivets and stone, clean lines and flourishes; one after another like a gallery of sculptures on a massive scale, proudly displayed between the banks until they too eased out of sight around the curving path of the city river.

"What were you looking at before?"

"Nothing really. The river. The movement of the water. The dam's open today."

Elisabeth sighed inwardly, although Daniel could not have noticed; there was nothing to see.

"Are you going to the ceremony?" Daniel nodded, as Elisabeth continued, "I saw the announcements on the screens as well; they were re-running all the old construction footage. I think I saw some film of you; a child in a red plastic hat by your father's side, beaming away at the cameras".

"Probably" replied Daniel, "I remember visiting a few times."

"You looked innocent."

"Thank you, I think." She had said the same words before; but the meanings had changed, as had they. "I should be getting up there. It starts in a couple of hours."

"In time for the speeches?" Elisabeth mocked with friendly scorn.

"Yes. Politicians trying to take credit for the vision of the previous generation"

"Credit?"

"Well it saved this city, that's for certain. We are closed more often than open these days" Daniel replied, before picking up his case and straightening up. "I need to get the rail from Blackfriars. Are you walking that way?"

Elisabeth looked as though she were considering it, if only to extend this happenchance meeting a little longer; but she shook her head. "I think I'm going to get the river-boat."

"It really is great to see you Beth"

"Yes. And you"

Daniel paused, as if struggling with how to say goodbye; then he put both arms around her shoulders. He hugged her briefly, but long enough to take in her scent and all the memories it triggered.

"And I'll see you at Bella's?"

"I hope so". She smiled, looking up into his familiar eyes for one last moment before walking back over the bridge the way she had come; back out of Daniel's life as abruptly as she had arrived.

Daniel watched her go; she didn't look back. Then he too left the bridge, up to the north bank and the station suspended fifty metres above, steel ropes hanging from four great masonry pillars, holding the ovoid metallic frame and its clear windowed skin in place as the air-rail pierced the cocoon-like platform structure before emerging again at the other end, an unbroken line stretching across the city on wrought-iron stilts, only punctuated by the great stations, each a work of conceptual and experimental architecture in its own right; and at the hub, the central terminus at Victoria, the most audacious of them all.

He stepped into the lift from the embankment, rushed swiftly and noiselessly into the air before the doors opened and he stepped out inside the hanging station, amongst the usual diasporic crowds of the city. It was busier than normal for a weekend morning, Daniel noticed, people heading out to the Dam as he was, going to see the anniversary celebrations with their children or parents or friends. Explaining to the young why the barrier was important; reminiscing with the elders as to why it had to be built in the first place; giving thanks. The recorded announcements were smoothly spoken, carefully calibrated so as not to antagonise; the train would be arriving in three minutes, ready to whisk them east of the city. Past the diminutive St Paul's to the station at Bank in the valley of glass betwixt the offices of the Corporation, and then down across the river again, past the old Olympic stadium and the manicured parkland, relic of a bygone time, back north of the river and east up to Southend, accelerating to full speed as the electromagnetic train raced up the Estuary to the edge of the Dam. He had made this journey countless times, the weekday routine repeated over and over; once inspiring sights increasingly lost to the unmemorable screenshots of the day's news; but today was different.

The train arrived promptly, effortlessly gliding into the translucent shade of the suspended station and gliding to a halt. Daniel stepped aboard a half-filled carriage and chose a seat by the window, the seat beside him taken by another man whose wife and daughter sat opposite, the child's excitement clear to see. As they pulled away, out onto the elevated line and towards the next stop, the father pointed out the buildings of the various companies and guilds, their architects seemingly caught up in an endless game of one-upmanship in bending and breaking the laws of gravity and possibility. Daniel part-listened for a while, unfocussed, as he thought about the chance meeting on the bridge, of the girl from his University years and what she had meant to him. There had been moments - when she smiled, when she laughed - that he saw that girl in the meadow; but the familiarity was tempered by the unseen and imperceptible changes of the years apart. Ever since receiving the unexpected invitation, Daniel had held a thought that he may meet Elisabeth again; but to do so by chance, and alone, had set him off balance.

The doors opened again; they had reached the next station without him really noticing. The carriage filled up now, standing room as well - unusual on the monorail but not unheard of for special events. They would be running extra services all day and all evening to transport visitors to and from the various events, fast trains that only stopped at the major city stops before passing through the eastern stations at speed. He looked around the carriage, observing the newcomers who had boarded at the last station. Another family, two children this time, one with a miniature London flag held tightly in excited hands, the other crying over a toy left on the platform behind the closing doors and probably lost for good; a group of students, apparent from the experimental colours in their hair and the uniformly distressed clothes, the latest failed attempt at originality amongst the young; an older couple, shuffling their way into seats given up by some women half their age; and a tall dark-skinned man, leaning on a cane, who seemed to be staring directly at him.

Daniel looked away, out through the window as the train picked up speed and started tilting as they approached the river; he looked back at the bridge as they crossed the water, half-expecting Elisabeth to be standing there still, but seeing only a crowd of walkers on the far bank. He tried to put her out of his mind; plenty of time to think about that later; now he needed to focus. Val Banerjee, his superior, would be looking after the Mayor; but Daniel would be expected to be on hand to talk to the various guests about his department, and no doubt answer questions about where all the money went.

The journey took less than a quarter hour, but in that time they had passed from the inner urbanity and its stalagmatic profile to the outer residential rings and finally the creeks and lagoons, the saltmarshes and flood ponds that existed for the times when the dam had to remain closed and the river water needed somewhere to drain so as not to back-up into the city. This was Daniel's world, more than the city would ever be.

As the carriage informed its passengers about their imminent arrival, Daniel readied himself to leave. Stepping out, he noticed an unusually large number of police lining the platform; although given the amount of luminaries and dignitaries who would be at the ceremony he realised he ought not be too surprised, particularly given recent events.

"Daniel!"

He heard his name being called. Across the concourse a young woman was waving her hand above the crowd, who were all moving towards the escalators that rose up the inside of the barrier like a concertina of cocktail sticks against the great concrete and steel walls, leading to the open expanse of the topside tarmacked surface which towered above the land inside and the North Sea without. The wall, whose base was only a few hundred meters away, loomed over the station; a perfectly manufactured concave cliff-face, its curvature hardly perceptible head-on, but clearly evident as it arched across to the far bank, twenty kilometres to the south.

"Hi Rachel", Daniel greeted his colleague, smiling. "There are more people than I thought".

"Of course people have come, it's exciting!"

"Yes. The bands and the fireworks, no doubt", Daniel replied with false solemnity.

"And you want them to come instead and admire the brickwork? To listen to a bunch of speeches?" she said laughing.

"I would, if anyone would say anything worth listening to."

"Come on Dan, don't be a cynic today," she replied warmly. "Aren't Saskia and Lexi with you?"

"No, they're coming up later" Daniel replied, before adding, "for the music and fireworks". He couldn't help but grin.

"That's better! You looked faraway when I first saw you"

"I was - I ran into an old friend back in the city"

"Oh really?" Rachel taunted, eyebrows raised.

"Nothing like that. It just took me back. Let's get up to the office; the suits will be with us soon"

"Come on then" she agreed, taking Daniel's arm in hers, "service elevators I think, it'll take ages going up the pretty way".

The lifts brought them out inside the administration offices, perched under the lips of the inner wall, with strengthened translucent windows cut into the uppermost reaches of the inner face. Although most Londoners had taken to calling it the Dam, it wasn't really an accurate name for the immense structure. Strictly speaking it was a barrier, designed to keep the sea water out when necessary, rather than to keep the freshwater in. The wall stretched from the hills above Southend on the north side of the Thames Estuary, through Sheerness and across the old Isle of Sheppey, and eventually to what was once Sittingbourne on the far banks; an arc stretching twenty five kilometres in all, and at points over one hundred metres tall. It was punctuated by eleven colossal floodgates that allowed low-riding sea traffic to enter and exit when open, but were closed for the flood tides and the storm surges when depressions in the North Sea funnelled water down the coast and towards London. The huge metal gates were driven by banks of mechanical engines buried deep inside the barrage structure itself, upscaled copies of their forerunners on the old Thames Barrier further inland, which looked more like a scale-model in a children's science class by comparison.

The office high within the Dam structure gave them a view back inland to the city and from this height the urban sprawl cascaded from the centre like a pile of sand. They could see the refineries to the south, and the greenhouses and chemical factories, and the patches of agribusinessland like biotic islands in an artefactual sea. Closer by was the river delta, its complex passages of inlets and culverts and creeks that gave them a biological defence against both river and sea to complement the brutalist primary construction; an artificial intertidal zone that Daniel and his colleagues attempted to craft, and monitored constantly. They both had the distinct impression that the construction engineers saw estuary management as somewhat untidy, an inexact science that blighted the majesty of their unrivalled masterpiece.

"I expect they won't spend very long with us" Daniel mused.

"You mean you hope they won't"

"Both, I think"

People were beginning to assemble on the top of the dam; the four lane highway that crossed the estuary on its walls having been closed for this one day, creating a giant promenade for the thousands who had come to celebrate. The main stage had been positioned on the road above the administration offices, facing the empty traffic lanes running south where the crowds were beginning to gather, some of whom had made the long walk up from the south bank and the station at Sheerness, enjoying a winter hike along what would normally be a busy highway.

As they waited they watched the small flotilla of river boats and water taxis that was beginning to assemble in the lee of the dam gates, in a prime position to view the celebrations from below. Saskia would be amongst them somewhere, bringing Lexi to see everything from the relative comfort of their river launch, and Daniel was looking forward to joining them after the official reception had finished.

On a different vessel, they were working to another schedule. Their craft had meandered downriver amidst the pleasure cruisers, private launches and chartered ferries. A darkened barge, one boat amongst many, whose deceptively-sluggish lines disguised a much faster machine beneath. Behind the blackened portholes and below deck, they were preparing for the task that lay ahead of them, confident in the moral-certainty of their intended action. The time for justification lay ahead of them; what mattered now was flawless execution.

Six figures dressed head to toe in subtle drab-cam; clothes that relied not on outright camouflage patterning, but instead looked relatively mainstream whilst still allowing the wearer to blend into an urban- industrial background. Six skin-coloured masks to subtly alter their features, disguising them from the ever-present cameras and the ubiquitous facial-measurement software. Six packs, each containing different elements of the package; none proscribed individually, but powerful when combined. Six heartbeats, quickening now with the anticipation of action; six minds, keeping them in check. Six is all it would take.

In the event, the party of politicians and their attendant tag-alongs did not have time to visit the office of Estuary Management. Val Banerjee's assistant had at least come by to let them know.

"Apparently there was some kind of security issue. They were all meant to ride the escalators up the wall, walk a little along the highway, and then come into the offices"

"So they could wave at their loving people?" asked Daniel sarcastically

"You arecynical today, Dan", Rachel said, returning his smile. She turned back to the assistant, asking, "What happened?"

"Some kind of demonstration near the basin-floor escalators. The Civil Guard had to make some arrests, but it took a while to sort out. The whole party had to use the lifts in the end, but security insisted on checking them as well so there wasn't enough time left to visit all the departments before the speeches" continued the assistant, before curtly walking out again.

"And before you say it, they probably did still go and see the gate engineers."

Daniel nodded. He enjoyed working with Rachel; her unswerving optimism was refreshing, all the more so because it wasn't grounded in naivety. She knew how their world worked, but had clearly decided to rise above it, at least as much as possible. "Come on, let's go and hear what he's got to say"

"Screens or highway?" she asked.

"Let's go topside. I prefer the real thing"

They put their coats back on to fend off the chill air of the sea breeze in winter, before walking along the internal corridors to the staircase. They came out onto the causeway through the main upper exit, emerging at the bottom of an arch that spanned the carriageway and housed more of the administration offices, these with views both inland and out to sea. The temporary stage had been erected facing away from this bridge-building, creating a separate area between them, off-limits to the public. It was filled with the retinue of the various speakers and their assorted security personnel; Daniel and Rachel had to show their passes a number of times to both uniformed municipal police and their Civil Guard counterparts. They walked around to the front of the stage, mingling with the diverse groups of Londoners who had made the trip out east, waiting for the ceremonies and celebrations to begin. The vast projection-speakers were, for now, repeating a series of safety announcements in the normal engineered-calm tones familiar to all who were listening. They made their way through this growing crowd towards the inward railings and looked back inland.

"This view never loses its magic for me" Rachel admitted enthusiastically. "I loved it the first time I came up here as a girl with my parents. I still love it."

It was a feeling Daniel shared. "I think it gets better as the years go by. It seems increasingly organic". Rachel smiled at the compliment

– that was what they had been trying to achieve within the Estuary Department ever since the Barrier had first been built.

"Less like a slab of rock blocking the river-mouth, you mean?" she joked.

"There's always the rock."

They were both intensely proud of the biological system that had been nurtured inside the walls of the dam. It was designed primarily to aid flood control and act as a pollution sink, but it had also become a refuge for natural life (or kind-of natural life) within an unavoidably urban environment. They could see the various streams and gullies they had planned and built, encouraged, cajoled even, spreading out like a complex venous system from the mouth of the estuary. What Daniel could not see, from this distance, was the darkened vessel carrying Elisabeth purposefully towards the barrage; her course determined many months before, planned and routed as precisely as Daniel had crafted the very tributaries that now carried her inexorably forwards.

Batista pulled hard on the tiller, swinging the barge gently in to the crowded wharf at the base of the barrier wall. Kanton's diversionary tactics seemed to have worked - there didn't seem to be many security people bankside. She watched the six gather their equipment before setting off, individually, in the direction of the wall-escalators. Separately, they each merged into the crowds heading for the concourse above. None were troubled by the detector-arches; each of their packs innocent enough, on its own.

The old-Portuguese sat on the wooden roof of the wheelhouse, drawing strength from her ancient solidity, watching them disappear, anonymous amongst the many. She opened a small, round, battered tin and twisted the top to reveal the tobacco nestling inside. She took a pinch, rolling it between forefinger and thumb before tucking it between her gums and upper lips. It would be her turn soon. Her task, as vital as the rest.

Her companion sat perched at the other end of the barge, a dishevelled grey-black spaniel alert on the bowsprit, ears cocked and nose raised to the scents of the mooring.

"Vasco" she called to the dog. "Vamos".

"Ladies and Gentleman" announced the banks of speakers, "Welcome to the Churchill Barrage!"

"Come on Dan, let's get closer." Rachel said whilst taking him by the elbow and moving forward through the now attentive audience.

The screens hanging above the stage sprung to life showing the same footage of the dam's construction that had been running all week across the city. It was being simultaneously cast on temporary screens along the entire length of the dam wall, as well as being projected onto the inner face itself, the mammoth pictures visible for kilometres around. The images came with commentary on how the barrage was conceived, designed and delivered, in the same synthetically assuring tones; no mention was made of why, beyond necessity. The documentary continued with a short history of the barrier's operation since its creation, the footage of the danger-tides and storm-swells being repelled by the steadfast walls leading to gasps and cheers along the length of its currently unthreatened defences. Finally, the screens settled on a picture of the dam filmed from above the sea; sitting proudly across the mouth of the estuary like the crossed arms of an ancient titan warrior.

The Mayor walked into the centre of the stage, and his picture was instantaneously transmitted to all of the public screens, both around the barrier and back in the city.

"Today is the thirtieth anniversary of the completion of the most important piece of civil engineering ever imagined", he began, his delivery immediately gripping the attention of the diverse audience. He was known for his passionate rhetoric, and today would be no different. He spoke slowly, pausing often, stressing each sentence to wring out every last drop of meaning and emotion.

"Today is a day we thank the ingenuity of the scientists and engineers who made it possible. We thank them now, as we thank them every time the tide rises and the wind blows. Every time the waters swell to threaten our beloved city, the Dam says no! We say,

No! This is London, and we will overcome! London is a survivor, as we are survivors.

Today is a day we should remember. Remember what would have happened had the barrier's creators not had the foresight, nor the skills, the expertise, the technical ability necessary to create this phenomenon. The wonder of our world. To build here, what was not built elsewhere.

We should remember the fate of the sea-cities. The great metropoli on distant shores abandoned. The late legendary Manhattan, once the greatest of all. Closer to home on our own shores. The list known to all, yet the cities forgotten.

Today I, like you, pay tribute to our defenders. They named this barrage for another great protector of this City. They, like Churchill, overcame the challenges. They made the impossible, possible. They gave breath back to a threatened dream. A dream of freedom. Of democracy.
Of a good life. The dream is London. I am a Londoner. We, are Londoners. We, together, say our thanks!"

Along the length of the dam the crowd erupted into a guttural roar of applause, a roar that echoed throughout the halls and corridors of the City itself. The Mayor had raised one arm to the sky, fist clenched and waving towards the sea as if to challenge Neptune's best. The screens focused in on his steely expression, his profile reminiscent of that on a roman sestertius as he stared defiantly at the distant waves, before turning slowly back to the still hollering crowd. He let them continue, nodding his head in agreement with the deafening cheers of the multitude.

As the applause began to subside and they could hear themselves again, Rachel leaned across to Daniel, saying, "You might not like his politics, but he can really work an audience".

Daniel didn't hear her. His attention was elsewhere. Standing near the back of the stage, a few metres from the Mayor, was a tall man staring straight back at Daniel. Their eyes had been locked together since half-way through the Mayor's speech. It was the same dark-skinned man who had ridden the transport from the Embankment earlier that day, the man with the cane.

"Dan, where have you gone?"

She squeezed his arm gently, and he blinked, looking away from his unknown watcher and back at her.

"Rachel, do you know who that is? Back-right of the stage, guy with the stick?"

"Where?"

When Daniel looked back the man had disappeared, probably into the wings of the temporary stand and out of sight. "He's gone." He shook his head, continuing, "It was odd. Everyone was watching

Haldane's speech apart from this one man, who I swear was staring at me through the whole thing."

"He was probably security, and was wondering why you weren't avidly watching our dear leader!"

"Didn't really look like security"

"Do they have a look? Aren't they just the ones who watch the crowd to try and spot troublemakers?" she teased.

Daniel didn't mind the joke, but still felt that something unusual had happened. The mysterious figure had not been looking in his general direction, Daniel felt. He was looking at *him,* directly; and not with the look of a concerned agent. It was something else entirely; but before he had time to think any more on it, a scream punctured the mellowing hubbub of the crowds, followed by another, and within seconds the crowd was tumultuous again, roaring with the shouts of people now frightened rather than excited.

"What the ..." Rachel started.

"Look - look at the smoke!"

She followed Daniel's eyes to the other side of the carriageway, a little further from the stage. Black smoke, like an improbable miniature thundercloud, was rising over the barrier wall at an increasing rate and pouring over the wall-top crowd; flowing like a half-speed river, slow but determined and rent with menace.

"Where is that coming from?" Rachel asked, confused as to the source, confused as to the seriousness of the situation.

Daniel was worried. The smoke might be a sign of a more serious problem with the dam - there was a small chance of something wrong with the structure itself that would put them in danger - but surely they would have heard an explosion? A noise of some form above the earlier cheers if something really serious had happened? No, Daniel realised that the more immediate danger was the smoke itself – if this crowd of thousands started to panic, packed tightly onto a four lane highway strung high above the water and land below.

"Shit; Dan that must be coming from the office"

In the absolute sooty black of their velvet cloud they worked by touch and feel. Radio silence; just the sound of their own compact breathing apparatus exaggerating each heave for air. A line tied to the barriers, knotted for distance. An elaborate dance, practised and practised, over and over; no mistakes. Each hand that of an artist, pointing and firing the paint-soaked accusation. No lines crossing, three steps for one and left-hand spray; two steps another and finish the arc; six strands of colour merging like a jigsaw into one.

"Rachel, we need to get to the fire escape, now"

Rachel was shaking, holding her head in her hands, grasping her hair as she kept looking wide-eyed into the approaching smoke cloud. Her voice, smaller now, "oh shit Danny. No. no…."

Daniel grasped both her raised arms, gently but firmly. "Rachel, we need to move, now. Wherever the smoke is coming from, we need to help people get down from here. We need to make sure they don't panic, Rachel. Okay?"

She blurred momentarily and then seemed to come-to. "Yes. Yes you're right." She nodded. "Where?"

Daniel felt strangely alert, and surprisingly calm; he could see the possibilities branching ahead of him and knew what needed to be done. "The fastest exits are behind the stage, past the arch on the inner walls. If we try to move people back to the other exits, back past the smoke, they'll get jammed by everyone coming this way".

Rachel followed his eyes towards the emergency barriers on the inner wall, and the drop beyond, and saw his full meaning in all its horrific detail. "Come on".

They managed to squeeze their way through the stunned throng, getting to the front corner of the stage complex before most people had realised what was going on and had started moving forwards as well.

They found their way blocked by a wall of Civil Guards, projectile rifles locked in their arms, each exuding the deadpan glaze of authority, and the confidence of orders given and understood.

Daniel approached the Sergeant, who was talking into his wrist-terminal.

"We need to let everyone through here, and the other side. The exits are behind the stage, past the arch, understand?"

"I'm sorry sir but this is a secure area. We are assessing the emergency routes as we speak"

"Can you see the smoke? We need to let people through, here, now, otherwise they are going to get crushed", Daniel explained quickly.

"Sir, we are dealing with the situation"

"Look, I'm Barrier Authority" Daniel insisted, holding up his security pass as Rachel did the same, "and I know where the exits are. Trust me, we need to let the people through here, and right away"

The sergeant looked to his wrist-terminal again, getting a message through his earpiece from the controller whose face had been replaced by a map of the dam-top on the view screen of the device sleekly attached to his arm.

"Listen, you two come through, but we are evacuating the public through routes south 4-5 and south 4-7" replied the sergeant, holding up his wrist for Daniel to see.

"That's not going to work," replied Daniel, shaking his head. "People will try and push forwards to try and get past the stage and onto the road behind. If we try and send people back we will create panic, don't you see?"

"We protect the security of the Administration sir, and right now that is at risk"

"This is madness" Daniel began, but was interrupted by the giant speakers coming back to life with the dulcet soothing tones of the announcer, the voice at odds with the message.

"This is an emergency. Please walk calmly to the nearest available fire exits. Do not use the lifts."
Then the localised message, "Your nearest exit is to the south, away from the stage. Do not push. Stay calm, stay safe. Your nearest exit is to the south, away from the stage. Stay calm ...."

Each set of speakers would be relaying specific instructions to the area defined by its own sound-field, moving the tens of thousands of people in elaborate patterns to each of the many fire escapes within and upon the walls, hundreds of separate snakes coming down from the immense structure. But near the stage, the smoke was getting worse, spreading with it the panic that Daniel had foreseen so clearly.

The cloud spreading across the dam towards the other side; the six-roped ballet following, step by step. Arms arcing through the utter darkness, joints locked and distance perfect, the message building with each and every stroke. Guilty colours pregnant behind the choking curtain, bright with righteous indignation, patiently waiting to be unveiled.

Daniel stood behind the cordon of guards, looking past them to the security fences under strain from the growing crush of worried faces. He realised the guards would stick to their orders, to their training, whatever happened. He needed to get the orders changed, and fast. The stage was still crowded with the official party of politicians who themselves were beginning to move back to the stairs in each rear corner and out to the empty escape routes beyond. Daniel saw what he needed, and shouted,

"Mr Mayor. Lord Mayor Haldane! I need your help sir, now! Daniel Mason of the Authority sir, and I need your help, now!"

Haldane heard him, heard the surname that had called him, and saw the eyes of the man speaking. He moved quickly over to the side of the stage, his aides and security men following with the same controlled speed.

"Yes?"

"Mayor Haldane, thank you. Security are trying to get people to evacuate through the exits south of here, but that's south of the smoke as well, look" he said, pointing to the smoke which had now spread across the entire width of the dam, and just a couple of hundred metres from the stage front. "People will not move towards fire, so if we try and send them that way they will get stopped by the rest coming this way. You do not want a mass of panicking people up here, trust me. If they get squeezed, well, look at the fall."

Haldane had listened intently, and nodded now to show he understood. He was proud of his ability to remain level-headed in a crisis, to listen to reports and then act on them decisively; skills born of less altruistic campaigns during the troubled years before. Haldane moved to the front of the stage, and summoned the sergeant to join him. Within a few moments a captain had appeared as well, and Daniel was being helped up onto the stage by some of the guardsmen. He turned back and pulled Rachel up after him; he was not going to leave her, not in this situation.

The sergeant had flicked his wrist panel to project a three-dimensional plan of their section of the dam in front of the group, complete with the stage, the offices that arched across the highway and those within the walls, and all the escape routes highlighted in red.

"These exits sir, we must let these people through the secured area and down through here" Daniel insisted, pointing out the route in the holographic image.

"I agree" concurred Haldane. "You're absolutely right. Captain, make this happen. We will stay here to make sure people can get out. Sergeant I want your team at the top of the stairs, make sure it is orderly and safe. Captain, do we have any people on the Authority doors?"

"Affirmative sir"

"Make sure the complex is secure"

"Sir", began Haldane's head of security, "We have to move you sir"

Haldane shook his head, and looked back to the captain. "Do we know the source of the smoke yet?"

"No sir. The lower Authority offices under the carriageway extend that far south but none of the alarms have been activated; we have teams checking each of the rooms manually in case. There is nothing at the base of the dam so that rules out ships. There are no engines for gates in this part of the dam, at least according to the plans."

Haldane and the captain both looked to Daniel, who nodded, "Correct, no engines, and I didn't hear any impact".

"Sound-fields from the speaker system could have masked something" replied the captain, which was true.

"Okay" continued the Mayor, "we stay and help the evacuation until such time as the situation changes, agreed." It was not a question, and both his personal guards and the captain knew as much.

The Mayor switched on the microphone transmitter in his lapel, selected the local speaker network only, and began addressing the crowds nearest the stage. "This is the Mayor. This is an emergency. This is a change to the evacuation instruction. I repeat: this is a change to the evacuation instruction."

Meanwhile, the sergeant had dispatched some of his men to the stairs beyond the archway, whilst the rest were hurriedly trying to clear a narrow path through the barriers on each side of the stage, two rat-runs through the lighting and sound equipment and through to the empty carriageway beyond.

"Please proceed North, through the passages to either side of the stage. Please proceed north, through the passages to either side of the stage". The Mayor's voice may not have been as scientifically modified as the artificial announcements, but given its familiarity and studied appeal to trustworthiness, it seemed to be having the same effect.

People were surging through the passageways, through and past the stage complex and down the wall-stairs beyond; the young helping the less mobile, a flustered teacher marshalling a scared-looking class of children, the sergeant's patrol helping and hurrying as hundreds moved out and down towards safety.

Haldane continued to direct the crowd, his instructions plain, simple, and unwavering; "leaders must offer certainty in a world gone to shit", as his own captain used to say in basic training. Daniel was monitoring the holographic real-time images with the sergeant, watching as the hundreds of people trapped between the wall of smoke and the stage began to bottleneck. They could both see what was going wrong.

"They aren't getting through quickly enough", Daniel said aloud. The smoke continued to move across and along the highway on the dam wall, and the people were trapped by the stage, the paths hastily cleared either side not wide enough to let them through fast enough. They were trapped like water in a blocked sink that continued to fill faster than it could drain, and if they couldn't fix it there would be a catastrophic overflow.

"Options captain?" Haldane demanded.

"We haven't got time for an airlift, and we can't make the paths any wider sir" he replied.

"Over the stage then", Daniel suggested forcefully, "it's the only option"

"Captain, he's right" added the sergeant. "We use the men to help people up, then they exit by the steps at the back. It certainly won't makes things any worse"

The captain looked to the Mayor, who nodded. "Make it happen Sergeant, everyone who can be spared to the front of the stage"

They began lifting in twos, each pair taking the arm each of someone trapped below and helping them up the three metres to the top of the stage platform. All of the sergeant's men, the captain, Rachel, some of the Mayor's aides, and in the middle Daniel and Haldane working together, hauling grateful bodies one after another up onto the platform as the smoke continued its incessant slow-march advance towards them. They were beginning to feel the effects of the acrid fumes now, eyes watering and coughing, shirt sleeves and scarves becoming makeshift breathing-filters for all.

Faces full of primordial fear looked up to them as again and again they pulled people aloft, salvation to the few whilst beseeched by the many. All along the stage front, two by two they hauled women and men and children to their safety, away from the suffocating embrace of the black wave beyond.

"My daughter, please my daughter!" exclaimed a soot covered woman as Daniel and Haldane lifted her up. They saw her below, being crushed into the stage-wall by the weight of the panicking crowd behind.

"The girl" shouted Daniel to the people below, pushing away people's hands who were trying to get themselves to safety. "The girl comes first".

Two men managed to raise her through the crush to the waiting arms above. As they pulled her up, Daniel and the Mayor caught each other's eyes, each understanding the other.

"Who's next?"

The last knot on the rope and the end of each line. Canisters returned to their pouches; no need for a trail. Six figures lined up along the edge of the great dam wall, still hidden. Six cloaks no longer masquerading, unfolded now to reveal semi-rigid wing-skin gliding packs. Six leaps of faith, towards the sanctuary amongst the lower marshes, where Batista waited patiently in the misty gloom.

Against their darkest expectations, it worked. The last people managed to get around or over the stage before the black clouds reached them; but the smoke itself showed no signs of abating, let alone retreating.

They left the stage area last, Haldane and the captain, Rachel and Daniel. They were rushed along the road behind the stage, under the arch-bridge of the upper Administration offices towards the emergency exit stairs beyond. The sergeant approached them, talking into his wrist-device as he crossed the carriageway.

"Lord Mayor, you are being air-lifted back to the City, and directly to the Cone. The lifter will be here in under a minute, sir", said the sergeant. He then turned to Daniel and Rachel, continuing, "Madam, Sir, if you will accompany me, we will proceed via the stairs".

Haldane turned to Daniel, reaching out to shake his hand. "Mason, you made a difference today. Thank you. I will not forget", and the glint in his eye showed he meant it.

"Thank you, Lord Mayor. We all did." replied Daniel, nodding to them both before setting off with Rachel to follow the sergeant to the stairs and off the Dam.

"This way sir; nearly there."

They reached the top of the stairs just as the lifter zoomed up and over the dam wall, before slowing improbably quickly and hovering above the road, descending close enough so that an extended gangplank allowed people to board quickly. They saw the Mayor get in with a small knot of military personnel, and the door slid closed. As the lifter rose away from the Dam surface, Daniel caught sight of a solitary figure behind where the lifter had come in, on the other side of the carriageway near another flight of stairs. It looked like a man, a man with a cane, and he was looking directly at Daniel.

"Please sir, we must leave, now!" exclaimed the sergeant, pulling Daniel to the stairwell and away.

two

The room was almost puritanical in its lack of colour; stark ivory walls rising from the polished marble floor. A bone china vase sat, solitary, on the ornately carved wooden table, its own grain buried deep beneath layer upon layer of matt white lacquer.

Isabella had always liked this room; its bright austerity lit from outside through the tall bay windows. She had cut the flowers that afternoon in the garden before coming inside; three tulips of different hues. She selected each carefully, lopping their stalks precisely with her antique clasp knife, ensuring no lasting damage to the plants that sacrificed such delicate beauty. Now the three magnificent blooms seemed to radiate colour, parching the room's optical drought with their dissonant array: one an indeterminate and changeable blend of oranges and yellows, floating above the vase; another deep, dark and uncompromising red; the third an incongruous ultramarine, fiercely individual. Three stalks the same lush green, disappearing down into the bulbous-bottomed vessel and its unseen sustenance.

A knock at the door disturbed Isabella's thoughts.

"Madam. There is a gentleman downstairs who desires to see you. He gave me this".

"Thank you", she replied, taking the small card in her hand and turning it over, slowly.

One side blankly black; the other white, and stamped with the words "ASSISTANT TO THE LIBRARIAN" in small type print. Her pulse quickened involuntarily as she read the words, but she showed no other visible reaction.

"Please can you show the gentleman into the conservatory; I shall be down shortly".

The butler hurried down the two flights of curving stairs and across the chequered entrance hall. "This way please sir. May I take your coat and cane?"

"No" replied the visitor, following the supplicant manservant through the double-doors, his unusual silver-topped cane echoing against the polished stone, "I suspect this will be a brief visit."

"The Senator will be with you shortly, sir. If you need anything further, please call". The visitor's eyes flickered comprehension, so the butler excused himself, leaving the nameless guest amongst the hanging plants of the many-windowed room.

Upstairs, after the butler had left, Isabella had allowed her cheeks to flush, blooming into the sterile canvas of the white room, the walls cooling her face and leaching away the emotion. She was not sure who would be waiting for her downstairs; she had certainly met agents of the library over the last few years, but none had ever titled themselves "Assistants". Maybe this man would be able to answer some of her questions.

three

Vasco was snoring now, his musty coat dull by the moonlight, his ribcage rising and falling with each laboured breath. Olof sat opposite, watching the small dog, silently thanking him. They had all played their parts today, even the ragged spaniel whose alertness had helped them evade capture during the escape through the maze of the Medway marshes. For all the Civil Guard's technology, the weather and the wildness could hide them still. He opened his flask, ready for the last few drops of the broth that had given him sustenance and strength throughout the day. He felt the warmness reach deep inside as he emptied the canteen, shaking it gently and then wiping his dirtied face with the back of his arm.

Past them lay the barge, stoutly moored and safely hidden under nets of dampening cam-foliage from the airborne scans. The two women sat in the wheelhouse, watching the portable screens whose modernity was sharply at odds with the rest of the bridge's almost antique instruments; the brass compass and wall mounted barometers all relics of an earlier time.

"Anything on the official screens yet?" Olof called up to them.

Batista answered, "Nothing yet." She turned to the younger woman, continuing more quietly, "suppressed you think?"

"I expect so"

"Do you think the independents will pick it up?"

"Maybe. They should do". Elisabeth paused, before continuing, "We knew this might happen; they suppress the story on the grounds of *seditious intent*, prevent the repetition of a 'terrorist' message".

Batista exhaled sharply, her eyes full of disgust.

"I know", Elisabeth continued. "But we both knew how they might try and spin this. The primary aim was always that they get the message. If the people hear us as well, so be it. But no matter".

Elisabeth turned off both screens, and held the wizened hands of the old Portuguese in hers, looking into her dark eyes. "We did a good thing today."

"Si sobrinha, we did".

four

Val Banerjee knew she was in trouble. The barrier was her responsibility, it was her jurisdiction; security accounted for a fifth of their budget and significantly more than a fifth of her role. Standing nervously in the foyer, her fingers continually smoothing her straightened shoulder-length black bob, she waited for the doormen to receive clearance for her to enter. She was frantic, unable to stop herself worrying about what might happen. It wasn't merely a case of losing her job, the lost pay and the inconvenience of finding another; she was a Council employee, and a senior one. She needed to calm down and focus, to convince them that she was capable of dealing with the situation.

Eventually she was collected by a faceless clerk who led her through a labyrinth of corridors before finally stopping outside the doors of a controlled lift.

"Stand here. Face the screen. State your name. Ask for level seventeen-deep", ordered the clerk before promptly exiting. She did as instructed, stifling a bout of nausea.

"No-one was hurt", she thought to herself. "It was embarrassing, but nobody died, nothing was damaged. Embarrassing, but not fatal". She knew, however, that this was exactly the problem. It did not do to embarrass the Council, or the Mayor. Involuntarily, she recalled a line that was popular for a time in her youth: "Harsh can be the hand that blessed". Its authors were not talking about her government, but she felt its relevance all the same.

The lift continued down for a surprisingly long period, before gently halting. The doors opened into a reception room, where a pair of near identical women with cropped blonde hair sat behind a desk opposite the elevator.

"Please", one of them instructed, "come forward Supervisor Banerjee. Follow me". The other woman remained seated, but gave them both a mirth-less smile.

five

The butler had retreated to the servant's passage immediately after closing the doors on the Senator and her visitor; he had long realised that any attempt to eavesdrop on her conversations would be a mistake. He was convinced she had the whole house electro-monitored, although he couldn't find any evidence and had stopped looking anyway: he had a comfortable life here and little interest in the intrigue of politics.

The conservatory service bell rang shortly afterwards; no more than six or seven minutes could have passed when he was recalled to show the gentleman out. He did so promptly, and returned swiftly to the Senator. In a face known for its inscrutability he thought he could trace the outlines of shock; but even he, so accustomed to his mistress, was unsure.

"I would like a glass of brandy please, in the study. And send Betsy to prepare my outdoors clothes. I will be going into town this evening."

"Yes Madam. Will you require the lifter?"

"No Mister Johns. I shall take the tramway. Clothes fit for the streets in this weather please".

"As you say Madam".

Isabella waited for the butler to set about his business before walking back across the chess-board entrance hall and into her private study. This room was as much a homage to the traditional as the white room was to minimalism; the aged panelling and shelves of hand-bound books circling an equally antique writing desk in the midst of a deep ruby carpet. She paced around the walls twice before settling at the desk, placing both hands purposefully flat on its matted surface, and shaking back her long white-blonde mane, taking the time to calm herself, to steady her breathing and centre her thoughts.

"Ask yourself this", the man had said, "Ask yourself 'where do I stand?'"

"Too simplistic", she had replied.

"And yet, at the end, maybe not so. We shall see."

She had so many questions, but she had to be careful. She did not know what the Librarian wanted; she had never even met the figure whose representatives had contacted her over the previous few years. They had never been explicit about what he wanted either; just frustratingly vague, their discourse meandering in mystery.

"What is it you want of me?" she asked, venturing the direct approach.

"We want nothing of you, but to show you something. You decide for yourself what it is you want to see."

"What will you show me?"

"This I cannot say. If you decide to find out yourself, go here." He handed her another card, similar to the one her butler had brought earlier; black on one side, black writing on the other.

Artur's, 14 Flood Street, Old Chelsea.

"Will the Librarian be there?" Isabella asked.

The stranger, dark-skinned, tall, obviously powerful and yet supple in his movements, merely smiled; his blue eyes twinkling as he pulled on two black gloves.

"What is your name?" Isabella tried.

"I am the Assistant. You are the Senator. This is as it should be."

As he turned to leave, the light from the conservatory's lamps reflected off the silver head of the man's cane, spraying the wall with shattered rays; and Isabella noticed, for the first time, the handle shaped like a dog's head.

Alone then, she turned the card over, and over again in her hands. She was curious to find out what these riddle-speakers wanted. She knew they had power, or at least influence at high levels – the previous agents had proved that without question; there was no other way for them to know the things they knew. She would visit this place; but not tonight. The Mayor had called an emergency Council session, and as one of London's three Senator's at the United Cities Forum she had been summoned to the Cone.

six

Haldane paced up and down the low-ceilinged subterranean crisis room deep inside the bunker; the table behind him packed with representatives of the various agencies, authorities, and the ever-present Council officials.

"How did this happen?" he asked in measured tones.

Val Banerjee blushed; she couldn't help it. Not knowing whether to stand or stay sitting, she opted for the latter, before saying, "we are still unsure exactly how security was breached Mayor Haldane".

"Davis?" he asked, turning to the shaven-headed Civil Guard chief, whose pugnacious demeanour was not in the least for show. This was a man Haldane trusted implicitly; they had fought together in the Migration Wars many years before, and carried that bond still.

"We don't know either. Yet. There are possibilities."

"Yes?" asked the Mayor. Val Banerjee had been focussed on her own hands and her own thoughts, but looked up at this; she wanted answers as well, hoping that they would not lay the blame on her people and ultimately herself.

"Pickering: explain", ordered Davis to one of the guardsmen beside him, who stood up before speaking to the room.

"A provisional chemical analysis of the device would suggest a somewhat artisan approach"

"You mean this thing was home-made?" asked Haldane.

"In a manner of speaking" continued the guardsman. "As such, the different ingredients themselves may not have alerted the sensors individually; they only become unstable when combined, so the system may not have recognised the threat."

"Then you think this is the work of dissidents?" the Mayor asked Davis.

"Dissidents or pragmatists. Hard to say"

Haldane sighed audibly. He didn't know whether to treat this as good news. The lack of any firm evidence pointing to any external involvement was in some ways a relief. London's foreign enemies would surely not resort to such an amateurish attempt, he thought, but the attack could easily have been designed that way to muddy the scent. Davis appeared to have been thinking along the same lines.

"Mayor Haldane?" broached a new voice. A gaunt figure of a man with sunken cheeks on his Asiatic face, he wore the uniform of the Pioneers, a special forces unit, independent of the standing army that existed to gather intelligence on external threats, and if necessary to neutralise them.

"Please" invited the Mayor.

The man did not introduce himself, but kept talking. "It depends on their aim. I think we may assume from this", he said pointing to the pictures which were now appearing on a holo-screen above the oval table, "that they intended to deliver a message".

"Explain."

"Look through the smoke, my Lord"

The picture was filmed from above the Dam walls, presumably by a security lifter; the remnants of the smoke now merging with a thick sea mist rolling in from the north-east and together obscuring the behemothic structure beneath. Occasionally, though, they could see the four-lane carriageway through breaks in the rolling bank of vapour. Every person around the table could see the same thing. One hundred metres from the stage where the prime minister had stood just hours earlier, the surface of the road was discoloured by an unmistakeable mural.

Four words were inscribed in technicolor glory across the black-tarred highway.

This is not freedom.

Haldane looked around the assembled faces, and grimaced. Davis returned the gesture.

"Make sure that picture does not make it onto the screens. Any of them. Are the Council members in the chamber?" Haldane asked an assistant. "Yes? Then let us begin."

seven

"The first thing a river engineer should learn", Daniel's father often used to say, "is to live on a hill."

The Mason family home was one of the few truly old buildings on Sawyer's Hill, pre-dating by centuries the modern developments that sprawled through what was once the great city park at Richmond. Daniel's grandfather had bought the former Ranger's building and comprehensively renovated it, making full use of the high ceilings and tall windows to keep the rooms surprisingly light, and adding an inner courtyard and hollow cooling tower that made the complex naturally comfortable in the heat of the summer.

Daniel had inherited the building the year he finished University; his own father's premature death hitting him hard. Every last piece of the building held memories. Every shadow spoke of games and shared triumphs, of rows and tears and joy and fear and all the rest a home sees over decades of habitation by the same tight-knit clan; for they were for a long time inseparable.

He hadn't moved-in immediately, preferring a small flat in Greenwich, oblivious to the ghosts of the western reaches and the memories of the last few years where his relationship with his father became increasingly strained. The nights they drank through the hours of argument about the rights and wrongs of barriers and laws and governments, of rights and morality and what should be done; should have been done. Daniel the young radical; blinded to his father's wisdom by the sparkling ideals of youth. Terrible rows, with words unmeant but all too keenly felt. Taken away, before either had chance to yield or remember or learn from the other; before they could make peace.

In a life with some regrets, he regretted this still.

Living here, in his Father's rooms in Richmond, had surprised Daniel; and for the better. As the days and months had passed he felt himself growing closer again to that absent figure; through walking the windowed halls, through the living walls themselves, and the bricks and the nooks and the aged boards, through the eaves when the night blew howling and the creaks in the beams that reassured like the ship's hammocks they once, centuries before, supported. He found some of his father's ideas becoming clearer, distilled with time; and he found himself understanding the man, sometimes agreeing, sometimes embarrassed at his own petulant certainty. Rapprochement, of a sort.

There was no wind blowing this evening; instead a curious stillness hung in the air, a temporary truce between the great weather systems, destined to be as short-lived as it was unusual. The air felt damp, hanging with moisture. Daniel and Rachel had been evacuated from the Dam via the monorails, whisked into the heart of the City amidst throngs of shaken and soot-dirtied Londoners. He had found Saskia and their launch at Blackfriars wharf, amongst a flotilla of craft of all sizes arriving from downriver. It was only then, only when holding his daughter Lexi in his arms that he allowed himself to relax, and was engulfed with the sudden realisation of how frightened he had been, not for himself but for those other children on the barrier wall. He felt physically ill for a few minutes, having to prop himself against the wharf's piles for balance.

Lexi didn't sleep on the slow trip upriver, but sat on deck with her parents, the sugary cocoa keeping her warm and awake.

"Did you see the smoke Daddy?"

"Yes, my dear. I saw it"

From the water, Saskia explained to him, it was not clear what had happened. First, the screens had stopped showing footage of the stage, as though there were a technical problem of some kind. Then they started to transmit an order to return to the western wharves because the Dam might have to do an Emergency Close.

"Isn't that a bit strange?" Lexi asked her father, parroting her mother's own words from a few hours earlier.

"Strange is right," he replied, turning to his wife and admitting, "I'm still not sure what happened up there and we were right in the thick of it. There was smoke coming over the dam wall, but I don't know where from and I don't know why. It makes no sense. None of the texts coming through from the Council say anything either."

"I saw the smoke daddy, it was far away but I used the bins and I saw it on the top of the wall by the offices"

"Really Lex? Well done you." Daniel said, smiling and ruffling her hair.

"Do you think they will call you in?" asked Saskia.

"I doubt it. It must be a structural issue. Although if the Dam's operations are affected, then maybe." He thought about it for a few minutes more as they continued slowly up the Thames, unable to keep up with the last of the light as the night chased them westwards. "No. No, I think I'll be working from home for a few days"

Lexi heard this, and smiled secretly to herself. She liked it when her father was home; she knew he wouldn't mind if she disturbed him – he'd pretend to be irritated, but she knew he wasn't really.

Unfortunately for Lexi, Daniel was wrong. The iron bell began ringing before the first glints of sunlight had appeared on the calm waters of the Thames. Saskia was first to hear it, and flicked on the screen on the bedroom wall. Two figures in plain suits stood outside the porch.

"Danny. Dan – wake up"

His blurring eyes were greeted with the same image. His mind immediately shook away the remnants of sleep. "I'll go. They must be from the Authority". Saskia grunted in agreement, rolling over and burying herself under the sheets.

Pausing to pull on an old cable-knit sweater over his flannel nightwear, Daniel made his way down the narrow front staircase to the front door. He flicked on the hall screen before opening it.

"Yes?"

"Council business sir", the shorter figure said to the screen on the outer door. If Daniel was not awake already, he was now; whatever they wanted, if the Council was involved, it was far from trivial.

He needed to check, and began, "Can you", but was cut off by their anticipatory acquiescence, both men tapping their wrist terminals onto the reader attached to the weathered, vine-infested walls. As the hall screen confirmed their identities as members of the Civil Guard, Daniel took a deep breath and asked for a minute to get dressed.

Soon afterwards they were aboard the patrol craft and heading downstream towards the city-centre. The Dam must have been left open because the tidal waters had retreated, exposing much of the mudbank and the reed-beds around Mortlake; they had to stick closely to the channel to avoid running aground.

All rational people had a healthy respect for, or fear of, the Guard; but despite this Daniel found himself warming to the two men sent to collect him. The helmsman clearly knew the river, and the other man, Walker, had made them all hot coffee to sup in the cold morning air. The light was getting better now as they headed into the sun that was just breaching the horizon, and Daniel sat behind the cuddy looking at the banks, watching a lone grey heron stalking fish in the shallow water, long-legged and long-necked with a devastating yellow beak that spiked and jabbed at the prey beneath.

He wondered why he was being summoned, but knew that asking the guardsmen would not get him anywhere – they were unlikely to know themselves. Delivery-men; and efficient too. They rounded the bend at Sand's End, the ghostly abandoned district that had been left to the ravages of the tides but now stood above the neaps once more; the night's water dripping from crumbling walls and rusting iron skeletons of old factories and warehouses and schools. Further down to the Wandsworth marshes; then the walled confines of Old Chelsea on the left bank, proudly defiant, hubristically so.

"Be there in a few minutes", the guard Walker said flatly, finishing his morning brew before climbing forward to ready the landing ropes. Soon enough they came alongside the Westminster pier, the guards tying-up before leading Daniel along the floating pontoon and into the government complex. The old Parliament took up much of the riverside area but was little used these days, replaced by the newer, flood-proofed London Council building to its west. Its official name was the Stephenson, honouring one of the city's military heroes; but most people called it the Cone, due to its conical shape that rose to a point ten storeys up, and extended deep and wide beneath the ground. Watertight and bomb-proof; that was the design brief. The structure housed the legislators in the Council chambers above ground, and the military and civil command centres in the basement levels, which were linked by tunnels to the various agencies and authorities housed in further outbuildings around the Cone itself. It was to one of these that Daniel was led, the Civil Guard headquarters known as Little Smith Street.

Inside, he was led through the various stages of security scans and searches before being taken up three levels and to the office of the Civil Guard Chief, Commissioner Davis.

"Wait here" said the guard who had driven the launch. Daniel could not help but feel anxious; he was all but certain that he was here in his capacity as an estuary engineer of the Barrier Authority, but being summoned to the office of a man like Davis made the mind wander. Could it be anything else? Could he, somehow, be under some kind of misguided suspicion? Did thinking this make him look guilty? Daniel swallowed, putting these thoughts to one side as his name was called from inside the open door of the room.

He walked through it to find a large office with an oval meeting table set in the middle, and a large desk towards the back. Around the table sat a number of the higher ranking Guardsmen, whose faces Daniel recognised from the security briefings on the screens, as well as the head of dam security, a slightly plump and red-faced character called Pennells who Daniel had never quite warmed to, and their superior Val Banerjee, head of the Barrier Authority itself.

She looked more tired than he had ever seen her, her trademark black bob looking unkempt, her eyes bloodshot and her shoulders sagging. Still, Daniel thought, they were all tired after yesterday, and he suspected that most people in this room would have not been home yet.

Davis stood at the head of the table, his stocky frame and aggressive demeanour combining to suggest pent-up yet tightly controlled violence. He was looking at a holo-screen map of the estuary, its myriad of channels and creeks, sedge plantations and saltmarsh, impenetrable except from the water and deadly to the ignorant on a rising tide.

"Mason. Firstly, you did well yesterday. I know the Mayor was impressed". Here Davis stopped, watching closely to see how Daniel handled the slightly loaded complement.

"Thank you. We did what was needed".

As the corners of Davis' mouth hinted at a smile, he continued to hold Daniel in his stare. "Quite so."

Daniel made a point of looking around the room, inviting an explanation if one was on offer.

"Yes Mason, I have not had you brought here just to say thank you, although maybe that would be justified. Yesterday's incidentwas, we think, the work of a terrorist cell."

Terrorists, thought Daniel. Not an accident then. That hadn't made it onto the screens yet.

One of the staff added, "This is classified information that you are not at liberty to discuss outside of this room."

When Daniel nodded his assent, Davis continued, "Were it not for the quick-thinking of individuals like yourself, and a lot of luck, the outcome could have been far worse, as I'm sure you understand."

Davis was trying to get him on-side, Daniel realised, and overcome the natural distrust most Londoners would have of the Civil Guard, given its reputation. "How can I help?" he ventured, keen to disguise his natural scepticism of the man and his methods.

"We suspect the terrorists are hiding in the marshes somewhere. We would like you to help us find them."

Daniel could not hide his surprise at this. He assumed, as did most of the city's citizens, that the Guard's monitoring systems would be more than up to the task of finding a few outlaws in the marshes, with all the heat sensors and auto-surveillance systems, not to mention a few lesser known pieces of technology, at their disposal.

Davis almost smiled again, as though he had been waiting for this reaction. "Mason, I remind you that this is classified information. The marshes pose what we could call a unique challenge to our methods of monitoring and recovery. There are certain systems that are less than effective in that environment, and there are also ways to deflect our attention. Obviously, it would not do to spread this information too widely."

Daniel agreed, wishing they hadn't told him. Too much knowledge could place a person in danger.

Davis watched the impact of his words, pausing before continuing. "My men know the river", he said, nodding at Daniel's companions from the earlier that morning, "but you know it better. Are you willing to help?"

Daniel knew it wasn't really a choice; the question was a form of politeness, nothing more.

"Of course."

Daniel noticed Val Banerjee's look of relief; she must have been worried that he would object, given his track record. She had always treated his questioning of Authority policy as tantamount to disloyalty, rather than as the objective independent science that he believed it to be; she might even have tried to force him out of the organisation, if he hadn't been his father's son.

There were times to question authority, Daniel thought; standing opposite the Commissioner, inside the most powerful security agency of the city-state, was not one of them.

eight

"It is time for me to leave", stated Olof in his clipped Scandinavian tones. The sun had risen as much as it would during the short winter's day, but the three of them were hidden from its betraying embrace inside the old riverboat and under the blanket of cam-foliage nets that hid them from more than just the naked eye. He clasped hands with both the women, saying, "Lycka till, good luck my sisters", before climbing up into the wheelhouse and over the side into his canoe. He slipped under the netting and paddled softly away, heading towards the wildfowl sanctuary several kilometres to the west where he could blend in amongst the other waterborne ornithologists.

The other four of their group had left at various stages through the previous evening; each separately, each to a different refuge and a different life. Only Elisabeth remained onboard with Batista, whose own sanctuary was the vessel itself; they hoped nobody would suspect an old lady and her dog aboard a houseboat as being a threat to the state; at least, not once they were safely out of the Medway marshes. Their current location, though well-hidden, was more difficult to explain away if they were found, so they would lie hidden in the sedge all day, and then remove the nets in the evening and head towards Chatham docks. Then they could hide themselves in the open, amidst the bustle of the busy river port.

Batista was in the galley heating some stew whilst Elisabeth monitored the portable screen for any news on the previous night's actions. The government were claiming it was a fire in one of the Dam Authority offices in the top of the wall, caused by a faceless bureaucrat and his defective portable heater. She checked the independent channels and they were all carrying the same story, none of them questioning the official version of events.

"Complete whitewash".

"What?"

"Whitewash – the information on the screens. No mention of a message. No mention of anything. Some cover story about a fire in an office."

"Moment – I'm coming back", replied the older woman, walking slowly and carefully through the cabin with two deep mugs of stew in one hand and a plate of bread in the other. She settled down next to Elisabeth, and they both watched the screen in increasing disbelief. They were watching a free broadcast, which was usually known for its independence and willingness to criticise actions of the Council.

"The fire in the dam", said the measured voice accompanying the pictures, "was a potential catastrophe. Although the blaze itself was easily dealt with by the automatic systems, the resulting smoke, itself magnified by the weather conditions, could have led to disaster".

The screens were showing footage of the crowds on top of the dam swarming towards the stage area and the crush that ensued.

"Were it not for the quick action of those on the spot, including the Lord Mayor, there could have been disaster".

Elisabeth bit her bottom lip as the pictures now showed Haldane – and Daniel - hauling people to safety.

"Whilst it is not normally this broadcast's policy to applaud the Lord Mayor, today we do so. Fortunately, most fortunately, the fire led to just one casualty."

The women looked at each other, and back at the screen. They had always known that there was a risk of fatality in the panic; they justified it to each other as an "acceptable risk", but had never felt comfortable doing so. They believed in peaceful protest, but a few too many leaders of the old movements had undergone sudden unexplained changes of heart, or had accidents, or had simply disappeared, for them to not suspect Civil Guard involvement. They wanted to wage the struggle without hurting the innocents, but it seemed they had failed.

The report on the screen continued, showing a picture of a young man and saying; "John Gates, a single twenty five year old law student from Herne Hill, was caught in the smoke and tragically died from asphyxiation".

Both women immediately knew the lie. They had not known his name, but they knew John Gates had not died in the smoke; the face on the screen belonged to one of six who had leapt from the dam and flown to safety; it belonged to the John Gates who had left the riverboat before it reached the Medway to make his own way back into the city. Their identities were reasonably safe − the operation had been put together as a cell with no names; only Elisabeth and Batista were known to each other, which is why they were still together; but John Gates, if that was his name, knew they were headed towards the marshes. If they had caught him, and made him talk, then the security services would know in which area to look.

Both women sat quietly, listening to the calls of the wading birds.

"Do we stay here or try and move?" Elisabeth thought out-loud.

"Why put his picture on the screens, but lie about how he died?" Batista replied rhetorically. "Claro. To make us panic and run. Only thing that makes sense. So we stay here, as long as we can".

nine

Daniel was still in Little Smith Street, standing near the door of a packed briefing room. Holo-maps of the estuary floated above the central podium, whilst the men of the Civil Guard River Patrol including Daniel's two companions from earlier that morning sat behind rows of undersized desks, awaiting instructions. Their leader was a Lieutenant known as Sparrow, a slight figure whose expression appeared almost permanently intrigued by everything around him. The moniker marked him out as ex-Military, like so many of the senior officers in the Guard.

"We have reason to believe that the terrorists, or at least some of them, are sheltering somewhere in the Medway marshes", he began.

Daniel did not know how they knew this; but this was the Guard, and they had ways of finding things out.

"With some decent electro-net camouflage and a bit of mist, they may be able to stay concealed from some of our surveillance systems. But not if they move. And we still have eyes. Gentlemen, this is Mr Daniel Mason of the Barrier Authority's Estuary management programme. He knows the marshes better than anyone, and will be assisting our operation."

Sixty sets of highly trained eyes locked on Daniel, assessing him, processing the body-language, sizing him up.

"We will cast the net and flush them out. Half the boats will proceed to the south-west of the marsh and begin the search; the other half will form the catch-net on the north-eastern borders. We will have air support from the lifters. I will direct operations from the Pike. Gentlemen, to work!"

"Sir", came the simultaneous reply.

As the men filed into a passageway that led to the central boathouse, the Lieutenant beckoned Daniel to walk with him. "Mason, you're with me."

Most of the patrol boats were fairly small, twelve metres in length but with powerful engines that made them some of the fastest craft on the river; they were designed to be operated by a crew of two but capable of carrying up to ten people if necessary. The Pike, or Hoodlum Class River Command Craft to give the boat its full name, was an altogether different animal; still fast but thirty metres in length, with a command cabin packed with screens displaying the tactical and surveillance information coming in through the dishes on the roof. It was also, subtly, well armed.

As they set off downriver towards the Dam and the Medway, the section tasked with searching the marsh shot off ahead. Inside the floating command centre, Daniel was being quizzed for information about the area – depths of the main channels at this stage of tide; how many of the smaller channels were actually passable, how

71

many were too clogged with organic material. As well as being fast, the patrol boat design included retractable propellers and minimal draught, allowing the craft to operate in very shallow conditions; but they were still too large to get into all the nooks and passages between the marsh grasses. As Daniel pointed to the areas on the holo-map that they wouldn't be able to reach, it was becoming increasingly clear that their quarry had chosen a good place to hide. There was a central zone, many square kilometres across, that they couldn't penetrate; and with the sea mist still rolling in, the lifters were unlikely to be much help either.

Daniel was in his element talking about the marsh system. It was, he was thinking, an astute move on their part to insist on his involvement, but he was still on edge; this was the Guard, and if you could avoid coming to their attention for any reason, all the better. He was being as helpful as he could, and was happy to do so – he had been on the Dam when the terrorists struck, had seen at first-hand how many people could have died if they hadn't acted when they did. He understood that the city's politics weren't perfect, understood that some of the protestors you occasionally saw on the independent screens had some credible grounds to complain; but putting innocent lives at risk was altogether different.

As he finished marking the passable stretches on the map, Daniel added, "You know, they were lucky with the timing."

Sparrow looked up from his tactical display. "How do you mean?"

"Very low tide today, the lowest for months. Normally, that impassable area in the middle of the screen would be much smaller."

"How fast will the waters rise?" asked the Lieutenant, his eyebrow arching like a flyfisherman's rod trying to coax out some trout from the safe waters below.

"Not fast enough in the daylight – you should have more water to move by the time it gets dark though." Sparrow shrugged his shoulders, and went back to his screen. Then Daniel had another thought.

"Things would be faster if the Dam was closed, but it isn't scheduled to close for another week – unless of course we get a storm swell".

He had their attention now. "What would happen if you closed the Dam right now?"

"Well", Daniel continued, considering it as a theoretical question rather than anything else, "if the upriver gates were all open, the river water would start to back up. Not enough to notice much in town, but you'd see the difference in the marshes. You could probably get into another half of that section before the light fails".

The lieutenant looked Daniel squarely in the eye, saying, "That fast?" before turning and speaking into his wrist-terminal. He turned back a few moments later continuing, "They are closing the barrier as we speak. Gentlemen, re-run your simulations."

Daniel could not quite believe what he was hearing. He knew the Guard were powerful – everyone knew that; but the fact that this man could get the barrier gates closed with a single call was, somehow, more frightening than any of the weapons so visibly displayed on all their tunics.

"Not so lucky anymore", the Lieutenant said to himself, straining to see the blurred rise of the distant saltmarsh; straining like a hound against the leash.

The Pike was keeping pace with the speeding patrol craft around her, an arrowhead carving through the still waters like a hungry pod of orca towards the feeding grounds. They were down past Dartford in no time, around the hook and past the Naval Defence base at Tilsbury, then into the open estuary with the Dam walls rising above the horizon and the saltmarsh spreading out on either side. Their wake rocked the transport barges labouring against the flow as they accelerated far beyond the ten knot limit, glorying in the privilege of the lawkeepers, lights flaring and sirens wailing as if the spectacle of the combined force of the River Patrol at full throttle was not enough on its own. Still the formation held, a phalanx with the Pike at the centre, pushing on past the flooded forest of Higham off their port rails, and around that lonely spit of land towards the Medway marshes themselves. The section tasked with beating through the rushes was out of sight now, encircling their targets and preparing to push through; the Lieutenant stood firm on the Pike's bridge despite the violent motion of the hull, directing his forces into action, ready for the hunt.

For all the fury of the fleet's rush to the east, the ensuing search proved to be a slow and frustrating operation. The group of craft beating their way through the maze of saltmarsh were continuously running aground on the sandy shoals or getting caught amidst the tangled clutches of the sedge-forests. As their markers on the holo-maps began to stall and reverse, Daniel had to try and find new passages for them to attempt as gradually, through trial and error, they passed across the expanse in a ragged, shifting virtual line. As the day progressed the sea-mist showed no signs of retreating making the lifters practically helpless to contribute to the search, and by the time the light began to drain out of the clouds in the late afternoon, they had only managed to search a third of the area. Sparrow could feel the opportunity slipping away, their advantage dissipating along with the daylight; but he remained patient, even allowing a wry smile to ease through his cheeks. Whoever was hiding in that marsh had a talent for evasion, and that was something he respected. There was no use in allowing the tendrils of anger any purchase; decades of uniformed experience taught him to remain cool and objective, and the men took the lead from their commander.

Daniel was less able to contain his frustration after hours of directing and re-directing the patrol boats on the virtual map in front of him. The rising waters had helped, particularly in the last few hours, but it was too late for them to complete the search before darkness. His disappointment had an edge; he didn't want to fail the Guard. For all his protestations of independence, at work or in the comfortable dining rooms of Richmond Hill, Daniel was also a pragmatist. His world had certain rules; they might not be desirable, they might not be right, but sacrificial opposition wasn't going to change them. If you had to speak to the Guard, Daniel thought, make sure you say "Yes."

"Searchlights on, keep your eyes open," Sparrow ordered over the comms. An arced pool of light flickered across the approaches to the Medway, intermittent islands with plenty of darkness between them. "Get those lifters to work as well," he continued. "The mist is thinner out here, and their lights would be helpful."

ten

Elisabeth felt unnaturally calm. That moment of fear-realisation, the sudden flush of blood and tightening of the diaphragm when they saw John Gates, had stretched into minutes and then hours of near-silent waiting. Batista had sat quietly on the bunk, sometimes sleeping, sometimes reading the withered pages of an old printed book, her fingers playing with the frayed ends of a knitted scarf. Elisabeth wanted to study plans of the marshes on her portable screen, but they had decided to turn off all the powered systems; they weren't sure if the Guard could trace them this way, and that was enough to not take the risk. There was no use in worrying about capture, but there was every reason to prepare for it – and they are different, she thought. Preparation of the mind for the assault that would come: the incessant questioning, the violent and the not-so violent methods of what they called "information extraction". Elisabeth had allowed her mind to drift gently before focussing on what needed to be endured; trying to stem her fears by inhabiting them, by knowing them and rejecting their power. She was at once relaxed and tense; lying inert but ready to move at an instant's notice. She had been here before.

It did not come. The light failed before their concealment.

"Soon my dear. Another day and they will find us surely"

"I agree", Elisabeth replied to her friend. "Which way?"

"West. If we go to the east, the marshes open onto the Sheerness channel. It runs inside the barrier wall down to the Swale Gate; it is too narrow and easy to watch. If we make a break to the north, maybe we get to the main river, but there is no cover if we get spotted, not at all, just open water. Going west means we cannot make it upriver tonight – we'll be hemmed in by the Halstow peninsula. But if we can get to the Chatham docks without being seen, like the original idea, we will still be able to blend in amongst all the other river craft. We have more of a chance that way – even when the marshes finish, there are still enough islands to hide between."

"Do you think that plan is secure?" Elisabeth asked.

"No reason why it shouldn't be. Gates"

"If that was his name", she interrupted.

"He did not know our route. Even the Swede did not know where we planned to go from here. Only the two of us."

They did not have to wait long for the darkness to smother the marsh entirely, and soon they were edging the barge from under the cam-nets. They would leave these behind like an empty cocoon; too incriminating if they were found aboard. Her motor purred gently, audible above the gently lapping bow-waters. Batista expertly threaded the boat through the narrows, her mental map of the area as detailed as any holo-projection and infused with the knowledge that comes from a lifetime of experience. Twice they saw the fragmented glow of searchlights filtering through the impenetrable marsh-grasses, turning off the motors and gently punting away before turning again westwards. It took five hours to thread their way gently to the edges of the Medway, the channels widening and the banks of grasses being slowly replaced by ever larger tracts of open water. They could hear the distant hum of lifters above them, none coming too close, occasionally recognisable by a ball of glowing cloud amidst the far darkness.

"Now things will get interesting," Batista muttered to herself in the darkened wheelhouse. Elisabeth knew what she meant – they both expected these waters to be well patrolled compared to the marine jungle where they had hidden all day. Passing between two small islands of sedge, they could see lights in the distance, a faint line of halogen rays slowly scanning the very waters they needed to cross.

"What do you think?" Elisabeth asked the elder woman.

"We have a chance", she replied matter-of-factly. "There are big gaps between the patrol boats – they must be spread all around the marsh. If we can get into one of those valleys of darkness, they will not be able to hear us. But if we get caught in one of those search-beams." She stopped there, both women knowing what that would mean.

"I think we give it a try."

"Then let us trust to fate."

Batista gave the engine a little more throttle, but not so much as to make the noise detectable. She brought the barge deftly through a narrow gap between the last grass-banks and then out into the open waters beyond. The patrol boats were visible from their lights and the scanning beams, spread-out like a thin line of floating buoys guarding a reef. She deliberately aimed between two near the south of the line, knowing that there was a network of small islets just past them and before the Chatham channel. If they were spotted, they might be able to escape into them, but she doubted it; the barge, albeit deceptively quick, was no match for the Civil Guard boats.

Closer and closer they came to the crossing searchlights; slowing up gently to let the two beams separate and go back towards their own craft; accelerating again through the gap, needing quiet speed now before the lights swung back between the patrol boats; accelerating before those two separate searchbeams combined to flush the gap between their lines; Batista's small aged hands tightly wrapped around the throttle, merging, the old Portuguese and her ancient craft moving purposefully through the darkened velvety water, hoping for one last escape, one final triumph against those who would hunt her down; and then through and beyond, shooting through a hole in the knotted net and gone.

Once in the Approaches they lit up the barge and the wheelhouse, hiding in the light. Elisabeth sat on the cabin roof, mending an eeling line, allowing her body to relax – properly this time, all the controlled tension working its way out, tears released onto her dirtied cheeks. Fate had decided, as the old woman had said.

eleven

In the library, the books lay pregnantly silent. A broadsheet ledger was open, patiently, on the Librarian's desk. A rap, the sound of metal on hardwood, echoed through the galleries.

"Come".

The man with the dog's head cane entered.

"It is done."

"Will she come, do you think?"

"She is wary but inquisitive. The latter is, I think, stronger."

"We shall see. There is another strand we must consider."

twelve

The country house had always been Isabella's favourite, especially as a girl. It was easy then to escape those watching over her and spend hours lost amidst the rambling grounds beyond the walled garden. She loved waking early and running through the kitchens towards the scent of the dripping dew, and listening to the flocks of airborne visitors singing on their way off to a day's foraging. There, hiding in the lifeless hollowed trunk of the ancient oak, what remained of its branches thick with vine leaves as if to mock its own misfortunes; or deep in the bamboo thicket, invisible to the outside, the tunnel of stalks closing neatly behind her as she crawled into its deepest heart; there, she felt free. Endless days exploring its secrets, before returning muddy-kneed to the red-faced guardians charged with her education. The estate was an island of unmanaged nature that was as rare within the confines of the vast city-state as a solitary edelweiss amidst the snowy alpine peaks; and Isabella embraced it, revelled in its very wildness, released from the strictures of her normal life and able to breathe it in.

Older now, she could but gaze at the wintry thicket from the house's upper windows. From here, high in the Chiltern hills, she could make out the limits of their estate, the far wall at the end of their grounds rising before the start of the agribusiness beds that ran all the way down to the great reservoir, packed with all-season crops. Her boundless childhood forest appeared small and self-contained from this view; yet still it stirred a rebelliousness in her, the reminder of feelings that had long since been safely locked away.

She brought her gaze back inside the room, and looked at her reflection in the long free-standing mirror. She wondered if she was doing the right thing in marrying Evelyn. She knew she didn't love him, but had given up on such pretensions early in her adulthood. Love was, in her position, an unnecessary requirement to marriage; desirable maybe, but inconvenient and desperately distracting. She suspected though that he had developed strong feelings towards her, which should at least make the whole thing more manageable. She was, at least, fond of the man.

But this was an alliance of families, a union of his relations who held such influential roles in the Corporation, with her clan, the Hardwicke political dynasty. Her uncle had been a prominent member of the council before he succumbed to the cancer, and Isabella had followed in his seat before being elevated to the United Cities Forum, sitting as one of London's three appointed Senators in what now passed for government in the Confederation of European Settlements. The seat, a lifetime appointment, gave her significant power and influence, and her family connections meant she also had access to a network of cousins working throughout the Council machine at home.

Evelyn's grandfather was still the titular head of the Corporation, although in reality each of his children ran one of the divisions; five organisations that dominated the economic life of the entire city-state, allied together in the federation that was the Corporation. His mother ran the Armouries and Defensive Capabilities section, and whilst it was his older brother who was likely to inherit the position, Evelyn was assured a senior role. It was a good move; it allied the families whilst not permitting any suggestion that Isabella was not the dominant partner. A sensible match, but by no means the only possible one, and there would be enemies made just by the act of overlooking them; yet she had considered all this before, and always came to the same conclusion – she should go through with it.

It had been Evelyn's mother, characteristically, who made the approach almost a year ago; and yet he had still insisted on courting her, on dinners and trips and walks by the river despite the decision being already made by those around him. He had even proposed, balancing on one knee whilst they punted on the Isis and nearly putting them both in the river. She smiled as she thought of it; unnecessary, but pleasant all the same. She wondered if the need to create this illusion of romance was for her benefit or his; either way, he seemed to have begun to believe in it, whatever his initial intentions. So be it; he was, if she was any judge of character, a good and moral man; she would let him keep his illusion.

The dress would do. Evelyn had dropped so many hints about the colour; the illusion of pre-marital purity as compelling to him as the illusion of his requited love. Isabella did not mind; she happened to like the way she looked in white.

In the corner of the room a screen lit up, signifying she had a message coming through.

"Yes, this is the one. Thank you", she told the dressmaker who promptly left her alone to change. Pulling on the legs of her thick country trousers, she opened the screen message with a flick of her hand. It was anonymous, which was very unusual – the net didn't allow them. The message, however, was clear – at least to her. It simply said, "Artur would still like to meet, if you are interested".

It had been three weeks since the strange meeting in her City house with the man who called himself the Assistant, and she had been stalling for time, trying to find out whatever she could about the Librarian and his organisation, putting out carefully disguised feelers and enquiries but all to no avail. They were like ghosts, people of whom she could find no trace in the system, but who seemed unfathomably well informed. The first woman she had met had known something that she was sure her uncle had told no-one but herself; something that made Isabella take them seriously. She had to find out what they wanted, what this was about, but in her position she needed to do so cautiously. Shaking her head in frustration, Isabella realised she would have to meet them soon, whether she managed to find out any more or not.

She finished dressing quickly and then turned to the screen, making the same movements with her hands to activate it at a distance.

"Call to Councillor Epstein".

"Calling", replied the disembodied machine voice. Moments later the image of an elder man appeared on the screen, the lines on his face like tree-rings, each signifying his long years of the struggle, each making him stronger still as his time ticked by.

"Senator, you look radiant"

She smiled at this, laughing "Bridal prerogative, you old charmer."

Yves Epstein had been her father's closest friend, and most dependable political ally; and when Wyndham Hardwicke had died suddenly, shortly before her sixth birthday, Yves had helped her to understand what had happened, how to cope with her grief. Always there in her childhood, he had helped educate her, teaching her the things she would not be learning from her tutors, the skills she would need to survive in the dangerous world that politics had become. It was he who had taught her how to control her emotions so they served her purposes; he who had demonstrated to her the power of empathetic understanding, the subtle ways in which people responded if you could understand their own perception of the world; he who had taught her how to use the white room, and the power that gave her.

"Yves, it is a fine winter's day. Would you like to come and enjoy a walk on the hills before this evening's dinner? It would be lovely to see you, and there are so many people coming tonight that I suspect our time together will be rather brief, what with the formalities."

"What a splendid idea," Yves responded cordially, as though there was nothing out of the ordinary in this sudden invite. " I should greatly enjoy getting out of doors for a while. I could join you in a couple of hours, if that would be convenient?"

"I look forward to it old friend"

Isabella flicked off the link, allowing herself a smile of appreciation at the old man's abilities. Not a trace, not even the slightest suggestion of surprise in his reaction, and yet she knew that he would be worrying why she had called on him so urgently. They had an understanding from the days of her childhood, and he would know that she needed to talk to him privately and with no chance of being overheard. She found herself questioning how much she should tell her old confidante; he was certainly trustworthy, she had no doubt of that; but she wondered whether he would be able to help.

In fact he arrived a little over ninety minutes later, whisked out from the city on the Oxford line but departing the train in the Chilterns where her driver picked him up and brought him back to the house. Isabella had not yet finished instructing the waiting staff on the arrangements for that evening's banquet, and he had to wait for some time in the outer reception room before she joined him.

"My old friend, sorry for making you wait" she apologised, embracing him warmly as he stood to greet her.

"Isa, what a pleasure to see you" he replied.

"Have you been offered refreshment?"

"I am sampling some of this tawny" he said, moving to the side to show a decanter. "I believe you will be serving it this evening? A fine choice"

"I'm glad you approve. Will you allow me to leave you here for just a few minutes more whilst I change?"

"Of course. I'm enjoying the glow of this old fire-place before we set out."

She kissed him lightly on one cheek, and left the room to dress. Yves Epstein sat in the comfortable leather armchair, watching the flames gently lick a fresh log that one of the servants had added to the burning embers. She had inherited her mother's beauty and learned her father's ability to control, he thought; what a devastating combination. It had not surprised him when she had succeeded to her Uncle's place on the Council, despite claims from her older cousins; nor when she was elevated to the Senate, at such a young age.

He wondered what she had brought him here to discuss. Maybe she would ask if he had perceived any disgruntlement about her choice; he had, but nothing that mattered. It could be about the problems the Council were having with the dissidents, but nobody he had conferred with on the matter thought it a serious concern. He took another sip of the tawny, savouring the thick sweetness on his tongue; he would have to wait.

Isabella returned wearing an old-fashioned oilskin, and having tied-up her long hair under a grey fur hat. They walked through the double-storied entrance hall and out through the bustling kitchens, where the preparations were noisily underway. Yves noticed the implied compliment, as she knew he would; only servants and family would ever walk these passageways. They walked through the kitchen gardens, past the regimented rows of winter vegetables and the translucent pods that insulated the less hardy foodplants inside neon-lit growers. Out past the old walls and the new greenhouses and into the parkland beyond, shying away from the open gardens with their views down to the vast expanse of water lying in the shadow of the hills, and into the narrow-tracked woodland where the boar would be found rustling in the roots.

"I think the woods instead. This breeze will bite on the hilltops".

Yves had expected no less; if anyone listening to their screen-exchange earlier had thought their meeting worth eavesdropping, they would hopefully have focussed their attention in the wrong area.

They walked for a while, Isabella letting her stride pattern match that of her more aged companion, her hands pushed deep into the fur-lined pockets of her old coat, and its collar turned-up against the cold.

"Are the wedding arrangements proceeding as hoped?" Yves began, waiting to see any reaction on her part.

"Smoothly enough. Evelyn is rather excited about the whole thing" she replied, raising her eyebrows.

"He is still, shall we say, enthusiastic about forthcoming events?" Isabella nodded; she had already confided in him about Evelyn's growing emotional attachment, treating it with a kind of gentle amusement. "Be careful my dear; powerful emotions can be powerful motivators; do not treat them lightly".

Isabella nodded again. "I understand".

"But I suspect", he continued, "that is not why we are here, having this walk?"

"No". Isabella kept walking for a few minutes, still unsure of how to start. Eventually, she began, "Yves. Do you know anything of the Librarian?"

He stopped walking, and seemed to be looking intently at the forest floor.

"Yves?"

He took a deep breath, held it, slowly let it out, and then began to walk again. Isabella followed.

"Shall we start with what you know?" was his eventual reply.

Isabella hesitated, but the reassuring look she received from Yves was enough to make her to tell him everything. She explained how it had all started, a couple of years ago now, in the Zermatt Stronghold – a fortress-like settlement deep in the Continental Alps, protected by the mountains on some sides and human-made mountainous walls on the rest. The city rose high within the walls like the corals on a reef – rooms built on top of rooms, buildings on top of buildings, so that all the structures merged into each other and were linked into one gargantuan hive-like settlement. The passive security provided by the walls and cliff-faces combined with the more aggressive types of defence – the protector fields and energy weapons – made it all but impregnable to any kind of low-technology attack, which was the type they most feared. There were still significant areas of the near and far continent dominated by the more barbaric tribes, and all of the City-States had to keep an open eye on their surroundings. Zermatt, as arguably the best defended outpost of what was still called civilization, had become its safe-house, acting as kind of store-room of technology and culture that bore strange echoes of the bank vaults that it had been renowned for in an earlier time. It was also, unsurprisingly, the permanent home of the United Cities Forum and its legislature which would sit in the city on the rare occasions that the full Senate had to meet in body rather than by screen-link, which tended to be once or twice a year.

It was on one of these trips, Isabella explained, that she had been approached by a woman of around her own age one morning on the steps outside the Federal buildings. The woman had addressed her not by her title but simply as "Isabella", which was enough to make her stop and listen.

"I would speak with you, if you will" the woman had said.

"May I ask your name, and why you address me so?" Isabella had replied.

"You may ask many things, but not here. Sometime hence, I will find you. For now, goodbye Chamois".

Yves looked puzzled and interrupted her, asking, "What did she mean, by calling you Chamois?"

"You do not know the name, Yves? Are you sure – it is important."

"No, I do not think so."

"You have never heard anyone called by that name for any reason?"

"Not that I can recall" affirmed her old friend.

"I thought as much. If you did not know it, I do not know who else would. It was the code-name my father gave me as a child. He was *Bouqetin*, I was *Chamois*. Our code, never to be repeated, never to be used except in an emergency. I have often thought what kind of emergency he expected a five year old to deal with whilst remembering her code name, but you knew my father." At this, Yves nodded solemnly; Wyndham Hardwicke was a very thorough individual, and was always prepared.

Isabella continued, "As far as I know, he never told anyone else these names, and I certainly never did. I had forgotten all about them to be honest until that woman used the name."

"Did you meet her again?" Yves asked.

"Yes. After that first encounter I kept expecting her to appear around every corner; never have I had to concentrate so hard on keeping my wild thoughts and distraction disguised" she said, reaching for her old tutor's arm and holding it in hers, "thank you once again for all that you taught me."

Yves squeezed her arm lightly, and asked her to continue.

"It wasn't until much later that I met the woman again, on my last day in Zermatt before I returned home. I was sitting in a cafe I had taken to frequenting on that trip, and was talking with the owner, thanking him for his service during my stay, when I saw the woman

94

approach from behind him. She smiled, looked out of the Cafe and across the outside roof-square towards a passageway leading into the buildings on the other side, and then left. I made my excuses and followed, but when I reached the passage she was nowhere to be seen. I walked through it until it opened out onto another roof-square between the tower- buildings, but again nothing – no sign of her and an empty square. Then I noticed a small shop-front in the corner, and walked across to find it was an antique bookshop."

Yves murmured to himself, as if agreeing with something, and Isabella looked at him quizzically.

"Continue, please"

She shrugged and went on, "The woman was alone in the store, sitting patiently behind a desk in the centre of the room and surrounded by shelves and shelves of old books. It was really musty", she said, remembering the smell vividly, "and dimly lit".

"You have many questions", the woman stated.

"Who are you?" Isabella asked.

"That is certainly one of them, but I suspect the least interesting."

"What was it you called me on the steps?" Isabella asked, remaining cool, remembering her training.

"You know what it was, but I will indulge. I called you Chamois, as your father the Bouqetin once did."

"How can you know that?"

"I can only tell you that I know of the names Chamois and Bouqetin"

Isabella could feel the frustration and anger rising inside her. How did this woman know these things, what kind of game was she playing? She thought of the white room, thought of its power to soothe, wished she were there now, held the thought in her mind.

She tried a new tack, asking, "Why have you brought me here?"

"Ah", replied the woman bookseller, "there I can be of more help. I have shown you a path to my door that you might take it. Now that you have, I would like to tell you something."

Isabella waited, desperately wanting to know what the woman would say, yet betraying not a flicker of her longing.

"I am a bookseller, but sometimes I visit the library. You will be welcome there too."

Isabella stood waiting for the woman to continue, but she seemed to have nothing more to say.

She turned back to Yves, continuing, "and that was it. Nothing more. I kept asking more questions, but she deflected them all."

They had walked some way through the wood now and come upon the forester's store shed. Isabella went inside briefly and came out with two folding chairs, which they carried some way off the path before settling in a small dell, surrounded by a dark low canopy of gnarled yew trees.

Yves had not yet commented on Isabella's account, pondering his response carefully as they found somewhere unobvious to sit.

"Thank you for allowing an old man to rest a little", he began, before turning his attention to the matter at hand. "You would like to hear my reaction no doubt, but this is not the only strange instance I think. Would you tell me some more before I speak?"

Isabella was confused. This must mean something to Yves, she felt sure of it, and yet it was impossible to tell by his measured reaction - the man was a master of emotional concealment. She had come this far, trusted him this much, that she felt she must continue.

"There have been other incidences", she confessed, "always unexpected, and always infuriatingly vague. In fact sometimes I thought I was imagining it. Once I helped an elderly man step up into a tram, and when we both sat down he opened a book and murmured something about the library and had I been there yet, but whether that meant anything at all I have no idea. Other times were unambiguous though. Always a stranger, usually passing me classified documents from the Council or the Senate – never anything explosive but often enough to give me an edge in a negotiation round, to help me see weakness or opportunity where I hadn't seen it before."

She could see the look in the old Councillor's face: this sounded a frightening risk, accepting information without knowing from whence it came, making herself beholden to some shadowy figures who had never declared themselves.

"I know, but it was never anything incriminating – just helping me to see things, to see people from a different perspective. Helpful, but not damning. Yet never would they answer my questions about the Library, where it is, what it is even. Clearly these people, whoever they are, seem to have penetrated some of our most closed institutions. I understand that I should be wary."

Yves still held her in his non-committal yet nurturing gaze, the professional listener working to find out what else she had to say, but Isabella was nearly done. She told him of her most recent visit, of the man who called himself the "Assistant", and of the invitation; although she was cagey enough to omit where it would take place, and Yves knew her well enough not to ask – she was protecting both of them.

The elder Councillor leaned back gently in the wooden chair, feeling the individual slats through his coat as he stretched his arms wide before letting them return to rest in his lap.

"My dear Isa", he began, "I have often wondered if we would have this conversation. You have told me a tale that frankly unsettles me to the very core. If this group, these people, whatever they are – if they have the sort of access you are implying, and yet do not explain why they assist you, then we must question what their motives really are. Are they benevolent, or is there something more sinister in their machinations? Why should they choose to assist *you*? Yet leave this to one side for a moment, for we shall return to it. First, I have my own story to tell, a story that involves a young girl, and a dear departed friend."

"Your father asked something of me, something that has often troubled me since. He asked me to tell you this if he died, but only – and he was very insistent on this point – only if you asked about it first. If you confided in me any concerns about an organisation called the Library, or about the Librarian himself, then I was to tell you that he, Wyndham Hardwicke, trusted them. I was also to tell you to be careful because within this organisation, like some others with which you are now well-acquainted, there exist different factions. Lastly I was to tell you that not everybody connected with the Library is always quite what they seem."

Isabella was rapt, and had long given up any pretence at disinterest. A message from her father! She had been right to talk to Yves, obviously she had been right.

"However," he continued, and saw her shoulders sag with the word, "that is all he said, and I'm afraid I can tell you no more. Not because I do not choose to, but because I simply do not know. I asked your father of course, but he would not tell me anything more, not even permit me to question him. In the years since I have attempted to find out what little I could of this Librarian and his associates, but they are like ghosts, as whispers on the wind. I hear the occasional rumour, the odd murmur, but nothing more. Whether or not you choose to find out is in your hands now".

Yves sighed, frustrated by his failure to discover anything more about these elusive figures, yet relieved that this last promise to his greatest friend had finally been honoured.

So, thought Isabella, her father had thought this organisation important enough to leave her an explicit message, to give her advice from the grave. He trusted them, and so should she; but the message also included a warning to be on her guard. So be it; she would accept the mysterious invitation to a meeting at Artur's, and find out who these people were, once and for all.

"And now my dear, this cold air is beginning to bite. Shall we resume our walk?"

They did so, wandering through the peaceful woodland, mostly in silence, feeling the changes in mood as they left the haunting power of the ancient yews behind them and emerged upright into the light environs of the undressed larch and shimmering birch. They found their way back to the path that meandered its way through the arboretum, taking pleasure in the sheer diversity of life they found even in this darkest of seasons, both quietly thanking Isabella's ancestors for planting the library of seeds that had created these towering bookshelves, this vast catalogue of the greats from across the ancient world standing tall as the statues that once adorned the temples of the Greeks.

Isabella had one more thing she wanted to ask of Yves before they returned to the house, a much simpler but no less pressing favour she needed of him.

"Daniel Mason and his wife are coming this evening," she began.

Yves nodded to show his recognition of the name, and what the name meant to Isabella.

"I haven't seen much of him over the past few years, hardly at all since rising to the Senate, but I would like to see them before the wedding. I doubt I will get to talk much to any of my old friends on the day itself, although they are all invited."

If Yves read anything into this at all, he would not be so insensitive as to show it.

"Yves, I am worried about Daniel. Haldane's lackey Davis has co-opted him to help the Civil Guard in their repeated searches for dissidents hiding in the Estuary waters."

"Yes, I had heard this also," he replied.

"Really?" asked Isabella, surprised.

"I maintain a watchful eye over your," he hesitated, looking for the right words, before continuing, "over those who have been close to you".

Isabella had not expected this, but perhaps she should have done, knowing the care her father's friend took over her well-being.

"Thank you," she replied. "I worry about anyone in such prolonged contact with the Guard; I worry about Daniel's naivety in dealing with these people."

"I understand your concerns", he replied. "You would prefer I spoke to him?"

"If you can; you will be seated opposite him this evening, and next to his wife."

"Saskia?" Yves asked, checking he had her name correct, "and the child is Alexandria I believe".

"They call her Lexi."

"Consider it done. I will leave no implication that this comes from you?"

"Thank you again, old friend", she confirmed, as they walked back through the ornamental gardens to the house where Yves made his apologies and retired to the guest-room that had been prepared for him, to try and get some rest before the rigours of the banquet that would follow that evening.

Isabella made her way to the house's white room, an exact replica of the one found in her town house – the very same dimensions, the painted table supporting an empty vase, one of an identical pair. Yet the vista from the tall windows differed, which affected the quality of the light in the featureless room; subtle, but enough for Isabella to know even with the view obscured by turning the panes to their frosted setting. She preferred it here; this was where she could get closest to finding peace, if only for a few precious moments.

She would need the power of the room today, she knew, to focus on what must be achieved this evening; a myriad of tasks to perform without ever appearing to be do anything other than enjoying herself and the company of her fiancé. There would be close to eighty people at this evening's dinner, and this would not be the last before the celebrations peaked with the colossal social gathering that would be the wedding itself. Several thousand guests: everyone that mattered in the political and commercial spheres of London as well as countless dignitaries, representatives, and people of power from their allied city-states across the continents. It would be far more like a summit-meeting than a festival of love; an opportunity to deepen the union between whole peoples rather than just two. If the girl of the nearby thicket mourned for the loss of her innocent dreams, no-one would ever know. Inviting Daniel and Elisabeth was perhaps the only indulgence she had allowed Isabella; for the rest, Senator Hardwicke would request their company. Despite everything that had happened between the three of them, despite all the pain, a part of her would always hold those University days most dear; a different life, when she could forget what had always been expected of her. She would speak to Daniel this evening, if briefly; she could not allow herself more. Elisabeth she would not see until the wedding itself, and even then she might not actually have time for more than a passing nod; but she would be there, and that was in some sense right.

With a sharp sniff she brought herself back into focus; no time for her thoughts to stray down that path today. Time to prepare.

thirteen

The pinnacle of the Stephenson building sparkled as sunlight glittered on the windowed uppermost layer of the cone-like structure; inside, it held the private office of the Lord Mayor, affording him uninterrupted views in all directions through this circular wall of tilting glass. Haldane often thought the room deliberately inappropriate; if it gave the incumbent Mayor the idea that he was master of all he surveyed, he only need descend three floors to the Council chamber to be reminded of his emasculation. Lately he was feeling the strain more than usual, and the darkness around his eyes was not the only sign; he had noticed himself becoming increasingly short-tempered and fractious, and was all the more frustrated to be aware of it happening and yet unable to stop snapping at the ineptitude of those around him.

Something needed to be done about their dissident problem, and quickly. Haldane's political senses, finely tuned through constant use in the military and civil hierarchies, told him he was losing the support of at least parts of the Council. Yet for all the might of their security apparatus, they didn't seem to be getting very far. He had called the heads of the various agencies to meet him here, in his private office, so that they could try and form a coherent strategy. Previous attempts, held in the always-crowded briefing room, had been plagued by grandstanding and rivalry between the different organisations, yet the Mayor was hopeful that they could achieve more in a small group, with just the real players present.

Davis was first to arrive, the feared Civil Guard Commissioner and well deserving of his reputation. The two men greeted each other as the old comrades that they were, a firm double-handed shake with their eyes locked. Haldane was one of the few people in London who felt comfortable in Davis' presence, the loyalty they had to each other running far deeper than any other; but even he didn't approve of all the man's methods. They had both risen to become powerful men in the civilian structure on their return from the Wars, thanks in no small part to their continued loyalty to each other, and the small group of officers from their former unit; but they had adapted to civilian life differently. Some would argue that Davis hadn't adapted at all, that his mindset of perpetual conflict was what allowed him to justify – to himself at least – the actions and tactics he used; either that, or he didn't see the need for moral justification at all, which worried them even more.

"You look tired," he stated gruffly.

Haldane shrugged his shoulders in response; he was. "Did you see the others on your way up?"

"General Lucas is on his way; didn't see the rest."

"Before they arrive, tell me what you think."

"About the terrorists?" confirmed Davis. He didn't need to think for long. "Find them, shoot them."

Haldane wasn't surprised by Davis' disregard for the niceties of courts and trials; but locating the dissident groups was proving to be their biggest challenge, after losing their only lead somewhere in the Medway. The Mayor didn't want to antagonise his ally and knew that he would be feeling this failure keenly, but still he had to ask. "Tell me; what happened in the marshes."

"I want to say it was a fuck-up and move on, but it wasn't. Sparrow did everything the way I'd have done it. We even had the river guy, Mason, helping us. The enemy had a good plan, and it worked. Next time they won't be so lucky."

"Mason impressed me on the Dam", Haldane mused, deflecting the conversation. "I met his father years ago, the engineer; he was a competent man. I hadn't met the son before though. "

"Me neither. Natural leader" replied Davis. "Wasted in his current post. We are going to keep using him on the river."

The Mayor indicated his approval; he had thought the same. "Do you think they are still using the estuary to hide?"

Davis seemed to think on this a while, before replying, "I doubt they have a permanent base. From what we got out of the one we caught, I think they use the river to move around unnoticed, or when they feel us getting too close. Either way, we'll make those waters hostile."

"Gates? The one you caught?" asked the Mayor

"Yes Gates; do you know, he was a teacher? Fucking primary. What does that tell you?"

"That they are living amongst us" the Mayor replied, "Probably organised in cells, harder for you to find them all"

"Exactly; but piece by piece we'll get there. You know how it is with these things."

"I think I would rather not know", replied the Mayor truthfully. He shuddered to think what Davis would do to any of these people they did get their hands on, all in the name of information extraction; Gates must have been lucky, to die as quickly as he did. He had seen the man at work, decades before; but in those days, Haldane thought, war changed the rules. In those days he had helped.

The stocky figure of General Lucas, head of the standing army, appeared at the door moments later, accompanied by the director of the municipal police and the last of the group, Julio Soon of the Pioneers, the special forces agency. Haldane thought of them as para-military spies, and was fairly shocked when he was appointed Lord Mayor to discover that they didn't really answer to him. Soon directed the clandestine organisation, calling on the other agencies when necessary for operational support, and answered only to a secret committee of the three Senators, the Mayor, and an appointed Council member combined. In practice, this gave him a very free rein.

"Gentlemen. Thank you for coming. Have any of your organisations made any progress since we last convened? Director, perhaps you can begin?"

The police chief, whose functional responsibilities meant that his organisation was usually more concerned with minor transgressions than internal security, had little to report.

"A few minor scuffles with students that led to some inconclusive searches; no, nothing of note."

"General?" asked the Mayor.

"Our sources continue to suggest that the incident on the barrier was not isolated, and that if anything it was the start of a likely increase in activity on the part of these dissidents."

Davis snorted and shook his head in disgust. They all knew his anger with the General for refusing to identify these sources to the Civil Guard, but even Haldane was careful to not put too much power in Davis' hands. A little competition between the agencies discouraged any of them getting complacent.

"Noted General, and we have stepped up the security level as a result of your recommendation", he replied, mollifying the man a little. "Mr Soon, then."

Julio Soon had been looking out of the window towardss the Western hills, an almost vacant expression across his thin-lined face, but now turned back to the group.

"Lord Mayor, gentlemen. In the spirit of co-operation", he began with a subtle reminder of the Pioneers' independence, "I can tell you that we have apprehended an operative aboard a cargo-carrier in the Dover channel following intelligence from one of our external assets. We suspect that this person has links to the group in question. Should conditions necessitate, we shall be calling on the various abilities of agencies represented here to further any lines of enquiry."

fourteen

The vast majority of the North Sea trawling fleet based themselves in Chatham docks; here they could shelter behind the Barrier from the vicious storms in their hunting grounds; here too they could lie in the safety of London's waters, protected from the lawlessness that plagued the seas and any unprotected settlements adjoining them. The need to defend themselves against piracy meant that all the fishing vessels were packed with armaments, and whilst all the city's security agencies were uncomfortable with the amount of weaponry in civilian hands in these communities, even the Civil Guard grudgingly accepted it as a necessity. In fact, London's Naval Defence leaders at Tilsbury relied on the merchant fleet to provide a significant part of their firepower in the unlikely event of an attack on the city's Dam-wall.

The *Arabella III* had arrived in port that evening after a fortnight at sea, their crew exhausted but content with a hold full of Atlantic cod; they knew they were lucky to have had such an uneventful run at this time of year, but the constant cold had been energy-sapping all the same. They tapped their last reserves to unload the haul, hoping the skipper would get a good price at the Corporation market before the shares were divided come morning. For now, the crew slept below as the ship lay peacefully against the wharf. On the bridge, a skeleton watch of one mariner and one marine drank bitter coffee to stay awake through the night; no use losing their pay for the sake of a few minutes doze.

"What's that bugger up to?" said the marine, indicating a figure approaching the bows of the ship in the night shadows.

"One of yours?" asked the sailor, a slight accent suggesting his Scandinavian origins.

"Shouldn't be, unless someone's hopped ashore to satisfy his thirst"

"Going to find out?"

"Aye. Keep an eye on the screens would you?"

"Yes", replied the Swede. It would be nothing, he told himself. One of the crew had been for a swift drink and perhaps some other business, hoping to be back before he was noticed. Or maybe it was some dockside drifter; you got enough of them in places like this, looking for something to steal or somewhere to stow away; people who had nothing left and nothing to lose. That wasn't supposed to happen in the city-states; everyone employed, everyone pulling their weight, that was the idea, but everyone knew it was far from perfect – and getting worse. Anyone who had been to the docks maybe, he thought.

Nevertheless, Olof watched carefully as the marine walked along the port rails towards the bows, flashlight in hand. He checked the screens for any signs of movement on the ship's cameras, but could see nothing. He looked back through the bridge windows, straining to see in the same darkness that the ship's night-vision so easily penetrated.

Where had that marine gone now, he thought to himself? Looking back to the screens, he couldn't see him anywhere; he watched the cycle again as the viewer showed first one part of the ship then another, all empty and in darkness. Wait, had he seen something in that last picture? He pressed the controls, bringing up the previous image – there it was, in the corner, a man's leg protruding from behind some tackle bins, the trouser-stripe of the marine's uniform clear to see.

Now it was time to worry. He moved quietly to the rear where he had stashed his gear under one of the consoles, ready in case of this eventuality, the small chance that he had been betrayed whilst lying low at sea; unlike the women, he had known John Gates, had been part of the same cell for some time. Opening the zipper he easily found the night goggles and put them on before quietly going down a level and out onto the decks.

There were four ways off the boat, and he didn't like any of them. The gangplank was too well lit, and jumping into the water to swim for it would make too much noise if anyone were watching; that left the fore and aft warps, the thick cables holding the vessel fast against the harbour, both of which would be obvious to anyone waiting for him to make a bolt for it.

He could sit it out and wait, try and move ashore with the rest of the crew in the morning, hope to lose himself in the bustle, but that carried its own risks; one watcher could become many by the morning, and they had only seen one. It was a dangerous assumption to make, but he had to take his chances; he would go now. He started out aft, moving slowly through the gloom and quietly lowering himself over the stern rails before climbing hand over hand down to the dockside.

Nobody waiting for him at the bottom, just a deserted quay. He moved into the darkness behind one of the loading cranes, and watched the Arabella for any signs of movement or alarm whilst catching his breath. Still silence. It could have been a thief, he thought, they might not be after me; maybe he should have stayed and raised the alarm?

No, too much of a coincidence; he couldn't risk it. Silently cursing, Olof slipped away into the raucous taverns of Chatham and the hills beyond.

fifteen

The babysitter had arrived on time, but Daniel had not. When he eventually walked through the door at Sawyer's Hill, cheeks blown red and hair thick with salt-spray, he only had twenty minutes in which to wash and dress.

"I'm sorry darling, but I'm here now; it wasn't easy to get away", he said, seeing the frustration in his wife's face. Like any woman confronted with her husband's past lovers, she wasn't completely comfortable with Isabella Hardwicke, and the prospect of an evening spent with the political classes in formal society hardly excited her either.

"Honestly, I'm sorry" Daniel repeated, taking the time to hug her properly before kissing her quickly and disappearing upstairs to dress.

Saskia followed him back into their room, checking her hair arrangement for the third time that evening whilst her husband showered, and then talking to him as he dressed.

"How much longer will you be working with the Civil Guard?" she asked.

"I don't know. I expect until they find these people they are looking for, or until they start looking somewhere else."

"Don't they have their own boat people? They make enough show of it screaming up and down the place," she said, her distaste clearly evident.

"They know the river pretty well, I'll give them that," Daniel replied, aware of his growing admiration for Sparrow and his team, as rivermen.

"Remember who they are Daniel. They might be afloat but they're still Civil Guard," admonished his wife, worried about the tone of his compliment.

Daniel nodded; he had to keep telling himself the same thing. He was an ecologist, a guardian and manager of the estuary's natural processes, and not a guardsman, he thought. Every liberal idea he held sacred, every memory of arguing against his father and the man's pragmatism, warned him against these people; and yet he found himself drawn to the hunt, and knew that the others aboard could see it, that they were accepting him as one of their own.

"I don't believe in terrorism", he said aloud, almost without realising it. Saskia looked at him, puzzled. "You know that. If they want me to help them find terrorists, then I will" he continued, taking solace in the power of the label; but still feeling uneasy inside about the alliance he had been forced to make.

sixteen

The Assistant walked through the quadrangle, the horseshoe of stone-columned study buildings with their tall squared windows facing onto the much larger Library itself at the top of the square. The courtyard area was mostly grass, with a single gravel path around the outside and two paths crossing at right angles through the middle. He took the central path that led to the steps and the vast Library doors, his progress slowed by the groups of scholars crowding both directions. On reaching the door, he raised his cane to knock on the smaller door set inside the larger one, preferring function over effect; before he could do so, it swung open, and the Librarian stepped out to join him.

"He escaped?"

"This time", replied the Assistant, "one of our number will follow"

"The Chamois?

"She will come, I believe."

"Let us hope so", the Librarian answered, taking the Assistant's arm and turning him to walk down the steps to the now strangely deserted quadrangle. As they reached the gravel, the old man listened, delighted, to the crisp crunching of his feet on the gravel. They walked together to the centre of the silent square, before the

Librarian continued, "Your colleagues have made some disturbing reports; I am sure you are aware."

"It has come to my attention, yes."

"Perhaps you should visit Soon".

seventeen

Like a many-tentacled octopus, the terminus at Victoria rose from the tangled confluence of incoming stilted rail lines, its central translucent dome dominating the adjacent skyline and bullying the neighbouring buildings so that they seemed to cower before it. There would be a special service this evening laid on especially for the Senator's guests, to cope with the number of high profile citizens and guests all making the journey to the normally quiet backwater. Daniel and Saskia barely made it to the platform in time, and even then almost missed getting aboard thanks to the queue of latecomers waiting to pass security.

They sat in uncharacteristic quiet as the train accelerated them eastward, watching as the line finally emerged from the urban cliffs and rose above the vast carpets of the industrial agriculture complex that dominated this edge of the city, all irrigated from the gargantuan lakes hollowed into the bedrock at Windsor and Slough which the train now rose above, its stilts supported on a narrow causeway that bisected the vast stores of water that kept London alive.

Saskia, concerned about the man she loved; Daniel, torn between the excitement of the chase and the hints of his own self-loathing, and no chance of an alcoholic release this evening, not in this company. Onwards they sped, past the aquaculture district and its salmony inmates, and then the real prisons packed with those judged to pose a threat to the state, row after row, acre after acre of character-less iron-barred boxes; and then finally through, and past the various rail-stop settlements occupied by those who could afford to live away from the centre, before beginning the gradual rise through the hills towards their destination.

In the next carriage Julio Soon of the Pioneers sat placidly watching the same view whilst calmly considering their recent capture. The man they had picked up was more mercenary than dissident, someone they had linked to a number of uprisings in distant cities over the years. "A man of no state who seems to flail against any kind of civilizing force", his subordinate had said, describing the prisoner. Soon knew better; the man was not uncivilized. In his own anarchist way, the man agitated for a different societal order than that chosen by the city-states of old Europe, but the man still believed in a society of sorts. Soon could understand his prisoner; in some ways they were alike, both labouring in the darkness to promote or protect their own chosen cause. It was a shame that the man's thinking was so one-dimensional, so dogmatic; had they made him see reason, see it all for the sham it was, appealed to his instincts of self-preservation, the man could have made a competent agent. As it was, he doubted they would get much out of him, any leads on the real forces in the underground; more likely scraps, bit-part players like the man himself.

The guests were collected from the station in a fleet of ten-seater short transit craft, the pauses between them allowing a staggered arrival at the house. Isabella was greeting their guests together with Evelyn at the entrance to the hall, her white-blonde hair cascading in ringlets down upon the tight-fitting black ballgown that so flattered her athletic frame. Their personal secretaries stood ready in the wings with little reminders: a title here, a child's name there; each welcome as seemingly warm and personal as the next. Evelyn was genuinely enjoying himself, she noticed with relief. Composure in society was more than a pre-requisite for the husband of a Senator, particularly during their trips abroad; but if he could find pleasure in the task as well, all the better. Yes, she was fond of his infectious optimism and bonhomie, although she had to stifle the image of a happy Labrador as it appeared in her mind; too cruel.

When it was Daniel's turn to meet the hosts, it was Isabella's secretary who whispered in Evelyn's ear.

"Daniel Mason, I's friend from University, Dam Authority, Estuary engineer, wife Saskia, daughter Lexi."

Isabella spoke first, according to custom. "My dear Saskia, you look wonderful this evening", which was more than an empty compliment as both women knew; she looked fantastic despite Daniel's making them rush to the station.

"Senator, it is lovely to see you and your lucky fiancé", she replied with a grin. Despite the tension lurking beneath their relationship, the women did admire each other; had the situation been different, they might even have been friends.

Evelyn spoke next. "Finally we meet Mrs Mason, and may I say it is your husband who is the lucky man" he said, unaware of the irony of his comment, "and Mr Mason, a pleasure to meet such an old friend of my dear Isabella."

Daniel smiled at both of them, replying, "Please, call me Daniel". As they were ushered on towards their seats to make way for the next arrivals, he couldn't resist glancing back at Isabella and raising his eyebrows. So this is the man, he seemed to be saying with an impish grin. She saw him and winked back, before enthusiastically welcoming a rather fat man and his fragile-looking partner, Corporation-types and cousins of Evelyn.

On the way to their seats, Saskia asked Daniel, "Did you think she would ever marry, Dan?"

"I'm not sure really. Seemed harmless enough",

"Yes, I know what you mean."

By the time all the guests had entered the hall, they were almost ready to serve; and the meal when it came was unfussy yet refined, somewhat like their host. Daniel and Saskia hardly had a chance to speak through all five courses; she had been subjected to an interminable lecture on the benefits of a new type of material by an enthusiastic designer, whilst Daniel had been involved in a more interesting discussion on the immigration laws further down the long-aisled table, doing his best to say nothing controversial in this unfamiliar gathering on this most explosive of subjects. It was not until the liqueurs that Daniel found himself being invited out for a smoke by Councillor Epstein, Isabella's old confidante. He glanced at his wife, waiting for her acknowledgement before following the elder man out onto the broad heated balcony.

"I am afraid your wife is rather suffering this evening, Daniel. I tried steering the subject away from fabric permeability ratios, but to no avail; I suspect she will only escape when the tables are cleared."

"Councillor, how good to see you again after all this time."

"And you Daniel. Congratulations on finding yourself such a remarkable wife; and I believe you have a daughter, Alexandria?"

Daniel smiled at the old politician; Isabella had taught him to spot all their tricks long ago. "Thank you, sir. I suspect you have not invited me out here to discuss Lexi."

"Indeed no, but the pleasantries are important, I think we both agree," replied Yves, eyes twinkling.

Daniel was waiting for it; was this going to be a warning? Isabella's old guardian testing the ground, one last check that nothing would upset this carefully choreographed match? Daniel had no doubt that the wedding represented some kind of strategic alliance between various clans, although he hoped for Isabella's sake that it was more than that as well. He thought of his own marriage, how it had been held together by his and Saskia's deep love for each other, particularly in the difficult times; he hoped Isabella had found something similar, although he doubted it now he had seen them together.

"She doesn't love him, but you already know that," said Yves, correctly guessing what Daniel was thinking. "With her, this may be the better way. Although not for the two of us, I think."

Daniel didn't know how to respond, so waited for the Councillor to continue.

"I had a different subject in mind, to discuss over these wonderful aromas", said Yves, surprising Daniel as he brought out a small pouch of cigars and they each took one, taking turns to use his cutter and then light them. The taste was subtle, a blend of rosewood and vanilla, with a slight hint of honey; rare, delicious, slightly narcotic but utterly harmless, their effect was to slightly relax the smoker, nothing more.

"As you may or may not know, I sit on the Council's internal security committee, and as such am privy to some of the less-celebrated parts of the government machine", he began, pausing to see the impact of this swift subject change on the younger man. "I understand that you are playing an active role in the waterborne segment of the current searches; seconded to the Guard's River Patrol." It was not a statement and not a question, and Daniel recognised as much. "I wonder if you fully understand who you are working with?"

Daniel wondered where the Councillor was going with this, and why. Yes he was helping the Guard, yes he wouldn't normally associate himself with the actions of the Council's internal security force, but why would a member of the Council have a problem with this?

"You know as well as I the rumours that surround the Civil Guard", Epstein continued, "and I can tell you this in confidence. Most of them used to be just that – rumour deliberately spread as a deterrent to any wrongdoers, using a carefully crafted reputation as a weapon in itself. This you may have guessed at, or maybe you think there is no smoke without fire?"

Correct, thought Daniel. "As you say," he replied, "I suspect they are not a force of innocents. But neither are those who seek to cause indiscriminate injury or death to ordinary people. There were children on the Dam when they let off that device," Daniel continued, articulating the very arguments he kept repeating to himself. "I think them the lesser of two evils; that is all."

"I understand your sentiment, Daniel, and I do not disagree with it. All I would say is remember who you are dealing with. Believe me, there are elements within our Civil Guard who make that manufactured reputation seem like a tale from the nursery. If you seek to balance one bad with another, keep an eye on which side you think worse."

"Surely you don't support the terrorists?" asked Daniel, unsure of what the Councillor was trying to tell him.

"Not for a moment", snapped the elder man, "not for a single instant. I have spent my life supporting civilised rule, and fighting those who would challenge it."

"I'm sorry, I didn't mean to imply" Daniel responded quickly.

"Accepted. But take heed of what I said. I tell you this in the spirit of friendship, as we have spoken before, some time ago".

Daniel remembered the conversation all too well. The paternal Epstein trying to tell a confused young man why he should leave his lover be, trying to appeal to Daniel's reason, explaining how they could have no future together, that the family would never allow it to happen; Daniel knowing that the old man's concerns were irrelevant, that he didn't understand, that he was too late, but furious nevertheless, and deeply devastated. How he had understood, much later, what Yves Epstein had really been saying, misinformed though he was; how he found himself belatedly realising that the words had indeed been in friendship and not in malice.

"I will be careful, although I have little choice but to assist on them on the river. Thank you for thinking of me."

"And now, let us speak of happier things," Yves replied. "Tell me about young Lexi; which of you does she take after?"

They both smiled, Daniel regaling the Councillor with his five year old daughter's exploits in river dinghies as they finished their smokes and wandered back inside.

Daniel stopped at the door; he might have frozen had the subtle effects of the smoke not smoothed his reaction. He could see a familiar figure on the opposite side of the hall, the man with the cane from the day on the Dam, the man he was sure had watched him throughout the Mayor's speech.

"Councillor," he asked quietly and indicated with his eyes, "who is that man?"

Epstein looked, replying, "You mean Soon or the other gentleman?"

"The one with the cane?"

"I'm afraid I do not know; which means he is probably one of the Senator's foreign guests. The man he is talking to is Julio Soon, head of the Pioneers, which would make sense if he is from abroad."

"I saw him on the Mayor's stage at the Dam, the day of the attack", Daniel confided.

"That is a little odd. Why is it you ask?"

"No reason really, just a feeling."

"I'll see if I can find out – I'll let you know if I do. Now I really must go and relieve your wife."

Unfortunately, Epstein did not have chance that evening to enquire of Isabella the mystery man's identity; for had he done so, she would have been as surprised as Daniel to find him in her house.

eighteen

Jonty was the last to leave, packing the books roughly into his tattered satchel, pushing the chair under his desk so that the legs squeaked against the lino flooring and then running after his friends, a rushed "seeya miss," aimed in the general direction of his teacher on the way out of the room. Elisabeth was exhausted, her head aching and her body weary after another long day in the classroom; eight lessons, two breaks and a half hour for lunch, six days a week, fifty weeks a year. She could have chosen an easier path, even in her profession; could have accepted one of the many posts she was offered amongst the Corporation schools, but she was blind to their promises of shorter hours, more support and better facilities. She had long decided that she would return to the streets of her youth, teaching where she was needed.

The sons and daughters of Corporation employees were entitled to attend their firm's schools, and the government kids were allocated places at the bigger of these institutions, but the Council was also supposed to provide an educational safety-net for the many children whose parents failed to qualify for places, or couldn't afford to pay for them. The criminally overcrowded public schools were the result, and they were uniformly inhabited by the poor, the displaced, the recent refugees and the unclaimed orphans. This was the world that Elisabeth had been born to; and to a life bereft of privilege, she had brought hope. Tarnished now, battered and bent by the grind of real living, but still it shone inside of her, a sparkling shield with which to face down disenchantment and despair.

She would be meeting Batista this evening aboard the woman's floating home, which meant an hour's walk down through the water-meadows to the towpath; if she set off straight away she could be there before dark, and then return with the frosty morning. She put on her winter coat, wrapping a thick scarf around her exposed neck to counter the biting breeze that would blow off the estuary, and left the classroom behind her. She had been looking forward to the walk; time to put her thoughts in order, to reflect on the last few weeks and try and make some sense of it. The way the screens had misconstrued their operation on the Dam; no-one would have been in danger if the evacuation planning hadn't been run by idiots. Errors by the officials of one agency or another, all turned and warped and mashed into something else entirely, the pretence of a dangerous terrorist attack when it was nothing of the sort; sure there had been some risk but more to them than anyone else, the way they had planned and envisaged it.

And then the escape, and poor John Gates, and their near capture in the Medway, and now living in fear that the organisation had been or would be compromised and that they would be the victims of the real terror merchants, Davis and his unreconstructed warmongering cronies.

She tried to clear her mind of these thoughts that had been swirling, ever-present in her consciousness for days now; tried to listen for the calls of the waders, to watch for them overhead, but the colour was draining out of the picture as the sun slipped silently away. She thought next of Daniel Mason. Of all the days to meet him, and then to see him again, centre-stage and centre-screen, side by side with that fraud Haldane; how her heart had lifted to meet him on the bridge, and how it had sunk again to see him woven into the propaganda assembled against them. How she craved to see him once more, to hear his voice tell her everything would be alright; how she disgusted herself with such childish desires. He was inescapably a part of her, but a part that she had survived well enough without. She made the choice years ago, although it wasn't much of a choice, and had finally closed that part of herself like a sealed locket; always with her, but never to be opened again. He was married now, she knew, and had a child; never to be opened again.

She could see the smoke rising from the barge's chimney long before she was close enough to see the blackened vessel itself, moored on springs and grounded by the retreating waters. Knocking first on the side, she clambered aboard to a chorus of muffled barking.

"Vasco, quiet", came her friend's voice from below. "Elisabeth, is that you?" She sounded weak, disorientated maybe.

"Yes it's me," Elisabeth replied, entering the wheelhouse door before descending the stairs into the aft cabin. Batista was sat on her bunk clutching her winter rugs around her old frame, her eyes red from rubbing and the tears still wet and salty on her cheeks. Elisabeth sat down next to her, wordlessly putting an arm around

Batista's hunched shoulders and gently smoothing the back of her head. "Tell me."

"I am sorry my dear, you must think me weak to be in such a state."

"No. But do tell me what has upset you, please?"

"I am worried about my brother."

"Why?"

"He has missed the last three radio contacts".

Elisabeth understood; although she had never met the Batista's beloved brother, she knew that the two kept in regular contact with each other when they could, through a code known only to them both. For one of them to miss a pre-arranged contact gave grounds for concern; to miss three certainly did. As far as Elisabeth knew, the woman's elder sibling was part of the international underground, dead as far as the authorities in the major cities were concerned, but in reality alive and well-hidden, and as active as ever.

"Where was he, when you last spoke?" she asked.

"Coming north, towardss us. We were to meet off the Kentish Coast and then go south; oh you must think me a coward for planning to run away" said the old woman, her tears starting to flow freely again.

"I will never think that of you my friend; your courage gives me the will to fight on."

"I was going to invite you to join us"

"But you knew full well I never would; my life is here, whatever it may lead to."

"Yes my dear, I knew. Now I fear for him more than I do for myself."

"It could easily be a safety precaution, radio-silence through the channel and the straits".

"Maybe" replied the old Portuguese, shaking her head as she said it, not believing her own words.

"What will you do now?" Elisabeth asked.

"Wait."

nineteen

"This is the one?" asked the woman.

"It is."

"Then let us proceed".

The man took a small device from his suit pocket, and tapped the screen a few times. After a few moments the front door swung open, revealing a small entrance hall lined with coats with three further doors leading off it.

"After you," he said.

They opened the middle door, and proceeded into a comfortable sized living room, three sofas arranged around an imitation fire-screen, and a dining table with chairs beyond them. They sat in the sofas, and waited.

Not much later, Pennells, the head of security at the Barrier Authority, arrived home from work to find the door to his apartment ajar. Puzzled and concerned, he entered with caution, his long-dormant training jerking rustily to life.

"Mr Pennells", began the woman, "do close the door and join us."

For whatever reason, he felt compelled to do just that, returning to shut the outer door and then taking a seat on his own couch opposite the strangers. They both looked to be in their late twenties, were both smartly dressed, and were both attractive; but Pennells had no idea who they were or what they were doing in his apartment. Their attire and brazen confidence suggested they were here on someone's authority he thought, probably the Council.

Before he had chance, the woman spoke first.

"You have many questions."

"Who are you, and how did you get in?" he asked in as reasonable tone as he could muster, given the intrusion.

"Both fair questions, but I suspect the least interesting", she replied.

twenty

The atmosphere in Little Smith Street deteriorated sharply with this latest admission.

"Let me get this straight," shouted an exasperated Davis to the corporal standing rigidly at attention in front of him. "You locate the Swede's trawler, you locate the Swede, and then you get the wrong bloody man?"

"Sir".

"Fuck-up"; turning to the rest of the room he continued, "we have to avoid them."

"That was certainly our best chance", mused Pickering, "whilst he was cornered. It will be harder now he's loose in the city".

"Could be anywhere", Davis added angrily. "Get out of my sight", he shouted at the corporal, who at least had the good sense to salute and leave as fast as he could.

"What now?" Davis asked the rest of the room, the senior officers of the Civil Guard, every one of them a veteran who had served with their leader in the campaigns, except for Pickering. He was the exception because Davis needed his intellect and technical ability; he might be more a scientist than a soldier, Davis had said to the rest of his staff, but he thinks like us. Now indeed, several years on, they accepted him as one of their own; some of his suggestions for improving the efficiency of information extraction had proved unexpectedly successful.

"He wants to hide. Let's flush the bugger out," suggested a captain.

"Agreed. Suggestions?"

"If I may?" Pickering began, continuing when bid to, "the sailor who met an unfortunate end at the hands of our directionally-challenged corporal; the Chatham community will want answers. Why not give them one, and issue a warrant for the arrest of his murderer – a certain foreign deck-hand"

"I like it" grinned Davis. "Suddenly we are the good guys. He won't find willing shelter with the mariners against him". He looked around the room, scanning the faces of his top men to see their reaction. His unit wasn't a democracy – far from it, but he valued their collective judgement, had learned to rely on it. "Any objections men?"

"Good plan" said the captain. The others nodded like a pack of hungry hyena.

"Do it."

twenty one

The people of Zermatt were having a tough winter; the blizzards rolled in, one after the other, for days at a time until the snow was drifting in the well-like roof-squares and rising to the second and even third storeys of the surrounding towers. The walls that kept them safe from other humans also kept them trapped in an ice cave that wouldn't ease until the temperatures rose. The outer doors and passageways that in summer opened onto these scarce patches of outdoors amongst the rising mega-building of the interlinked city, were for now sealed closed and the cafes and shops had to rely on their inner entrances.

A man carrying a wooden staff, its end curving back like the crook of a shepherd, walked towards one of these doorways. He stepped inside the bookshop, and found the woman he had come to visit.

"It has been some time", she said in welcome.

"Always too long. And yet also, just so", he replied.

"You have a task for me?"

"If you are willing; and if you agree."

"Then let us talk freely.

twenty two

Isabella kept an office in the Stephenson Cone for when she was required to work with the Council; all three senators did. Hers was on the floor directly below the Council chamber, high enough up the slanting side of the building to ensure a decent view, and fortunate enough to be river-facing so as to avoid the tower-shadow that afflicted the rooms on the other side of the floor. She had decided that she would visit Artur's in Old Chelsea this evening; a discrete search on the net told her that it was a small private members club set up by a charitable foundation, that it was licensed to serve alcohol and light narcotics, but very little else.

Normally she would be very wary of visiting somewhere like this without having her official security team check it out first, but buoyed with confidence from her conversation with Yves and the message from her long-departed father, she felt it an acceptable risk. Anyway, she would not be totally defenceless; to survive the rigours of inter-city politics, the travel and intrigue and constant plotting, she like her colleagues had been extensively trained in self-defence, and armed with some very subtle and very deadly pieces of weaponry that were all but invisible to most types of search-equipment.

She was roused from her net-search by the familiar tone of an incoming screen-call.

"Identify incoming caller", she instructed the screen.

139

"Julio Soon"

"Answer" she said, and moments later she was looking at the unmistakable features of the diplomat-soldier-spy.

"Senator Hardwicke"

"Mr Soon"

"I was hoping to speak with you, privately."

This was not unusual, if not that common. Soon often briefed the three Senators on the status of international security risks as well as providing valuable intelligence on allies as well as enemies in the United Cities. For some reason he preferred to do this individually rather than to them as a group, although it made little difference to them as they always shared information, acting in concert as much as they could.

"I am in my office in the Stephenson, but have an evening engagement. Would you be able to come over now?"

"Certainly Senator. Ten minutes."

Isabella leaned back in her seat as Soon's image disappeared from the screen and it resumed displaying her earlier search results. She stretched her arms behind her head, before clearing them and turning it off. She wondered what Soon would be coming to tell her;

she knew it would be fruitless trying to guess, she had never managed to predict it correctly before, but it amused her to try. Of all the people she dealt with, Soon was the biggest enigma, the most inscrutable and impervious to analysis. On the one hand, he was a master of emotional understanding; she had seen how he could read people instinctively, and then deftfully steer them towards his direction or use; and yet in his own person there seemed to be such unemotional control, with a complete lack of vanity or self-regard. That is not to say he didn't concern himself with his own appearance or standing or the impression he created, but that he only cared about these things for the effects that he could generate in other people through their use; and it seemed to Isabella that the effects were solely to reach whatever goal the Pioneers had decided upon, never for any selfish reason that she could discern. Where did the Pioneer finish and the man begin? Whatever it was that motivated him apart from the efficiency with which he carried out his loosely-defined duties, she could not ascertain. A most remarkable individual she thought; remarkable and frankly quite frightening. She mentally prepared herself for the meeting, hoping that she would not be a subject for Soon's immense powers of manipulation, but wondered whether she would even know if she was.

"Senator Harwicke. May I begin by thanking you for your hospitality last week."

"Of course", she replied.

"But I wonder", he continued, "if you had the chance to enjoy the company of all your guests."

She kept smiling, but was unsure what he meant by this. He likewise seemed to be watching her reaction, she could tell.

"However, this is not a social visit", he continued, as if to draw a line under the previous exchange. "I am afraid I have received some most worrying intelligence. At this stage I have not been able to verify any of its particulars, but it comes from a source that has proved remarkably accurate in the past."

Isabella listened, careful to remember Epstein's training; she should give nothing away in her visage, even if there was nothing to give. Underneath the placid-mask, she was intrigued; where was he going with this?

"I will tell you this in the hope that we might co-operate, that you might tap your own sources on this subject" he continued. Isabella knew he was referring to the edge she had gained from the information passed to her by the nameless representatives of the Library over the past few years; she knew that Soon could not work out where she was getting it from, and knew that this had gained her the man's respect, if there was such a thing.

"Please, go on" she replied, implying her agreement.

"As I say, this is unverified, but there is the possibility of a most serious plot against the very fabric of the city. I am not sure who or what the target is, and whether the threat comes from home or abroad, but I have been warned that something is coming."

Isabella was, on the inside, dumbstruck. For Soon to have come to her with such vague information was so out of character that she decided he must be genuinely worried. If he was, so should she be.

"I have not heard of any credible or present dangers", she replied, "but my eyes are open".

"Thank you. For once, may I ask you to indulge my secrecy in this matter and not share this information with your fellow Senators, at least not yet? I speak to you this evening as someone who has a knack for coming upon information, and not as a city representative."

Isabella was surprised by the subtle complement from the spymaster, but understood his reasons.

"You may."

"Then again, I thank you. You know how to find me", he said, before half-bowing and walking, backwards at first, to the door.

The Thames was sparkling with the reflected light of the City by the time she pressed the shutters closed and locked up her office. It would be quicker to get the tram to her destination but she preferred to walk along the illuminated riverbank; it would give her time to prepare for whatever lay ahead of her at Artur's, time to focus on what she wanted to find out, what mattered most.

The evening air was still chilled by a resurgent winter, unaware that its unbreakable grip was really its final glorious bloom. She watched as her own breath appeared, caught for a second in childish amazement before the spell was broken. A grown woman now, her own wedding a handful of days away. Would she have children of her own? Would they be fascinated too? Strangely, she hadn't really thought about this before, at least not recently; not in the context of marriage to Evelyn. Would she have his children? How did she feel about that?

There would be a time to meditate, she told herself, but not now; now she needed to ready herself. But if not now, when? Would there be a time, if Soon's suspicions were founded? She should ask the Librarian, or whoever she was meeting, if they knew anything of a plot against the City; Soon was right in thinking she had been well-informed in the past.

She was still uncharacteristically lost in thought when she arrived at the old district's sea-wall and had to make her way inland from the river bank to one of the three gates that still controlled access into and out of Chelsea. A walled city within a walled city, a protected haven built with the wealth of its once powerful residents, the old district survived intact as the repeated inundations destroyed the

144

less fortunate neighbouring boroughs years before the great Dam was built to protect the City, the skeletal frames of Sand's End testament to the battle lost just as here the living walls spoke of a siege endured. Within, the traditional two-storied brick streets remained untouched by the whirlwind that had wreaked such destruction around them; their delicate pink and yellow shading incongruously cheerful.

These days, with most of the old residents long since departed for higher elevations, the defences were becoming increasingly dilapidated, but the buildings themselves were kept in good order by their new occupants – those who couldn't afford, or didn't want to live in the Corporation towers with their regulated environments and ever-present screens, and security and concierge and on-site restaurant, their integrated transport links and no need to leave their closeted covered comfortable world. It was home to the craftsmen and women who kept the old skills alive, the watchmakers and carpenters, sculptors and artists, the seamstresses and tailors, and the booksellers; but most of all it was home to the poor. The King's Road was lined with emporia of the reclaimed and restored, a vast recycled bazaar where most things could be found if not today then give me a week sir and see what we can do. It was an enlivening, and sometimes dangerous, place to be.

It was also the most closely monitored area of the city, the Civil Guard's electro-surveillance systems targeted on what they considered to be the cradle of political protest; so predictably, most underground movements avoided coming here. This made the

Librarian's choice of meeting place all the more intriguing to Isabella; it was a combination of meeting in the open, and yet whispering behind their hands. It didn't take her long to find her way through the markets and onto Flood Street, a name that had survived for hundreds of years; didn't they think even then, she thought, it wasn't the most sensible place to live?

It didn't take long to find number fourteen; it was the last one before the street abruptly came to an end, blocked off by the towering flood-wall that loomed above the tiled roofs of the terraced buildings. A plain white door, with a black-painted iron knocker and a small plaque with the establishment's name. Isabella took a deep breath, and knocked.

The door was promptly answered and a nondescript suited doorman led her into a kind of reception area, a hall with closed doors to both sides and some stairs leading to a galleried area above. A door opened on her left, and the man she knew as the Assistant came through it, his ubiquitous cane muffled by thick carpets.

"You are welcome here, as has been promised," he said, beckoning her to follow him up the stairs. He led her round two sides of the open gallery, finally halting by another door.

"You may find what you seek through here; that is your choice".

Isabella could not help but feel wary, despite what Yves had told her, but it was clear that the man with the dog's head cane had nothing more to say so she turned the handle and entered. She found herself in an oak-panelled room, with two armchairs arranged to enjoy the warmth of a fire that was gently sizzling in the hearth. In one of the armchairs sat a small bespectacled man reading from a tattered, ancient-looking volume; the other seat was free. She was aware of the door being closed gently behind her back, but did not feel threatened. She waited patiently behind the empty chair for her host to speak, although he hadn't seemed to notice her arrival; only when he came to the end of the page did he gently close the book, having first placed his flattened marker carefully between the pages.

"Chamois, please sit."

Isabella did so, still holding her tongue, forcing him to take the initiative.

"You are wary", he said, smiling knowingly; "your father was the same."

"I am wary" she affirmed; "with good reason."

"Quite so." He seemed to decide something, putting the book purposefully on the table between them, and then beginning to rise from his seat; Isabella could see that this was not easy for the man so she stood quickly and offered him an arm which he gladly took.

"Perhaps I should show you something, before we speak", he said, his darting eyes scanning her features. Yves would be proud of her; totally calm, fully inscrutable.

"If you so choose, please do", she replied.

"Which door would you prefer?" he asked.

More riddles, she thought; if this man was the Librarian, she could see where his staff got it from.

"I would follow you," she replied. Let him choose, she thought.

"Then this one," he said. "I like the sound of the gravel."

Through the door, Isabella could feel her mask of neutrality shattering, leaving her naked and exposed; this didn't make any sense whatsoever; it was too strange to not react.

They had walked through the door of a sitting room on the first floor of a building in Flood Street, and suddenly she was standing in the open air at the edge of a bustling quadrangle, with five-storey stone buildings making up three long sides and a still bigger structure completing the square, crowds of people walking one way and another, mostly with their arms stacked with piles of thickly bound books.

"My library" said her companion matter-of-factly, "as I suspect you realise".

"How?" she asked, almost choking.

"How?" he replied.

She was dizzy, her placid-mask long evaporated, wishing she were back in the white room. "How is this possible?"

"Go on,"

"We can't be inside the Chelsea walls; you could see this place from all around if we were; and according to my sense of direction", which is very good, she thought to herself, "the river should be where that building is standing."

"It is possible, and that is enough, although I apologise for the presenting it to you like a cheap magician. It seems to help with some; I thought maybe with you, although now I am not so sure", he said, watching her intently.

"I do not know what to think," Isabella said honestly, looking at her feet and gently scraping at the gravel.

"Then let us walk here, and talk", said the Librarian, this time taking her arm, standing straighter and taking the lead himself. When

Isabella looked up to follow, she realised that they were suddenly on their own, the square now somehow deserted.

"The people", she began meekly, straining to widen her eyes.

"Were here, and now are not so. This is as it should be, but it need not concern us. Perhaps I should do the talking, for now"

Isabella just nodded weakly.

"Your father Wyndham, also known to us as the Bouqetin, was one of my assistants, like the man who invited you here. Do you remember that your father often carried a walking stick?"

Isabella, concentrating on her steps, her head bowed and resolutely refusing to look at the buildings that shouldn't be there, did remember. In a small voice she replied, "Hazel branch".

"Ah yes, so it was. All my assistants carry one of some shape or form; it is if you like their tool, or their badge of office, or something close to both. No matter; it is enough to say that your father, a great man, came here often, walked these very stones with me."

Isabella was breathing deeply now, trying to re-assert control over the waves of vertigo.

"You can choose to follow him, if you wish", continued the Librarian, again watching her intently, seeing how his words settled.

"And do what?" she asked.

"Join us, become part of our Library"

"What does that mean", she asked again, lost in her confusion.

He stopped walking, and took both of her hands in his, waiting patiently until she lifted her gaze to his and held it.

"In your case Chamois, it means a choice. You have the power to save your city, if you so choose; doing so, I am afraid, may cost you dearly."

So confused, she felt her legs sway and yet was unable to break away from this gentle man's eyes, seeing in them that his words were somehow true and yet how could they be? What did they mean? Save the city from what? She felt tired, unsteadied and uncentered, but deep inside her mind something had clicked into place and despite all the strangeness she knew that this was right, that this should happen and here, in this place.

"And now we should return to the warmth of our hearth, perhaps?" said the Librarian, sensing the impact he had created in the young woman. Isabella's long-studied self-control had been obliterated, her greatest weapon and constant shield evaporated by the power of her host.

She struggled to walk, having to use the Librarian's arm for support as she concentrated on placing one foot in front of the other in the crunching, crackling gravel path. He stopped them at the side of the building, where he picked up a woman's cane, polished maple with a white marble head; she looked at it, sure she had not seen it on the way past, but accepting this latest incongruity along with the rest.

"Yes, I think perhaps it will do", he muttered to himself, smiling.

"You may find this of some help", he then said to Isabella, handing her the stick. She took it gladly, and holding his arm with her right hand and the steadying cane with her left, they returned to the room in Flood Street.

twenty three

"Thank you General," Haldane said, dismissing the leader of the standing army.

"Sir" he replied, saluting and making for the door to the penthouse office.

Haldane stood by the window, looking out at London and wondering what was causing it. General Lucas had come to him with yet more intelligence reports that all pointed to a markedly rising threat level; small-scale events that individually were nothing much to worry about but that combined were a real cause for concern. Theft from military stores, rising desertion rates in the conscripted ranks, even a full platoon rebelling against their commanding officer and demanding – yes demanding – a replacement. It would not have happened in his time in the military, but in those days they had a war to keep the troops' discipline intact. He was hearing the same worrying message from the municipal police commander as well – vandalism, theft, violent crime all on the rise in the City, and in the wrong parts of it as well. There was always a background level of lawlessness in the slums, that was to be expected; but this was different, the criminals were targeting the Corporation neighbourhoods and even government buildings. And then there was the rise in *organised* unrest, that gaudy message on the wall of the dam just the most provocative of countless examples of silent protest from these dissident groups and their supporters. The very City seemed to be fermenting, a simmering brew of opposition that constantly threatened to turn into violence, and even the ordinary law-abiding citizens were beginning to notice that something was amiss.

Why were his security forces so incapable of identifying the ringleaders? Haldane, perhaps because of his own populist success, perhaps because of his lifetime in uniform, firmly believed that people were led to do things; take out the leaders, he thought, and that would defuse the situation. The protestors were mostly just ordinary people, misinformed by some gifted malcontents and led astray; the people did not really want to challenge the Council. Their society might not be perfect, maybe he could have spent more time and resources trying to improve the conditions in the less affluent districts and less time pandering to the Corporation, but he was sure this was a matter of degree. In the end it was better to be a poor Londoner than to live in the violent, anarchic world beyond the city-state's borders; and slowly they would improve the conditions for everyone. No, he said to himself, these problems are not of our making; they are created by the agitants, by the terminally hard-done-by who would have us all live in misery. They must find the leaders, and cut them out.

The screen on his desk lit up with the face of his secretary, another ex-soldier from the same cadre of officers who dominated his inner circle.

"Commissioner Davis to see you, sir."

"Send him in", he replied.

The mayor's attack-dog came brustling in through the door, his pent-up menace evident even here.

"Tell me some good news, Davis."

"Nothing doing," replied his old ally. "We are still investigating Gates' background, but we only have one firm lead, and he's gone to ground".

"Then find him, man," replied the Mayor angrily.

"Sir," replied the obedient soldier-policeman. The Mayor was the only person who could speak to him like that, and not find his throat ripped out come morning; and Haldane wasn't sure that the Davis hadn't considered it.

"I assume you are not here to tell me about your failures Commissioner?"

Davis grunted, stifling his anger. "We might get somewhere if our own side didn't keep holding things back."

"We have already talked about this; Lucas has his own sources, talk to him" the Mayor replied instantly.

"I mean Soon", Davis snapped back, to Haldane's surprise. "He has one of them in custody, remember. We need to question that man, using *our* methods".

"Have you requested access?" asked the Mayor.

"Denied."

"Then ask again."

"No point. You know he won't give him up."

"So?" asked Haldane.

"Let me raid them, take the prisoner, question him properly."

The Mayor took a sharp breath. He knew what Davis was asking – permission for the Guard to raid the Pioneers wasn't something Haldane could give; that would require approval from the Senators and the Council leaders, and they wouldn't get it. Davis knew this as well, he realised. The man was asking for permission to break the law, to do it in the Mayor's name.

"Sir. Extreme threat requires extraordinary measures; you taught me that sir."

"Do it" replied Haldane, looking at the streets below. He had stepped over a line, but if the Council kept frustrating his actions what was he supposed to do? As a jubilant Davis left him to his own thoughts, the Mayor began formulating a political strategy, one that he had often considered over the past few years. The constitution might not allow him to declare martial law, but he didn't need to, not with the Civil Guard packed with his own men.

twenty four

Elisabeth studied her reflection closely; she could see the tendrils making their subtle marks, advancing onward each morning just that little bit further, always imperceptible and yet always she knew. Today they looked worse because she had been crying the previous evening; tears born of frustration and fear. She had seen the screen-casts of the hunted Chatham murderer, and she had recognised her comrade the Swede; the net was tightening. She had visited the houseboat twice this week but no sign of her friend, and Vasco barking crazily when she came near. She had fed the dog both times from the store of tins in the galley, but when finished he returned straight to his rooftop vigil and his whimpering. Walking back through the darkened fields, she felt the chill fear against her neck; where was Batista?

This morning, though, she must cover the facial lines and the things that caused them; she must take a page from the bride's book and hide her own feelings, her own fears. There would be all manner of people at the wedding, she knew, and not all of them sympathetic; Isabella's position demanded she invite even the people she must, surely, abhor – the Corporation drones and the populists with their lies, the guardsmen and their civilian spies. Although she wanted to avoid it, Elisabeth knew she must attend; her cover story was her own life, and she needed to hide.

As she thought of the wedding itself, the old guilt started to creep up on her; she could see its ghosts looking back at her from the mirror, the hints of the girl she once was. Was she responsible, in part, for this marriage? Isabella had visited her six months before at her public school, come to see her old friend, and see for herself what kind of education the Mayor's policies were providing. Elisabeth had thanked her for that, and they had spoken long into the night, both glad to be together again. Isabella had laughed when asked if she loved Evelyn; and maybe it was the smoke, but Elisabeth was sure she could see real tears in her companion's eyes. Had she caused this? Had she condemned this woman, the beautiful girl from her own past, to a lifetime without love? If she had, she had not meant to.

It was in their last term that it all happened, although perhaps it had been coming since the three of them had met, young and carefree on their first day at University; independent at last, consciously forming their own identities through friendships and fun and wild experimentation. They had become close almost immediately, three children with such different lives bonding together to march into adulthood as one. Daniel, vibrant and radical, the son of the famous engineer whose marvel, the Dam, had saved London; Daniel, so unlike his father, so idealistic, always rejecting the practical in favour of the right. And Isabella, oh Isabella! The scion of the Hardwicke clan, orphaned like Elisabeth and yet born to such a family that she was never left wanting; destined for politics and single-mindedly networking her way through college, and yet always Isabella had cherished her friendship above all, she who would never be able to open any doors. The three of them as unlikely a set of friends as could be imagined, and yet as devoted to each other as they could be.

But then, in that last term, everything had changed. Elisabeth had not realised it was happening at first, had not known the signs to see that Daniel and Isabella had become lovers; although perhaps she had known from the start that Isabella desired him.

Elisabeth only finding out when Isabella insisted they tell her; and only then that she started to see Daniel differently. Only then that she had wanted him too, hating herself for feeling it but unable to stop. Only then that he had fallen in love with her, not with Isabella who loved him so deeply. Only then that she realised she could never do that to the girl who had been so kind to her, so selflessly kind. Only then that she had to deny her own love, to lock it away, never to be opened again. Better that they were both heartbroken, than she betray Isabella.

All these years later, and the subtle aftermath still with them, part of them. Neither of them wanted to embrace Daniel, to take him away from Saskia and his child; the Daniel they both held in their hearts existed only then, lost to them both but alive in their memories. The once overpowering emotions had mellowed with time, but the scars remained. Isabella, her emotions so tightly controlled; she would never allow herself to be hurt like that again, Elisabeth knew. And herself? She wasn't sure, but she knew it must shape her as surely as it shaped her friend. She wondered if Daniel had ever felt it as keenly as they, the tragedy of this abandoned love? The wedding,

Elisabeth thought, didn't call an end to this story; this love-lacking union would confirm it.

Daniel was avoiding his own mirror; he had slept badly, despite being exhausted after another night spent searching the estuary with the River Patrol. Saskia had tried to ask him again the previous afternoon when it would end, when he would be going back to work, but he couldn't tell her the answer. He didn't know, and a part of him didn't want to ask his new taskmasters. Like a narcotic addict he found himself at once both exhilarated by the hunt and disgusted with himself for needing it; and like a an addict he managed to overrule the nagging part of his mind that told him there was something wrong, that told him this wasn't what he, Daniel, really wanted. He could tell his wife was worried, but snapped at her concerns before they had time to settle in his mind; hated that he was pushing her away, yet powerless to stop himself.

At least they could spend this day together, he thought; although the occasion could hardly be less appropriate. Elisabeth would be there, he knew, the Elisabeth whom he had once loved so dearly and who had walked away. He had hardly had time to think about their chance meeting on that bridge, almost the last moment of sanity before his life had been turned upside down by the terrorists and the evacuation, the Guard and the darkness of night after night on the river.

Elisabeth the dreamer, the idealist, the girl who had allowed him to imagine so much was possible in the days of their innocence, with whom he could fly as the birds in the morning sky before he learned the cynical reality of the world. Elisabeth who had broken him, brought him crashing down into the meadow-mud and left him to wallow in his own misfortune. How, he winced to remember, he had found Isabella in the same place by his own hand. Then, how he and Isabella helped each other back to solid ground, but never flew together again. How indulgent we were, he thought, how blind at that age to everything but ourselves and each other.

He had discovered in Saskia a different kind of love, an understanding between them as they grew intertwined like the roots of maturing trees, forgiving and supportive and stable, bending with each other in the breeze. He should be the one holding her on this day, he realised with a flush of shame, he the one taking her hand as they walked in the land of ghosts.

He walked into the bedroom where his wife was sitting at her dressing table, playing again with the arrangement in her hair, a hint of sadness in her smile. Wrapping his arms around her shoulders from above, he said simply, "I love you". It was enough, this time, because she knew he meant it; when they left twenty minutes later, they did so arm in arm.

Isabella was also examining her own reflection, alone in the safety of the white room to gather her thoughts before the dressers and their battalion of stylists arrived to lay claim to her body. She had sat here for a full day after her visit to Flood Street, gripping the maple cane and staring fiercely into the whiteness, only allowing Mister

Johns to enter with a tray of food and instructions that she was not to be disturbed again. Slowly she had regained control over the tempestuous storm of emotion the Librarian had created in her mind; slowly, she had collected herself, and to her surprise felt stronger, more focussed than ever before. She tried to make sense of the meeting with the Librarian, playing it over and over again to look for some meaning she may have missed, but finding only the simple truth – Soon was right, the city must be in danger, and she must try to save it if she could. The Librarian's assistant – at least, the one she thought of as the assistant, for she supposed now that she could also be described in such a way – was to help her. He was downstairs now, the man with the dog's head cane, the man she now knew as Helio; her ally and, she suspected, her protection.

The wedding seemed like a distraction from somebody else's life, an inconvenience, a triviality even; and yet Helio had assured her she should continue as normal, that her role demanded it. Alone amidst this blank canvas she had accustomed herself once more to the idea of the union with Evelyn, reminded herself why she had chosen him above all others, the sense in the match, and although she found her own logic somehow incomplete, she was determined to see it through. Isabella stood, her long locks dancing against the bare skin of her back, allowed her features to settle once more into their familiar pattern of calm, and left her sanctuary behind.

The ceremony itself was to be a simple affair, a pledge from both parties in front of a small group of witnesses and a registrar; although given Isabella's position, the role of the registrar had to be filled by the most senior official possible which according to the Constitution meant the Lord Mayor himself. The real celebrations would begin once this formal proceeding had been completed; food for five hundred and drinks for many times more.

Evelyn stood in the decorated courtyard of the Stephenson's formal garden, an oasis of tranquillity wedged between the monumental Cone and the riverbank. He had not expected to love her as he did; but he couldn't help himself. She was so beautiful, but it was not a fragile beauty for she was strong and confident and always so controlled; and yet he had also seen another side to her, kind and gentle and compassionate even. He was sure that somewhere inside that guarded exterior was the real Isabella, if only she would let him past the mask. Despite everything – the agreements and arrangements and the celebrations planned for a Senatorial wedding, Evelyn still worried that she might not go through with it; in the end, when all titles and positions and families were forgotten, she was still a woman pledging herself to a man. She could still say no. He could feel himself getting clammy in the chill air, feel his own nerves stretched tight.

He had no need to worry; Isabella finally arrived, adorned in the white that he so desired, in a dress that was at once both sleek and flowing, with layers of silk seeming to float over a high-collared and fitted inner gown. She read the expression on Evelyn's face, his undisguised delight that she was there at all, and found herself smiling with genuine warmth. She might not love him as he loved her; but she had chosen a good man, and maybe that would be enough.

She greeted each of the small group assembled there, Evelyn's parents and brother on his side, Yves Epstein and Helio on hers, and then they walked together to the stone dais where Haldane was waiting for them. When the time came to make their vows, to pledge themselves to each other for the rest of their lives, Isabella surprised herself by actually meaning them. Evelyn seemed to sense this, and he felt himself flush with a new strength; yes, thought Isabella, I have chosen well.

The only venue capable of hosting the wedding ball was the New Albert Hall near Hyde Park, a scaled-up replica of an historic building that had once stood on the site but that had been destroyed by fire during the troubles. It had been many months in the planning, and the teams of serving staff, hundreds in uniformly-starched whites, were nervously awaiting the first arrivals, none more so than the Hall's principal function co-ordinator who had been having nightmares about this day for months. Waiting too was the vast army of security people, assembled to protect a guest-list that included the entire ruling cadre of the City-State and its Corporation. The Civil Guard had enforced an exclusion zone that extended far away from the building, and within the cordon the municipal police, the Guard, the Council's own security, a number of individual Corporation protection teams, and even some units of the standing army were all checking and re-checking every possible potential threat.

Within the galleried ovoid interior the normal banked seating had been replaced by a series of terraces, the lower of which held rings of dining tables, followed by smaller standing areas as the gradient increased towards the impossibly high ceiling. In the central arena were more tables, encircling that of the wedding party itself that stood proudly in the centre of this vast auditorium. Thus arranged, all of Isabella and Evelyn's many guests would be able to see their hosts during the supper, and they would both tour the galleries together after the meal.

The guests began to arrive long before the newlyweds themselves, so that the hall would be packed when they made their triumphant entrance, and by the time Daniel and Saskia found their table it was already almost full. They did not have to wait long, and when the floating folds of Isabella's dress came into view on the arm of her blissful husband, the whole chamber erupted in spontaneous applause. They walked to the centre of the arena, where both stood and bowed to their guests, holding each other's hands as they did so. Then Evelyn took a step back, raising his arm to his wife as the applause reignited in an explosion of white noise. Isabella raised both arms, slowly lowering them and with them the volume in the hall.

She began to speak, her voice captured in a localised sound-field and amplified throughout the hall as she uttered the traditional address.

"My friends, for such you all must be; my husband and I welcome you and ask you to celebrate with us".

With this came the loudest cheer of all, and when it finally subsided the strings of the orchestra began to play, as the waiting staff entered the hall from all directions in a carefully choreographed dance of their own, weaving and spinning between the tiered tables so that from the balconies above it almost resembled a Viennese waltz. It was later, when the supper was long finished and the tables quietly removed, that the guests began to mingle more freely, with those on the highest balconies beginning their descent through the tiers towards the arena itself. It was when Daniel's table finally made the move down that he found himself being approached by the Lord Mayor.

"Daniel Mason; and this is your wife?"

"Lord Mayor", replied Daniel, taking the man's offered hand and shaking it warmly, "yes, my wife Saskia".

"I have not had the chance to thank you for your assistance during the evacuation from the terrorist attack. And so once again", he continued, partly for the benefit of the small crowd watching the exchange, "London's Mayor finds himself thanking one of the Mason family." Then Haldane put his arm around Daniel and took him to one side. "Commissioner Davis has also been impressed by your work on the river, Mason",

"I am helping where I can, sir."

"Keep it up", said the Mayor in parting, winking conspiratorially before moving on towards the next citizen he needed to greet. Out of the corner of his eye, Daniel noticed Yves Epstein had been watching the whole exchange intently.

Still in the balconies, Val Banerjee had smoked a little too much and was feeling too lethargic to join the societal whirlwind below. She knew she was only here as a matter of protocol, here as the office of the Barrier Authority rather than in her own person. She harrumphed quietly; that wouldn't last much longer, she was sure. Ever since the attack she had been losing her grip on the vast bureaucracy under her control, and she was sure that Haldane was going to remove her soon. Maybe one more smoke wouldn't hurt, she decided, one more to ease her nerves. As she gingerly rose from her seat to make the short walk to the dispenser, she found herself being helped by a young man and woman. Both very attractive, she thought through the drug-induced haze, slightly aroused.

"Would you like to go somewhere a little more private?" the woman asked suggestively.

Val Banerjee found herself agreeing, and let the couple lead her out of the auditorium and towards an elevator bank. They stepped inside and descended to the basement where they helped her into the back of a private transport. As it left the complex, Val Banerjee was surfacing enough to get worried.

"You have many questions," said the woman.

"Where are we going?" asked Val Banerjee; "why have we left the party?"

"Both fair," replied the woman.

Also sat in another of the balcony bars was Elisabeth, but she had avoided any of the free-flowing chemical aids on offer; she needed to keep her mind clear and on guard. She could not get Batista's sudden disappearance out of her mind. What did it mean? Had she been captured? Was she, Elisabeth, at risk? She felt claustrophobic in the giant hall, surrounded by guardsmen and security personnel on every level; if they were looking for her, she realised, there would be no escape from here. She decided to leave, and began to collect her things when she was suddenly grabbed around the waist from behind; as she wrestled to turn around she could smell the alcohol.

"Come on my love, where do you think you're going?"

"Kindly release me, now", she said firmly but unable to shake his grip.

"Nothing doing. See this uniform?" he drawled, moving around in front of her whilst never releasing the hold, "well it entitles me to a dance"

Elisabeth realised with horror that he was Civil Guard, and an officer as well. That made him dangerous.

"Please", she said again, raising her voice and hoping that someone would come to her aid, but promptly falling silent as he indicated the knife held to her stomach, hidden from view within the folds of his jacket.

"One dance I said my love; come on, let's go for a walk."

He pushed her slowly towards the back of the balcony, knife pressed gently into her dress and beginning to cut through the fabric, before pushing her against the wall and groping between her legs with his other hand. Elisabeth felt nauseous, her head spinning with hatred and fear.

"That's right," he whispered in her ear, "let's be a good girl. Come on."

Now he was pushing her again towards the exit and whatever lay beyond, but as they reached it she kicked back as hard as she could into his knee and felt his grip fail as he fell behind. Elisabeth bolted, reaching the elevator bank before he could steady himself and escaping into the safety of its closing doors. The guardsman, a lieutenant with river patrol insignia on his uniform, just laughed.

Oblivious to his old friend's terror, Daniel had been scanning the crowd for her face, hoping that they would at least get to meet before the night was over. As he was doing so, he spotted with a jolt the now familiar features of the unknown man with the cane; for once, however, the man was not watching him back. Instead, he was transfixed by a couple of men who seemed to be arguing, partially obscured by a hanging curtain from the first tier of balconies. As he strained to see who the men were, he realised that it was Mayor Haldane and the man that Epstein had identified as Julio Soon, and the latter looked to be furious about something. When Daniel looked back towards his watcher, he found that once again the man had disappeared from view.

"Daniel! Saskia!", exclaimed the bride.

They both turned to see Isabella approaching them from behind, and took turns to kiss her.

"You look wonderful," said Saskia.

"Thank you, you are most kind"

"Congratulations Bella", added Daniel, with a genial grin.

She returned the smile, holding both their hands warmly. "I hoped I might find you two with Elisabeth, but it seems you haven't found each other yet?"

"We haven't seen her all night", replied Saskia, "have we?"

"No," confirmed Daniel.

"Well I want to have a drink with the three of you on my wedding night. When I find her, I'll come back and find you," said the bride, feeling uncharacteristically enthusiastic. "But first, I'd better find that husband of mine."

Elisabeth, however, was nowhere to be found.

twenty five

They had gone to the country house after the wedding, and Isabella had the odd sensation of realising that her home was now their home, that she was now we. She had asked the servants to install Evelyn's things in a suite of rooms in the upper west wing close to her own; but on their first night together she had decided to stay with him. The experience, she reflected, had not been at all unpleasant; he was a gentle and unselfish lover, and that suited her own tastes perfectly.

In the morning she had risen early and, maple in hand, gone for a solitary walk whilst the frost still crackled beneath her boots, listening to a sparrowhawk call to her mate. On her return to the house she noticed Helio strolling alone in the ornamental garden, and went to join him.

"As one becomes two, so both become stronger. Congratulations, Chamois".

"Thank you. And now it begins?" she asked.

"It began long ago" he replied, walking a little before turning back to her and asking, "did you notice your Mayor talking to Mr Soon at the supper?"

"No, I did not."

"Intriguing. The normally unflappable Mr Soon seemed somewhat animated. I would suggest that you might want to discover why."

Isabella nodded. "Will you stay with me now?" she then asked.

"I will be here when you need me. I can advise and give you information, although what you choose to do must be entirely yours to decide. It is, after all, your city."

"I understand", she replied. Whatever it was she must do, she must do it alone.

"And now I must leave, for a time. Look after that maple-stick; you will need it."

As Helio walked away, disappearing behind the boxed hedge, Isabella turned the cane in her hand, feeling the strange coolness of the white marble head in her ungloved hand. Always the mystery with these people, she thought, but after her father's message and her incredible experience with the Librarian she knew she must trust them. She returned to the house, where her new husband was waiting for her in the breakfast room; to his surprise, she kissed him lightly on the cheek whilst squeezing his hand, before settling at the table. It would not be long before their closer friends and relatives would be arriving for another reception, this one a more intimate affair after the extravagance of the formal celebrations, and she was looking forward to having a chance to talk to Yves about her conversation in the gardens.

Later, when finally she did manage to get Yves alone, away from the rest of the gathering, she could tell something was wrong.

"What is it, my old friend", she asked.

"I am not given to overreacting, I think," he began, looking for her agreement before continuing, "but I must admit to being significantly worried". Isabella realised this must be important; Yves was certainly not one to exaggerate either.

"Tell me."

"I am afraid that the Council is at threat. Subtle things, it always begins with small actions, slight infractions, but the course is clear for us to see."

"What do you mean, Yves?" she asked.

"Let me ask you this, Senator", he replied formally. "Are you aware that the members of the Civil Guard have raided the headquarters of the Pioneers in order to secure a prisoner for questioning?"

"No, I was not."

"Or that the Civil Guard did so without the agreement of Mr Soon, or quite obviously his governing committee, on which we both sit."

"No", she said again, her surprise evident to her mentor if to no-one else.

"That in fact, they did so on the authority, they claimed, of the Lord Mayor."

"That is not within his prerogative" Isabella said.

"And so," continued Yves, "it starts. Our executive branch of government overstepping the mark."

"There is more?" Isabella half-asked, half-stated.

"Indeed. I have for some time been concerned about the concentration of power within the executive and the Civil Guard in the hands of a small cabal of ex-officers from the same former war-units of the military."

"This we have spoken about," she agreed.

"I have been concerned that this group of men, for they are all men without exception, have increasingly demonstrated a lack of regard, a contempt even, for the institutions of this City and the inherent checks and balances built into them. That there are tendencies within this group, borne out of their time in the military, towards a disciplinarian centralisation of power."

"I know your concerns".

"Then mark this act – for this is the start. By instructing the Guard to flex their brute power against the Pioneers, the Mayor's office challenges both the Council and the Senators to stand up to him or pale weakly into the shadows by his side. It is not the first move they have made to strengthen the executive, not by far, but it is the first time they do so against the laws and norms of the state. And so we move towards a creeping coup d'etat – unless they are stopped."

Isabella knew the Councillor well enough not to ask if he was serious; of course he was. For him to make these statements to her, he must be more than convinced of his analysis. This must have been what Helio had witnessed the previous day, the heated exchange between Soon and the Lord Mayor. No wonder he was furious; his treasured independence challenged by the Guard; she could well imagine the man's anger. Isabella imparted to Yves her morning's conversation, finding herself caressing the whitened tip of her new cane as she did so.

"This man, Helio you call him. He is from the Library?" Yves asked.

Isabella nodded in response.

"What is their role in all this?"

"I believe they, like you, are concerned about the threat to the city".

"Then we must move carefully," Yves eventually responded. "I must challenge this action in the Council, but we must all watch out for snakes in the Chamber; they will not, I am sure, have been as foolhardy as to start this and not have a plan. Mind yourself, Senator; I will watch over you."

"And I you," Isabella replied, completing the old oath of alliance between friends.

twenty six

She lay still, the sheets damp from a night of dark dreams, her body feeling the sharp edges of the blue-tinged morning air. Yet even through this sunrise, Elisabeth had woken to find the darkness all too real. The sounds of the city jabbed and jerked at an opened window that she couldn't bring herself to close; she couldn't face the silence. Sitting up now, arms locked around her knees in the cramped studio flat that was all she could afford on her public school allowance; one cluttered room in a ramshackle tenement. She had escaped from the would-be rapist guardsman, but not from the fear.

Had they been betrayed? Olof hunted and Batista missing - were the guard looking for her now, were they walking up the crowded narrows below and forcing their way in? No; if they had been after her, she would have been snatched at the wedding, not left to herself, not left to be abused by one of their own simply because she was alone. So that was safety in this city was it? That was the protection afforded by the citizens' guards? She could feel his tightened grip on her arm still, could sense his gluttonous arousal, could see the look of entitlement spread across his smoke-reddened features; she felt herself shudder with the thought. Forcing herself to rise, she waited for the searing water to substitute her pain.

She had to make the trip to the riverbank, had to look for her friend, yet walking through the meadows she was oblivious to the sunlight's dance, glittering and shimmying in the frosted air; deaf too to the ringing calls of the redshank as they took to the skies. She could think only of Batista; where had the woman gone?

Approaching the barge, she listened carefully for Vasco's barking but strangely heard none, and when she emerged from the tall sedge grasses and the boat came into view, he was nowhere to be seen. The hull looked strangely lifeless; nobody on deck, no smoke rising from the chimney, no smell of frying breakfast on the moistened air. She climbed aboard, carefully and quietly, and let herself into the wheelhouse before slowly descending the stairs into a main cabin still darkened by curtains drawn tight.

Through the shadows, Isabella could see the old woman sitting on her bunk, cradling the sleeping body of her companion, stroking his fur gently.

Too still to be sleeping.

Before Elisabeth could speak, the Portuguese raised a finger to her mouth indicating silence, and then stood slowly, carrying Vasco's lifeless body towards her. Elisabeth stepped aside and allowed the woman to climb out onto deck with the dead dog. Batista had prepared a heavy mud-anchor weight with a length of chain, and she attached this to the dog's collar before easing both into the waters below. Still she indicated silence, returning to the wheelhouse to collect her pack before leading them both ashore and away from her home.

The elder woman set a swift pace afoot and showed no signs of either slowing or speaking for a couple of hours as they threaded their way first downriver and away from the city, and then slowly heading into the wilderness of the northern marshes. Elisabeth followed in silence. This had long been one of their evacuation routes, known only to the two of them. They had scouted it together three years before under the cover of a camping holiday, plotting a route to the north-eastern border of the city-state and the wastelands beyond, in case they ever needed it. If her friend was leading her on this path, she thought, they must have been discovered. As they walked on, Elisabeth slowly understood what had happened to Vasco; remembering the half-eaten bowl of food on the cabin floor, and the anchor waiting above. They couldn't have brought him with them.

A brief stop, some water and nourishment from the pack and then onward; Elisabeth angry that she had come so ill-prepared for a sudden flight, although glad for the winter clothes she had worn for the walk to the riverbank. A few more hours and they would know if their equipment cache had been discovered, buried in watertight bags beneath the unmarked rushes. Then they would be able to scan each other for tracking bugs or listening devices; then they would be able to speak.

They found their marker without much of a search and each took one of the shovels from Batista's pack, digging methodically through the dampened earth before slowly uncovering their stash. They hauled the bags free of the cloying soil and set up the tracing equipment, soon discovering a beacon and microphone in Batista's clothes, before Elisabeth found another beacon somehow inserted under the skin on her friend's bruise-coloured back. For the first time since the barge she really looked at the old woman, and could see how wasted she looked; reddened eyes and a large welt rising on her left cheek; what had happened, she asked herself again?

When the search was reversed, they thankfully found Elisabeth to be free of any devices, but still they kept silent as Batista reached into her pack and pulled out a rectangular wooden box that had a grill at one end. She placed a sack over it before opening the grill-door, allowing the creature inside to dart into the bag. Then, motioning Elisabeth to hold the animal tightly, she attached the three electronic devices they had found on her to a collar that she then fastened around its neck, before removing the bag and letting the otter run free.

The two women divided the remaining equipment and stores into the two packs they had prepared in the cache, before setting out again towards the city for an hour, laying a false trail before doubling back partially and then striking out, as invisibly as possible, to the northeast. Batista led the way, her wiry fitness more than compensating for her age. It was dusk before they both felt it safe enough to talk.

"My brother had been captured alive," began the elder woman, "at sea, in the Dover Straits. He was betrayed to one of the Pioneers."

She began to sob; quiet tears on a worn-out face. Elisabeth waited, silently, for her friend to continue.

"They brought him to the city for questioning, but the Civil Guard found out and they seized him themselves. They have a different form of question" she said, shaking her head.

"He gave them nothing, my brave brother gave them nothing at all; he would not break, no matter what they did to him. But they took his blood, and they traced me. He had never been caught before you see? Never been on their system. They found me soon afterwards, aboard the barge. They took me to see him, made me watch as they ...". Her voice started to crack as the words would not come; stuck in her throat like the nausea they inspired. Elisabeth patiently held her friend's hands, not interrupting.

Batista took a deep breath and pulled back her shoulders, wiping the tears from her eyes.

"They tortured him. Mediaeval torture. Jodere", she cursed. "They made me watch but they could not break him. So they kept him alive. They are not sure if I am involved but they tell me to go to his friends; they will watch. They tell me they will not release him unless I lead them to his people. They inject me with that bug, they send me out, they keep watching me."

At this, Batista looked straight into Elisabeth's eyes, before continuing, "I had to find you, do you understand? They would have made a link between us, no doubt about that. We are known to be close. If I had not led them to anyone, they would have come to you anyway. They chase everything, like pack-hounds. I had to give you a chance to escape them. Do you understand?"

Elisabeth nodded with the sudden realisation that her life as she knew it was over. She could never go back, never hide in her schoolteacher's skin when her alternate role became too overwhelming, too dangerous. With Batista's story her two lives had merged into one; a few minutes passed and her identity forever altered. She was an outlaw now, and it had been her own choice.

Batista continued, grimly. "Those bugs were not their only way to trace us. We must move fast. We have a chance, if we can reach the Shepherd."

Elisabeth looked at her questioningly.

"Let me tell it to you as we walk."

twenty seven

Far across the wide flats of the Estuary, beyond the honking and shrieking flocks returning in the dusky light, the Swede lay hidden deep in the rushes. He had been running from the Guard for days now, hounded from the havens of Chatham by the lies on the screens. He had cursed them for that; the fishermen he knew had no love for the Civil Guard and would gladly have secreted him away in one of the many secret compartments aboard the ships or in the storehouses, let him hide in the tunnels and the lairs of their smuggling sidelines and evade the guardsmen just as they evaded the Excise. Now they thought he had murdered one of their own, he was not welcome; they would have betrayed him to his pursuers in a moment. Forced then, to run from the docks and choose: to try and make it to the border through the well-guarded swathes of agribusinessland that surrounded Chatham, or to hide-out in the estuary marshes. He had chosen the first but had not made it, frustrated at every turn by the looming presence of Corporation Security forces more concerned about keeping people off the land than capturing anyone trying to pass through it. Twice he had nearly been caught by these privateers as a trespasser and food-thief, and countless more times he had given away his position to their surveillance equipment. He had been forced to turn back and to try and conceal himself in the Medway for as long as he could, stealing what little food, water, and equipment he could on the way.

He had spent days looking for a place deep in the marshland to make his den, somewhere well-hidden and well-protected where he could disappear for as long as his food and water held out. He set trap-lines ashore and fishing lines in the nearby waters, and had managed to fix a small desalinator he had stolen along the way; but its power supply was already depleted ad he knew he would have to rely on rainfall before long.

At first he thought he had thrown them off the scent, that so long as he could stay alive here, he would be safe; but they must have realised where he had gone to ground. Every day now he could hear more lifters searching from above, and every minute he lay in fear of the sound of a patrol craft engine coming towards his burrow. What had at first seemed a perfect hideout had now started to feel instead like the inside of a trapper's cage; if they caught him here, there would be no escape. As the lifters got louder and he no longer dared to check his water-lines, the claustrophobia began to grow.

Aboard the patrol craft, Daniel could sense they were getting closer; could feel the cold sweat of anticipation cool against the back of his neck. They had searched the denser areas of the Medway marshland methodically, focussing on those areas where Daniel, with his unrivalled knowledge of the estuary's more remote parts, thought fugitives most likely to seek shelter. They had nearly completed the block that he had marked out on the holo-maps aboard the Pike as their primary target; and he felt sure in his own judgement. Either they would find him here, or the Civil Guard's information was wrong and he was not in the marshes at all.

Sparrow could see the look of the hunter growing in Daniel's eyes; recognised and respected it. The Commissioner had been right about this man, he thought to himself; he was a natural leader, fitting easily into the team of river patrol guardsmen and directing the boats as though he had been one of their officers for years. Davis had ordered him to involve Mason in the capture and interrogation of the suspect, if possible; then they would see for certain if they could use him as one of their own. The Lieutenant was not sure which way he would react; they would see soon enough, he thought.

Daniel himself had left the Pike and was aboard one of the smaller craft with the patrolmen who had come to his house on Sawyer's Hill the morning after the attack; men he now knew as Walker and Stiphons. Using his wrist terminal's holo-projection, he could still watch the overview they would be seeing on the bridge of Sparrow's command craft, the depiction of each patrol craft and their respective locations in the map. Even from here, deep within the reeds, Daniel was directing the hunt, bringing his boats through the creeks like the beaters on a pheasant shoot; if it was an analogy that had come into Daniel's mind, he quickly stifled it.

His wrist indicated an incoming communication from one of the other craft; Daniel flicked it reflexively, allowing the guardsman to proceed.

"Found some fish-lines set up on the bank. Recent," came the incoming message.

Daniel felt his heart beating faster; they were close, he could feel it; the terrorist must be hidden somewhere near here. They had discussed what to do when they had him cornered, and the Lieutenant had ordered them to flush him out; there was no chance of surprise in the marsh, their engines and lifters made too much of a racket. Daniel gave the orders firmly, holding back his own excitement, bringing the patrol boats in towards the small dry-land area from all sides, calling in the lifters above their location, loosing the hounds ashore.

Olof knew he had no chance; the down-draft from the lifters hovering directly above destroyed his reed-den in seconds, and he could hear the ferocious barking as the pack found his scent.

twenty eight

Another unsettling piece of information, thought Julio Soon, to add to the already tangled web held so precariously in his mind as he tried to see the unseen links between them. It was the return of his operative from the continental fortress of Zermatt that had brought this latest little mystery to his attention. He had long suspected the bookseller to be an affiliate of the Library organisation, although he was still no closer to discovering what the latter actually was. Sometimes they gave him information, and less often he gave them some in return; but who they were and why they existed he could not, after all these years, fathom. Where he suspected their involvement he had his agents silently observing, trying to find out what little they could, but still it amounted to nothing.

The bookseller was one such hunch, and he had alerted the Zermatt station to keep a gentle watch over her activities. Now they reported that she had disappeared. The shop boarded closed, and no forwarding address. The only unusual visit they could report was with an unknown man; and all they could say about him was that he was tall, lithe, and walked with the assistance of a long curved stick that bore a strong resemblance to a shepherd's crook. Nothing more, and Soon was confident enough in his own people to realise that if this was all they could find, it was all that likely could be discovered.

He could not see how this fitted-in, could not see if it was relevant; what use was knowledge if he did not understand it? He would seek out the man with the dog's head cane; they had long ago agreed a means by which he could contact the man who consistently proved to be so well-informed. He would watch how the man reacted to the news; try to glean from him whether it mattered.

First, though, he needed to warn the Senators about the activities of the Civil Guard; if they dared to challenge the Pioneers in the Mayor's name, then no institutions of government would be sacrosanct. The Council itself could well be challenged by the power-base that Haldane had assembled around him in his para-military security force, and they needed to be forewarned.

twenty nine

The Commissioner's office in Little Smith Street was filled with palpable tension as the officers kept their leader appraised, all heads turned towards the holo-maps that showed in vivid detail the two chases, both nearing fruition. Two chances to find these dissidents and crush them, Davis thought; then their actions would prove justified, even the cowards on the Council would have to realise. He could feel his own barely restrained anger rising inside him, holding it in check just enough so that he could control its power.

On the northern banks of the Estuary, the gamble with the old woman seemed to be paying off. They hadn't known if she was involved with the actions of the prisoner they had commandeered from the Pioneer's custody; hadn't known if she even knew of the existence of this man who, according to the DNA tests, was definitely related to her by blood. It was possible they had never met; the upheavals of the last century had split many families apart across the torn continent.

It had been worth finding out; seeing her reaction when they showed her the sight of her broken relative, she clearly knew him well. Whether she was involved with the underground movements they could not tell, but the probabilities certainly pointed that way. It had been Pickering's idea to set her loose; hold the male prisoner hostage and see where she would run, who she would lead them to. The flashing lights on the holo-map, threading a course north-east through the northern marshlands, suggested she was running somewhere, and their surveillance had identified another suspect accompanying her: a schoolteacher. A squad of men had already been dispatched to the new woman's address to learn what they could.

The adjacent holo-map showed the progress of the River Patrol, closing in on the fugitive in the southern estuary. Davis grinned with satisfaction as he watched the markers of the different craft slowly converge upon a single spot, sure they had the Swede in their grasp this time. They would destroy these dissidents, he said to himself, relishing the prospect of seeing how they reacted to Pickering's new techniques of interrogation.

Haldane had trusted him to deliver the terrorists; now he had to deliver. If a few of the Council's precious laws were broken in the course of their action, so be it. He had had enough of their interference, their constant weak-willed cowardice. In his opinion, it was the Council's softness that encouraged these vermin to think that they could challenge the power of the city in the first place. That had to change, the officers had agreed. There was no room for compromise if they wanted to keep discipline; no space for ill-considered pandering to the troublesome. The city was in decay, the city that for so many years they had fought for, that so many of their comrades had died to protect. He would not allow it to happen.

He worried that the office of Lord Mayor had weakened Haldane's resolve; that the politicians had infected him with their own cancerous sickness. He had been allowed to raid Soon's headquarters, and Davis had enjoyed seeing the preposterous diplomat emasculated so unexpectedly; but he wondered if Haldane still had the balls to take on the Council when their inevitable remonstrations began. It would be easier with the Mayor as their figurehead, he thought; but if necessary, they could continue without him.

thirty

"My brother was once a soldier", Batista continued, telling Elisabeth her story as they continued the yomp through waterlogged reed-land.

"He fought in the Migration Wars, joined the Coalition. We both did, trying to protect our family from the marauders and savages who would have taken our lands. We were not successful; our countryland was abandoned. We found ourselves refugees in the Northern Cities. You know the history; how the promises made in wartime were so easily forgotten once the cities were secure. You know why we both made the choices to be here; this I have told you before."

Elisabeth did; they had talked about it aboard the barge many times.

"During the Wars, we met a man of great but subtle power. It is hard to explain. A man of no country; of no city. He fought not for his land nor for his family like we did, but for his ideas. Others fought with him. They fight with him still. His name is the Shepherd."

Batista stopped and opened her pack for a sip of water, and Elisabeth did the same.

"Do you think the Civil Guard are trying to find this man, this Shepherd?" she asked.

"Yes and no. They search for the leaders of those who would oppose their tyranny, and in a sense that is what he is; but they have no idea. He is a ghost, a whisper, nothing more to them."

"Is he part of our protest?" Elisabeth asked. They had always been divided into cells for their own protection in case the organisation was compromised, so she had never known who the leaders of the movement were; even if there were any. She had thought they were part of a loose federation of like-minded protestors rather than part of a hierarchical secret army, but Batista had always known more.

"In some ways yes, in others no. He and his followers give advice, protection, sanctuary where they can; but they do not control anything. The protest is as you always thought – devolved and dispersed. You and I have always acted according to our own beliefs, not as the puppets of some shadow-figure. Of course, our enemies cannot understand this and so they continue to hunt for the *ringleaders* as they call them. In the Shepherd, they would find the closest thing; but they will never discover him. You, however," she said to Elisabeth, "must."

"Is that our plan, to meet up with this Shepherd beyond the city's borders?"

Batista nodded, although her head was turned and her face shielded behind her ragged locks of hair.

"Now we must continue."

Both women shouldered their packs and set off again through the rough country of the marshland, shrugging off their fatigue, thankful for the thick winter jackets which protected them from the slicing edges of the reeds as they pushed their way northward. Soon enough they were clear of the marshland and had begun to follow the course of a freshwater stream that ran along the floor of a narrow gully between the raised agribusiness beds on either side. It was deep enough that the tops of the trees growing by the brook only just cleared the steep banks, a hidden canopy of refugees whose upper leaves danced with the raised crops above. They would follow this narrow corridor of tolerated wildness until they reached the end of the food production areas and the relative safety of the timber forest that lay just inside the City's walls, a vast monoculture of grid-planted conifers whose densely packed groves should afford them greater cover.

The air was growing cooler as the clouds blocked out the sun, but both women were soon glistening with exertion as they continued to trek for hours without break. At this pace they would be over the border before the end of the coming night. What awaited them outside, Elisabeth could only imagine. She had never left the confines of the city-state; never ventured beyond their well-protected walls. She had been brought up to fear the wilds, convinced by her childhood's mythologies of the dangers and darkness that lay beyond. A land without law, where humans fought with the beasts and each other for food and sustenance and more; a land with no trust and no hope, abandoned to those who chose savagery above civilisation. Elisabeth shuddered at the thought. She hated what London had become, hated the betrayal of the people by their leaders, the creeping fascism of the security forces and their corrupt masters; but the thought of leaving filled her with a deep-set anxiety. The screens still told of the border skirmishes, of the periodic attacks on their outer walls by the bands of outlaws, yet she had come to realise that she didn't know where the propaganda finished and the truth began. Often she had asked Batista of the lands beyond London, and the old Portuguese had responded with epic tales of wonder and despair; but as to what lay directly beyond the northern borders, Elisabeth could only guess. She merely understood enough of the realities to know that they were headed from their pursuers into a land no less dangerous.

The light had almost completely gone by the time they stopped to rest and re-fuel, breaking open the long-life rations they had stored in the buried packs. Neither spoke as they chewed their way through the rehydrated food, pausing only to wash it down with what remained in their canteens before re-filling them in the stream. They had nearly reached the forest now; another couple of hours and they would be into the woods; then they could worry about how to tackle the border walls.

Batista had pulled a map from the inside of her coat and was spreading it out on a large rock, using the soft illumination of a night-light to pore over their route.

"I must show you the way, in case we are split." Elisabeth didn't want to think about that possibility, but knew her friend was right; they were not clear of the city yet, and even without the bugs the Civil Guard may have extrapolated their likely direction and be searching the surrounding area.

"When we reach the forest, we must head towards this escarpment. It is a vertical rock face, ten metres high and hidden deep within the plantation in one of the older-growth areas. If you search carefully along the base, you will find three holes cut into the rock in a pyramid shape. In the top hole is a handle. Pull this handle and whilst doing so reach into the lower left hole and pull the handle you find there at the same time. Do you understand Elisabeth, the order is important?"

"Top handle, then lower left."

"Good. This map is for you; I can find the place without it."

Elisabeth accepted the folded papers from Batista and tucked them safely inside her jacket, before they gathered their things together and set off along the sunken gully once again.

thirty one

The triumphant release when they finally captured the Swede had not lasted, and Daniel could feel in its place a sense of growing emptiness. The guardsmen had not spared any violence when dragging their prey aboard the launch and dumping him in the back of the cockpit, firmly trussed and bloodied. Daniel looked away from the man and the deep gash across his cheek that was leaking interminably. Walker lowered the bucket overboard, pulling on the rope to bring up a pail of saltwater with which he doused the prisoner, temporarily washing away the red stains. Olof began murmuring, unable to form words with his smashed jaw, but a swift hard kick in the ribs from the other guard soon silenced him again; now there were just whimpers.

Walker could see Daniel looking again at the state of their captive.

"He'll be feeling a lot worse if he doesn't answer Pickering's questions", said the man. Daniel wasn't sure whether the upturned corners of the guardsman's tight lips signified resignation or pleasure.

It did not take them long to reverse course through the culverts and creeks of the Medway; finding their way out of the maze with the aids of the holo-maps was much easier than finding the way in. They rendezvoused with the Pike in the deeper Estuary waters and transferred their prisoner and Daniel to the bigger vessel. As Olof was bundled below decks into the ship's brig, Sparrow clapped his arms around Daniel's shoulders.

"Well done Mason. Well done."

"Thank you", he replied, not returning the officer's smile.

Sparrow laughed at his protégé's earnest expression, and shook him by the arm. "Does it feel like an anti-climax, now you have won the chase?" he asked, laughing again when Daniel didn't reply. "I know how you feel."

The Lieutenant returned to the command bridge, leaving Daniel alone momentarily on the deck. Was that why he felt so hollow, Daniel thought? Or was it something else? He wasn't sure, but could feel the involuntary shivers of unease branching out from his spine.

The atmosphere in Little Smith Street had improved immeasurably; finally, after all the failures and mistakes of the previous few weeks they were making progress. Another of the Dam attackers in their grasp, being rushed upriver ready for questioning. They would break this man, but carefully. They couldn't allow him to die before they had extracted the information they needed. They would avoid using the rash violence that led to the premature death of John Gates before he could finger his associates. That had been Davis' fault, he knew; he should have given the man to Pickering. Their traditional beatings did not seem to break these dissidents, but the new recruit had ways of making people talk. His subordinate had already left the office to prepare the equipment, Davis noted with satisfaction.

When the Pike docked at Westminster, Sparrow and Daniel proceeded directly to the Commissioner's rooms, where they were greeted by a re-energised Davis.

"Well done men", he began, returning the Lieutenant's automatic salute, "and thank you Mason, for helping us with this matter. Perhaps you would like to see it through, before returning to the Barrier Authority?"

Daniel felt torn. Part of him wanted to be away from these people and back with Saskia and Lexi and his job at the Authority; but he was still enraged by these terrorists and their indiscriminate disregard for life, had been driven by this anger ever since the near disaster on the Dam. Davis could see a glint of the latter in his eyes, and took it as confirmation. He would have Mason sit in on the questioning of the captive he had helped to bring-in; then they would see if he had the stomach for a commission in the Guard.

"Lieutenant, I would like Mr Mason to assist Pickering. Please show him the way."

"Sir".

When the two of them had left Davis' still crowded office, he turned back to the holo-screens and focussed his attention on the other pursuit, still flushed with their recent success. One in the bag but two still on the run. Not for much longer if he could help it.

"Update".

The Sergeant who had been co-ordinating the northern hunt had been dreading this; it never paid to give the Commissioner bad news.

"Our tracking devices may have been compromised, sir."

"Explain", Davis ordered in barely measured tones.

"The movements of the markers have become increasingly erratic, sir. It reminds me of something I have seen before, in an exercise." The young guardsman could feel the stares of all the senior offices in the room, but he had to tell them this; if he was right, they would thank him for it.

"Go on", said Davis.

"It was during an evasion test sir", he began, referring to the part of basic training that all recruits to the Guard had to endure. "The guardsman somehow discovered the tracker beacons we had inserted in his equipment, and removed them. He then attached them to a small mammal, sir. We did not realise for some time, but the movements on the screen were very similar to what we have been observing, sir."

Davis seemed to ponder the suggestion for a few moments before responding. Much to the sergeant's surprise, he did so without losing his cool.

"So they know what they are doing, these two. That confirms that they are worth finding. Gentlemen, I want scenarios. Where do we think they would head?"

As it happened, Elisabeth and Batista were still in the stream-gully between the acres of latticed crop fields; they still had at least another hour's walk before they reached the relative safety of the plantations. Both women were beginning to tire now, Elisabeth more so than her exercise-hardened older friend. They had stopped to rest again, taking on water and nourishment from the stores in their packs. Batista looked up towards the sky through the thin canopy that rustled in the breeze.

"The clouds are beginning to lower. There will be rain before morning."

Elisabeth nodded; the old woman had spent a lifetime outdoors and on the water, and could read the weather like a familiar book. She dug into her bag to locate her waterproof gear, readying it for when it would be needed.

"You remember how to open the stone?" she was asked.

"Yes. I pull the top handle and then the one on the left"

"Good. We should reach the cliff before first light, if our luck holds. Let's go."

They hauled the kit onto their backs once more and continued their trek towards the trees at the border, their eyes now adjusted to the darkness of the path, able to pick their way through the silhouetted roots and rocks and branches.

They were not to know that lifters had been dispatched across the entire area, packed with heat-sensing cameras and night-vision equipment for the spotters. Davis thought they had a decent chance of finding the two women. Their trackers in the marshland were following a trail back towards the city but that made no sense; they wouldn't be able to hide amidst the electro-surveillance of the urban quarters. No, he thought, they had surely laid a false trail just as they had muddied their scent with the animal trick. He allowed himself a wry smile; he liked it when the enemy were good. It would make his eventual victory all the more pleasing.

Their options, Davis decided, were to head for the border on foot, to go to ground in the marshland, or to be picked up by a boat on the Estuary. The last was unlikely; the northern side of the estuary was nowhere near as accessible by boat as the Medway, and they had blockaded the few passable routes in and out. If they went to ground, his trackers would find them within a matter of days, if not hours. He felt certain that they would realise this as well. The border, then. Davis instructed the guardsmen by the holo-maps to focus their attention on likely escape routes to the north-east. It did not take them long to report.

"Sir. Scaling the border wall is very unlikely to succeed, it is too well monitored. However, if they were desperate enough to make the attempt, it would make sense to do so in as remote a section as possible. That would suggest this region here," he continued, indicating a densely-wooded area on the holo-screen. "To reach the plantation, they would have to cross these areas of agribusinessland. Given the time of year, sir, they would find little or no cover in these particular fields. If it were me, I would head for one of the streams. They tend to run ten to fifteen meters below the level of the surrounding land, and are usually wooded which would give you some cover."

"Agreed" snapped Davis impatiently. "How many are there?"

"Only seven sir."

Davis leered towards the screens, feeling the adrenaline wash through his system as he realised they were within his grasp. "I want seven teams at the northern ends of these gullies, waiting. Another seven start making their way through them from the south."

The officers replied with a sharp simultaneous "Sir!".

In another, lower, basement room of the Civil Guard headquarters in Little Smith Street, Daniel Mason was struggling to breathe. He stood with Walker behind a screen, looking into a high-ceilinged chamber with walls of brushed metal and a tiled white floor. In the centre of the room was a chair of sorts; made with steel and adorned with restraining straps, it was occupied by the prisoner. On a trolley to the side of the chair was a surgeon's tray, covered in shining instruments from a more barbaric age of medicine. To the left, a door opened, and they watched as Pickering started to work on the man they had brought back from the Medway.

"The aim", Pickering had told them before entering the sound-proofed cell, "is not to cause pain but to engender fear. Real, inescapable, terrifying fear. A person's imagination can, when manipulated, be turned against them. Allow them to think about what you will do before you do it. Subjects can lose themselves in pain, it is place they can hide. I offer them no such sanctuary from the horror. Short-duration local anaesthetics are the key. I let them see what I am doing before they feel the pain. Take them apart, piece by piece". The Guard had said this matter-of-factly, as though it were merely a matter of efficiency.

After a few minutes, Daniel could watch no longer. He could not bear to see Pickering slice into the Swede with such precision, nor the deadened eyes of the man witnessing his own disfigurement. He could feel himself sweating, feel his balance starting to weaken. As he glanced at Walker, the man returned his look with a smile. The Guard was enjoying this, Daniel realised with re-discovered shock.

He pushed past his companion and through the viewing room's door, making for a sink which he soon filled from his own insides. Walker shrugged, and turned back to the action.

The wind was beginning to build across the exposed winter fields, and the high wispy tails of the morning's cloud had been replaced by a thickening layer closer to the ground, its jagged underside illuminated by the distant glow from the city's night-lights. The women were glad of the noise it made rushing through the sunken tree-tops, even the bare branches of the deciduous trees sprinkled between the rogue spruce were starting to whistle. There had been more lifters crossing the skies in the last hour and although none had flown overhead, both women were increasingly nervous. They had been forced to slow their pace as the terrain began to steepen, but were glad because of what this meant: they were near the edge of the fields. They could not see the wall of fir looming above them yet, as the stream was still running metres below the level of the land, but they knew it must be close.

Suddenly, Batista raised her right arm, indicating silence. She pointed the fingers of her right hand to her eyes, and then pointed to a spot some way ahead of them on the right hand bank. Elisabeth could see it too; something was moving in the darkness, although she could not make out what. Both women lowered their bodies to the floor, crawling off the path and into the undergrowth as quietly as they could. Batista reached gently inside her coat and brought out two compact projectile rifles, passing one to Elisabeth as she silently assembled her own. Elisabeth tried to remember the instructions her friend had given her on how to use the gun. She had not wanted to know at first, did not believe in violent protest; but Batista had insisted, if only for her own protection from an increasingly militant Civil Guard. Now she felt thankful to have the weapon in her arms, but still doubted whether she would be able to use it. She would soon find out.

Batista motioned to her to follow, and the two of them slowly scaled the bank to their left, climbing up its steep sides in the darkness as quietly as they could. Ahead of them, where Batista had seen something moving, they could now make out several figures moving into position above the stream. Somebody was setting an ambush, and it was meant for them. When the women reached the top the slope levelled out quite suddenly onto the empty field. They crouched in the shadows, trying to control their breathing after the exertion of the climb.

The options looked bleak. They would be completely exposed if they left the cover of the gully, but that route was now un-passable; the two of them couldn't take on an armed patrol and hope to prevail. They were outnumbered, and Elisabeth had never fired a weapon in anger. Batista frowned, uncertain of their next move. They had little choice, she realised, but to try and cross the featureless winter field. They would attempt to do so unobserved; hope that they could crawl in the gloom and pass unnoticed; but they would have to be ready for flight.

It was not easy to crawl across the muddied surface of the crop-less beds, the weight of their packs forcing them deeper into the waterlogged soils. Batista led the way, exhausted but not letting Elisabeth see her own pain, forcing this one last push towards the tree-cliff and the sanctuary that lay beyond. So the Guard had guessed where they were headed, she thought; guessed they would try to cross the border and leave the city-state behind. Clever, but not enough; they would have no idea about the three holes hewn into the rocky escarpment, no idea of what lay beyond. She had to get Elisabeth to safety, she told herself; that was all that mattered.

They set off at an angle, trying to cut the corner and reach the tree-line a half-kilometre from the stream-bed and their would-be ambushers. They had nearly reached cover when the lifter flew overhead. It traced the course of the gully from above, showering the treetops in the light of its search-beam and throwing deflected shadows across the neighbouring fields. Twice it followed this route as Elisabeth and Batista accelerated their shuffling progress towards the forest, but then the aircraft turned towards them, letting its beams widen to light up vast tracts of the unplanted field. They froze, lying still and hoping in vain that they would not be discovered. The searchlight narrowed once again, pinpointing their position for the patrol waiting in the gully.

Batista jumped up, dragging Elisabeth with her, and shouted to her friend, "Run. Run for the trees. You must save yourself."

Elisabeth replied instantly "No! Together, come on!", but the older woman pushed away her arms.

"Run I said. Go!"

As they both fled for the welcoming lines of tightly packed conifers, Batista started to drop behind. She had used all her energy to get this far, disguising her fatigue from her companion in case it came to this, She knew what it would mean to run, the instant she had been released from the dungeon where they held her brother. She knew what she had to do to save her friend; and the likely consequence for herself.

"Run Elisabeth!" she shouted again, as the schoolteacher reached the edge of the plantation and disappeared from view.

Batista stopped running, her profile caught in the lifter's bright beam. She could see the men emerging above the banks of the stream-gully now, running towards her with their weapons raised. She lowered her pack and reached into it one final time, pulling out the grenade she carried for this one purpose. Attached to the firing pin and wrapped around the shell was a length of fishing wire. She removed the safety, placing the miniature bomb in her jacket pocket, and holding the translucent wire in her right hand.

"On your knees, on your knees, hands in the air!" came the barked orders as the riflemen came closer, their dull outlines slowly taking form and colour from the lifter's light.

Elisabeth, scrambling up the plantation's incline, looked back through the branches of the outer trees to see her companion surrounded by guardsmen. Trapped by a shrinking circle of armed men, illuminated from above, she could see there was no escape for her friend. Elisabeth turned, cocking the rifle as she had been taught and started back down the bank. She would not allow this to happen; she would not leave Batista behind.

The old Portuguese knew she would not have much time. She waited, arms raised, for the riflemen to come closer; kneeled as instructed as they brought the dull-grey lifter in to land by her side.

In the trees beyond she saw a hint of movement, knew her friend was returning; Elisabeth, full of unlikely hope. Batista had known her own life was over when they had shown her the broken shell of her brother. She would not allow this young woman to suffer the same fate.

As the guardsmen raised their captive to her feet, she pulled the wire.

From the tree-line, Elisabeth watched as her friend erupted like a vengeful dragon's flame, consuming everything in a fire-cloud which left no survivors.

She turned her back on the smouldering hulk of the lifter, wiping away the tears as she ran back into the murky grove.

thirty two

The clouds had begun to assemble above the quadrangle, but the flagstones were yet dry. A dim light shone from the upper window, the flickering illumination of the Librarian's fire. His door opened, and Helio entered the study, the dog's head cane reflecting the flame-light across the mapled walls.

"Tell me."

"It is as we suspected", Helio replied. "The Mayor Haldane has started to make his move. He seeks power for himself. He will challenge the Council, perhaps soon. "

"And the Chamois?"

"Her eyes are opening."

"Is she ready, do you think?"

"She has the will."

"Assist her, where you can; but she must make her own choices."

"Of course", replied Helio. "There is another matter."

"Please?" the Librarian encouraged him to continue.

"Mister Soon felt it important to inform me of the disappearance of a certain bookseller from the Zermatt stronghold. Why he suspected this particular shopkeeper would be of interest to me, I do not know. And yet you know of whom I speak."

"A keen mind, Julio Soon", said the Librarian, almost to himself.

"I find the disappearance, if true, more concerning than the manner in which it was revealed to me." Helio added.

"As do I", replied the Librarian, closing the ledger on his desk as he moved to the tall window and watched the darkening skies. It was some minutes before he spoke again.

"It is time to tell you of my suspicions, Helio", he said. "I believe that one of our own may have turned."

"A reader?" asked Helio.

"One of the twelve", replied his master, to his companion's evident shock.

"You suspect an Assistant of this?"

The Librarian nodded. "I believe Bastien no longer desires a seat at our table."

Helio, for once, was speechless. This Bastien, the Shepherd they called him, was the wisest and most powerful of the Librarian's assistants, the first of the twelve. None had ever turned, not in all their history.

"You must stay with the Chamois. She is young, and needs your guidance. But you must also be on your guard, for both your sakes."

"I understand," replied the shaken staff-carrier, leaning on his cane for support.

thirty three

Davis could not quite believe his own eyes as they watched the screen-images recorded by the lifter's cameras moments before its destruction. The old woman had taken them all out; the whole patrol, the flight crew, everything. Moments earlier he had been feeling jubilant; his hunch had proved correct, and the women would soon be joining the Swede in their interrogation suite. They had been good opposition, but he had been better.

"Fucking terrorists" he murmured angrily to himself; they played by different rules. The old woman had killed herself and all her pursuers rather than being taken alive. Her brother was still barely conscious in the cells; he would be made to suffer in her place, as would this schoolteacher when they finally caught up with her.

They had six teams heading for the crash-site, and Pickering had already been summoned back to the Commissioner's office to devise a cover-story for the explosion in the fields. Now he had to wait as the men tracked this woman through the plantation. She had no chance. In the next room, one of his officers was leading the team who were busily researching her background. They would find out who mattered to this woman, and pick them up as leverage. The Civil Guard had its own rules as well.

Pickering had been watching the screens in silence, making it show the lifter's demise over and over again. As the edges of his mouth rose fractionally in his own economical version of a smile, Davis knew his strategist had found the answer.

"Well?" he asked.

"We tell them the truth", Pickering said simply.

If this was a joke, Davis was not in the mood for it. He could not tell the Mayor that he had failed again; one suspect dead, another on the run, and nine of his own force dead or dying in the wreckage.

Pickering could see the fury rising inside his superior, and continued quickly, "in a manner of speaking. We release the screen-images from this point only", he said, indicating the frozen image behind him. It was from one of the lifter's cameras that had been focussed on their own men rather than the old woman. It showed the troops from behind, approaching the trees; Batista was not in shot. Then, when slowed to quarter-speed, it showed them consumed by an exploding fireball before the picture itself crackled and died.

"Go on" ordered Davis brusquely.

"The plantation is close to the border; we say one of our patrols was attacked by insurgents. Well-armed and violent insurgents. It strengthens our hand, sir."

The fury began to subside, replaced by something else entirely. Davis could see the genius in Pickering's suggestion. The army were responsible for border security; this would make the pacifist General Lucas stand up and take notice. It would help the Mayor as well, he realised. The city-state under attack from armed invaders; it was all the excuse Haldane would need.

"Do it", he instructed. "Now let's get hold of that schoolteacher before she screws it up. Where is Lieutenant Pieterson."

"Here sir," responded the research officer returning from the adjoining room.

"Tell me about her."

"Not much to tell, sir. Elisabeth Hope, orphan, grew up in the East End projects; academic type it seems and won a scholarship to the University; graduated near the top of her class but instead of joining the Corporation she returned to her childhood district to teach; has never come to our attention before so no detailed records."

"What do the neighbours say?"

"Nothing much useful. Known acquaintance with the boatwoman Batista, friendly enough with the other staff but not that close to any of them from what we can make out. This is interesting though: she attended Senator Hardwicke's wedding at the Hall. Found it in our security files. Spoke to the Senator's protection team – I served with one of them in the regiment, sir – and he asked a few questions.

Turns out they were students together, and very friendly at the time."

Davis was frowning; he could hardly haul the Hardwicke woman down to Little Smith Street under duress; even the Civil Guard's powers had limits – at least for now.

"Sir", continued Pieterson, "there was another University friend at the wedding, according to my source: Daniel Mason."

Davis' eyebrows instantly arched in recognition. Very interesting, he agreed. "Mason still here?" he asked the room.

"Yes sir," replied Walker, who had just returned himself. "In the canteen sir."

"How did he fare downstairs?" asked Davis.

"Squeamish sir" replied the river patrolman with a grin, "decorated the enamel."

Pickering could see the faint look of disappointment in his boss' expression, so said quietly, "It often happens the first time people see my work. He could still be useful"

Davis shrugged. "About to find out where his loyalties are."

Daniel was struggling to manufacture an appetite. He felt nauseous still; kept replaying the scene in his own head. Had he done this? He had captured the man, had brought him in; did that make it his hand on the scalpel? Was he responsible for what happened within these walls? Was he as good as the torturer himself? He shook his head, trying to dispel the cloud of horror spreading through his own consciousness. The small voice inside of him that had been gently whispering for all these weeks was turning into a roar. You know who they are, it told him; you know what the Civil Guard are known for. Are you sure you want to be part of it? What would your father think? Where were your precious principles when the man you captured was held in that chair?

Terrorists, he told himself again. The attack on the bridge; the smoke and the panic and the fear; the faces of the children crushed against the stage. How close they had come to catastrophe. They could not be allowed to do that again. He wanted them caught; he wanted them stopped. It was the right thing to do, whether he was involved or not. If he could help, he should.

But this? What must he become to protect the innocents? Did it justify this? What he had just seen?

"Mason. Mason!" came a voice from across the empty chairs of the half-lit eating hall.

Daniel shivered as he came back into the room. "Yes", he replied.

220

"The boss wants you upstairs", Walker told him.

"Coming".

When Daniel finally left Little Smith Street a few hours later, he was having to grip his hands together to stop them shaking. Now they were after Elisabeth. The lieutenant had explained why; had told him about the prisoner they had seized from the Pioneers, about how they had traced his sister and tracked her through the marshland; how she had tried to escape with the help of a schoolteacher. He hadn't mentioned the explosion, had just stated that the older woman had been killed whilst trying to flee their patrols. Elisabeth was still on the run.

Daniel had answered all their questions about her − he had not seen her for years apart from the chance encounter on the bridge, and he was keeping those few moments to himself. Lieutenant Pieterson had grudgingly accepted that he could not be much immediate help, and he had been sent home to get some rest. He would not be returning to the Barrier Authority just yet though, Davis had told him. They would extend his secondment until they had found this woman as well, if he wanted to help.

How could he say "no"? He had spent the previous few weeks enthusiastically helping them on the river; if he walked away now, they would guess that Elisabeth meant more to him than he had admitted. He could not allow that to happen, could not let them use him to get to her; he could not betray Elisabeth to these people, not now that he knew what they would do. He screwed his eyes closed as he thought again of the fate of the Swede, still tied to the surgeon's chair in the lower levels.

He was exhausted physically and mentally from the hunt in the marshes, but could not face going home to sleep. Saskia kept asking him when he would be free to return to his own work, when he would be away from the Civil Guard. The distaste and bitterness in her voice was so clear, and yet he hadn't heard it, not when his obsession with catching the terrorists in the Medway had seemed so important. Instead of listening, he had pushed her away. Now, all he wanted was to hold her and their child in his arms, but he could not go to them this evening; not after what he had done. He felt dirty, undeserving of their love as he remembered the Swede's bloodied face.

He needed advice, and hoped that she would still be in the compound this late in the winter evening. As he turned towards the Cone, he was unaware of the surveillance cameras closely watching his every move.

thirty four

Isabella had turned down the lighting and was sitting quietly in her office, reflecting on the events of the past few weeks: the warning from her long-dead father, the mind-shifting meeting with the Librarian, her marriage so closely followed by Yves' stark warning. She had since made a few discoveries of her own, finding that the hints were there if only she looked for them. Critics of the government quietly disappearing, outspoken Councillors suddenly losing their tongues; it seemed that those who opposed the Mayor were silently melting away into the background.

She had met up with one of her informants earlier that evening, a well-placed Colonel with the Intelligence section of the standing Army; one of Lucas' men. He told her that they were concerned about a threat to the stability of the City, but were not sure where it came from. Isabella, however, recognised enough of the vague warning to suspect she knew the source. No matter; they both agreed something was happening in the background. They needed to find out what.

"There is something else that worries me," he had continued. "I can't prove this, and it seems outlandish I'll admit, but I think the Army is being deliberately divided."

As Isabella asked what he meant, the soldier had pulled out a hand-drawn map. The man was clearly taking no chances if he thought his wrist-projector could be being monitored.

"This is how our forces are normally positioned around the city. As you can see, the six Regiments each have a section of the border to protect, and each keeps roughly one third of their troops near the Walls at any particular time. The rest of the men are stationed in their urban barracks or on leave. Now look at this map," said the Colonel, turning over the sheet. "This is from today. You'll note that all of the Second are back in the city, with their border responsibilities being shared by the Fourth and First. That is not unusual. But the Sixth are also in reserve in their Chiltern barracks, their sections of wall being spread between other Regiments as well."

"And you find that surprising?"

"For two Regiments to be in reserve at the same time, yes," said the Colonel, "it does happen, but very rarely, and usually for good reason."

"The Second was Haldane's regiment?" she asked him.

"And Davis'. A lot of the Civil Guard passed through their barracks as well."

"What about the Sixth?"

"Very different, I'll admit. Lucas' men."

"You have a theory?" Isabella asked.

"I wouldn't call it a theory. An idea, maybe. I'm not sure if it involves the Sixth, though. Lucas is a traditionalist; believes in honour, respect, that sort of thing. Believes the role of the Army is to do what the Council decide."

Isabella nodded in agreement. She had worked with General Lucas for years since his appointment as Head of the Standing Army, and knew he was loyal to the Council.

"But the Second have always been different to the other Regiments," continued the Colonel. "They believe in themselves. They will do whatever needs to be done for them to prevail, which is why they were so feared on the old battlefields. In the early days of the Council when there were still murmurings of discontent from the returning soldiers and whispers of coups and military rule, they always revolved around the Second. The Regiment has never quite lost that tradition."

"You suspect they may be planning something?" she asked, her blank face giving no indication of her own thoughts on the matter.

"I know it sounds outlandish. But I don't believe in coincidences. The Second in barracks and the Civil Guard packed with their ranks, at the same time as our sources suggest the City faces an internal threat?"

"Thank you," Isabella had finished. "You have given me much to think about. We should speak again soon."

She had been meditating on this development all evening. The Colonel was certainly a shrewd analyst, she decided. If the Second were still loyal to Davis and Haldane, which she suspected they were, then the fact that they were massing their troops within the urban areas was certainly worth knowing. But why the Sixth as well, she wondered? Had Lucas been turned, or did he suspect something himself? She would have to try and talk to the General, find out where he stood. She was readying herself to leave, when her secretary's face appeared on the room's screen.

"I have a Mr Mason to see you, Senator. He does not have an appointment,"

"Send him in", she replied, wondering what he could want at this time of night.

The hunched figure that shuffled unsteadily into her office was not the confident Daniel Mason that she had seen a few days before on her wedding night. He looked awful; red-eyed and sunken.

"Is it Saskia? Lexi?" she asked quickly.

"No, no, they're fine," he replied. "Sorry to turn up uninvited".

"You are always welcome here. What is wrong?"

"The Guard are after Elisabeth."

Isabella was genuinely shocked; she took a moment to contain her surprise, before asking in measured tones, "Do you know why?"

"They have linked her to one of the terrorists involved in the Dam attack, at least that's what they are telling me."

"Do you believe them?"

"I have no reason not to, but it must be a mistake?"

Isabella led Daniel to the couch, helping him sit before pouring two glasses of brandy from the decanter on her desk. She passed one over, swilling her own in the cup of her hand to warm the syrupy liquid and release the vapours. Inhaling it first, allowing the strength of the spirit to clear her head, she then sipped slowly before speaking again.

"You have seen something that has upset you, I think?" she asked.

Daniel just stared into his glass; he had not yet tasted it.

"Please; you may find it helpful to talk."

He knew she was right; this is why he had come. He could not talk to his wife about what he had seen in Little Smith Street, did not want her to be sullied by his memory. He needed to talk to someone else, somebody with clearance who would not be endangered by the knowledge of events in the Guard's headquarters.

"Do you know what the Guard do to their prisoners?" Daniel asked.

Isabella understood immediately why Daniel had come to her. They had made him sit through one of their interrogation sessions; made him a witness to the torture. She had been keeping herself informed of his progress with the Guard, out of concern for the man she once loved. Had been worried when reports had reached her of his enthusiasm; of how he had taken to the hunt on the river like one of their own. She had lately discovered that Davis was even considering making the secondment permanent, giving Daniel a commission in the Guard.

Probably this had been some kind of final test, seeing how he would react to their questioning techniques. Perhaps even the hunt of Elisabeth was part of it – it would not be unlike the Guard to actively test where a new recruit's loyalties really lay.

"They made you watch?" she asked in return.

Daniel nodded, his eyes not leaving the swilling liquid in his hands.

"You think you are responsible for this happening?"

"Of course I am," he spluttered, before going silent again and rocking gently, forward then back, forward then back.

Isabella moved to sit beside him on the soft leather seat. Placing an arm around his shoulder, she said quietly, "you did not do this."

For a while, neither of them spoke, Isabella softly stroking his back as he continued to gently rock, his knees pulled together and up towards his chest, his arms reaching around them and clasping the untouched goblet. Eventually, Daniel took a deep breath, relaxed into the chair, and took a sip from his glass.

"I am responsible for what happened to that man. I can't escape that."

"You did not do it knowingly"

"I had my eyes closed."

"For good reason", she replied. "You sought justice"

"I didn't find it. Not with them."

"Now you know"

He turned towards the Senator, noticing her as a woman for the first time since he had arrived, seeing how the white-blond ringlets of her long hair cascaded softly down her torso. Her eyes, so full of life, always so full of answers, held him firmly in her gaze.

"Isabella", he said, taking her hands in his. "Thank you."

For once, she looked away. Daniel took another sip of the aged cognac.

When she rose to refill their glasses, she sat instead behind the desk, allowing its firm back to hold her spine erect.

"What will you do now?" she asked.

"They want me back tomorrow to help them search for Elisabeth. I have no idea if she is involved in this, but I don't think they do either. It won't matter. They'll put her in that bloody chair, whatever she says."

"You must return." Isabella said, reaching for the maple-cane propped up against the wall and slowly caressing the polished marble head.

Daniel looked surprised. "I can't help them catch her, Isa. You know what they would do."

"Nevertheless," she replied calmly but firmly, "you must return."

"Why?" he asked, genuinely puzzled.

"Daniel, my old friend. There is more at stake here than you imagine. There is a plot against the Council, against the city itself, and I believe it involves the Civil Guard. I need someone on the inside."

"Isa, surely you don't want me to?"

"You do not have to betray Elisabeth," she continued. "You must appear to be helping as much as you can. You have not seen much of her over the past few years I believe?"

"Hardly since University", he said with a touch of sadness,

"Then you are unlikely to know anything that will compromise her. If you do not arrive at Little Smith Street tomorrow morning, it will be you who falls under suspicion. You and Saskia. You know now what they are capable of."

Daniel looked truly horrified; it had not occurred to him that his own family would be drawn into this, but the instant Isabella mentioned it he saw the truth. They would use Saskia against him, just as they had used Batista and her brother. Would they stoop to involving his daughter as well, he asked with a sickening feeling?

"Can you protect them Isa? Saskia and Lexi?"

She pondered this for a moment, thinking of the best way.

"Of course. They must come and be my guests at the country house. They must let it be known that I have invited them due to your prolonged secondment to the Guard. Daniel, you must go home now, get them to pack. They should come to me in the morning. It must not look like they are running away."

"I understand. Thank you Isa," he said, moving round behind the desk to hold her hands again as he spoke.

"Now you must leave."

thirty five

The morning light was long overdue as the thick clouds rolled in from the turbulent sea, their ragged undersides hanging like daggers from a lowering ceiling. Val Banerjee was alone in her Dam-top office, watching the waves build as the wind continued to grow. They would have to close the gates within the hour, she knew; ride out this winter-storm like all those before it. The forecast, for what it was worth these days, was not good. A vicious low pressure system was developing overhead, which meant they might have to close the barrier for days. The danger then would become rising waters on the inside of the walls; the marshes could only absorb so much, especially at this time of year when they were already water-logged.

As she sipped on her third caffeine-laden brew, she tried once again to piece things together. She remembered being at the wedding, standing in the balcony bar and letting the drink and smoke wash away the problems of the previous few weeks. She remembered everything, fairly clearly, until the food had finished and everyone began to socialise freely; but then it became confused, a few hazy images but no order to them, no narrative. She could picture herself talking to beautiful people, but after that remembered nothing at all. When she had woken the next morning, groggy and disorientated, she had no idea how she had made it to her own bed.

"What happened?" she asked aloud, clenching both fists as her frustration overwelled. Even now that days had passed she was still wracked by the anxiety of not knowing; and that in itself worried her yet further. She had not allowed herself to get that wasted for years, at least not without intending to, not without being surrounded by friends. Surely she would have heard by now if she had done something bad; somebody would have told her? But would they, she wondered; she hadn't known any of the people there particularly well.

In the corner of her bedroom at home sat her clothes from that evening, neatly folded. She had not touched them since. Something about the symmetrically laid garments was wrong: she would have thrown them in a pile on the floor after even a few drinks. She couldn't arrange clothes that tidily even if she tried. It did not make sense. She had even used her clearance as a senior Council employee to access the security logs of her building, but they did not help. She had entered the building at four in the morning, they stated, alone. Nobody else had used the turnstile for an hour on either side, and the stile only admitted one person at a time. She must have been on her own; although strangely enough there were no screen images of the lobby available. Apparently the cameras had been de-activated for maintenance that evening. Was that a coincidence?

Eight hours then, a complete blank; another problem for her to worry about. The Civil Guard investigation had not gone well either, criticising Barrier Security for allowing the breach to happen. At first she had thought that Haldane would make her take responsibility and resign, but he seemed more concerned with catching the terrorists than apportioning blame; still, she worried that when it all calmed down, she would find herself pushed out of the Authority.

Pennells, her security chief, had not seemed himself for days after being questioned by the Guard, and had called in sick two weeks ago. She made a note on her desk to check up on him later in the day. Banerjee did not know his deputy particularly well, but had warmed to her as they worked together in his absence on tightening procedures and surveillance along the vast length of the Dam Wall. Perhaps she would have to promote this Sarah Jones, and let her superior be the scapegoat; better him than me, she thought to herself.

thirty six

It had been a long night alone in the plantation. The endless lines of fir trees seemed to make the darkness somehow blacker than normal, and Elisabeth had struggled to navigate towards the hidden cliff. Some hours before dawn she had given up, deciding instead to rest and gather her strength before trying to find her way in the pre-dawn light. She had managed to stay ahead of her pursuers, helped by the head-start that Batista's selfless sacrifice had given her. It had taken them some time to get more teams into the area after the explosion of the lifter, which gave her the opportunity to use the chemical masking agents in her pack to disguise her scent as she made her way into the forest. The Guard's dogs, when they finally arrived, could not pick it up.

She had taken shelter in a small dell, nestling under the needled branches of two great firs and leaning her tired frame against the buttress roots. Despite wearing waterproofs, her clothes were soaked through from the worsening rain, so she changed into a fresh set from her pack; it was dry enough where she lay under the trees. Sleep came quickly, but she only allowed herself an hour, waking when the silent vibrations from her alarm gently roused her. She was happy to wake, leaving behind the troubled dream-images of vengeful fire. Steeling herself to make this one last effort, she set out again in what she hoped was the right direction. She owed it to her old friend to try as hard as she could; if she could escape their clutches, the woman's awful death might at least mean something.

As she came nearer to the border wall the terrain began to steepen, and with the hills came outcrops of rocks. Here the neat lines of the grid-plantation gave way to a free-for-all, as the trees grew where they could. This was the oldest part of the forest, first to be planted along with the construction of the city's outer defences. Exhausted, her legs gained strength from these ancient trunks, their thick evergreen bodies protecting her from the worst of the driving rain that lashed against their upper regions. She kept climbing the slopes, scrambling where she needed to, running where she could. Her new clothes were damp now with effort as the sweat leached her body dry; she would need to collect some drinking water soon if she could not find her way.

Crouching once more under the spiky boughs she brought out the map from her inner pocket, examining it carefully in the half-light. It should be ahead of me, she thought, just a few hundred metres more. The branches were too thick for her to run now so she pushed her way through the sharpened arms of the steadfast firs, keeping her head lowered to push through the thousands of needles all raised like miniature pikes to protect their own lines. Soon she could not even force her way past the trees and was forced onto her stomach, crawling through tunnels between the trunks, silently hoping that there were no snakes in her path.

Ahead she could see the faint promise of light and towards it she slid, arm after arm, dragging herself along the softened forest floor. Her strength was nearly gone now but still she moved, propelled by the trees themselves as they wafted her forward like oversized cilia, until eventually she emerged from the darkness into a small clearing in front of a sheer wall of granite.

The rock was almost glimmering as the first rays of the morning found their way through the upper reaches and bounced off the rain-soaked moss that covered the entire face. Elisabeth lay where she had emerged, the tears streaming down her face as she sobbed for arriving here alone. There was no chance of the rendezvous they had planned, no hope that they would laugh together again when this was all over.

The familiar drone of a lifter above the canopy roused her to action; it did not sound close, but they were searching for her still. The dogs would find her trail soon enough, she knew. She must discover what her friend had stashed in this rock-wall and then continue towards the border. It must be something to help them cross, she reasoned, but she could not think what the Portuguese could have hidden here that would get them both through the concrete barrier. Tunnelling equipment would be too heavy for them to carry, even if she were here as well. Elisabeth suspected it would be explosives of some kind; she hoped she could figure out how to use them.

She loosened her pack and set it against the base of the cliff, before letting both her hands come to rest on its mossy surface. She could not see any holes in the mossy curtain, so began to feel her way along, trying to locate something hidden behind the veil. She moved all the way along the wall but could not find them, becoming more frantic as she repeated the search in reverse. The lifter was getting closer now, she could tell; she did not have much time.

For a third time she made her way across the rock-wall, moving her hands across the living surface and trying to find a spot that would yield to pressure but still nothing. She slumped to the floor exasperated, talking to herself as she tried to make sense of it all.

"This is the right place. I'm sure of it. What did she say to me?" she asked the trees before starting to sob again. Inhaling deeply, savouring the sweet smell of the damp woods, she steadied herself.

"Search along the base for a pyramid of holes", she said aloud; that was Batista's instruction. Maybe she meant along the very bottom of the cliff? Elisabeth started to feel her way along the wall again, this time on her hands and knees.

"Yes!" she whispered to herself. Pushing her hands through the matted moss she had found three holes in the rock, arranged with one around knee height and two just above the ground to either side. She remembered the order Batista had taught her; had spent most of the night's escape repeating it like a mantra to ward off the chasers. She reached into the top hole and felt her fingers close around a handle. She pulled it firmly and it responded, smoothly sliding out towardss her; holding this in place she reached into the hole on the left and did the same. As that too responded to her efforts, she heard a wet thumping noise to her right. Turning her head, she saw that the moss covering an area of the rock-face around two metres in height by a metre wide had begun to sag-in slightly. She released both handles, and stood to investigate. The moss gave way as she pushed her hands through, and where moments ago had been solid rock there was now just air behind! She pulled the green blanket apart, making a tear large enough for her to step through, but she could see nothing in this newly opened cave. She walked back to her pack, digging out the torch before returning to the wall and shining it through the gap.

She had expected some kind of cave; a hidden cache of equipment secreted somehow in the granite outcrop. As the torch-light lit up the interior, she saw instead a passageway hewn through the rock and running for at least fifty metres before it started to bend away to the right. Whatever this door had opened, it was not a simple hiding place for explosives. She didn't like the idea of trapping herself in a tunnel, but the Guard would find her soon if she stayed in the forest and she had no idea of how to cross the border on her own. Batista had told her to come here; had died so that Elisabeth had a chance to reach this place. She knew she must enter.

She moved away from the doorway to gather her pack, and then stepped into the tunnel. Once through the mossy entrance and inside, she could see another handle set into the inner wall. Carved into the rock above it was the simple inscription "Close the door". Elisabeth weighed it up in her mind; if she closed it she might be trapped in here, but if she did not, the dogs might follow. She took a deep breath, and pulled the handle.

A section of rock rose with unexpected smoothness from the floor, filling the entrance completely. Elisabeth shone her torch back towards this solid door, giving it a shove with her free hand: firmly closed. She noticed the silence immediately; the sudden absence of the wind blowing through the trees that had been her only companion through the long night in the forest. She did not know where the tunnel led, but was beginning to feel safer for the first time since they had left the city, standing in this still air whilst the storm continued to build on the outside. Her pursuers would be closing on the escarpment, she knew; the spittle-mouthed hounds pulling their beastly masters ever closer. Let them bark, she thought, let them rage against the unmoving rock face; it would not betray her now, hidden deep inside.

The walls were roughly cut to begin with as the passage arced gently away from the entrance. After no more than a hundred paces she shone the light back towards the door but it was already out of sight around the slight corner. Onward then, through this underground burrow. Soon the walls began to flatten out, the jagged edges of hand-cut granite being replaced by a smooth white wall on either side, almost like plaster but firmer to the touch. The floor had changed as well, the gravelly stones of the entrance giving way to what looked like neatly laid flagstones; separate metre-square blocks set into the ground one after the other. Elisabeth kept walking for almost an hour as the tunnel wove gently through the earth, always a slight curve to left or right stopping her seeing too far ahead. Soon, though, the exhaustion of her flight from the Guard returned; in the calm quiet below ground, the adrenaline had started to ebb away. She was too tired to go on for much longer, but didn't know how far she had to go. Unshouldering her pack, she sat down to take a rest, leaning against it for comfort. Within minutes, she was asleep.

thirty seven

They had not had much time to prepare before the transport arrived, and Lexi had not been much help; she was still half-asleep. The driver had helped them load the hastily packed cases into the trunk, before taking his seat up front for the journey to the Hardwicke country house. As they pulled away, Saskia looked back through the rain-mottled window at her fast-receding home, wondering how it had come to this.

The previous evening she had decided to have it out with Daniel; he was scaring her, spending all this time with the Civil Guard. If only she could get through to him, make him realise how unlike himself he was acting. He had always been so disparaging of the city's internal security forces, considered most of them a serious affront to liberty. That fierce independence had been one of the things that attracted her to him when they first met; yet he had become obsessed with hunting for these terrorists, and she didn't recognise the man he had become. When he finally arrived home, however, he looked terrible. His complexion was almost translucent, and his eyes were puffy and bloodshot; she even thought he may have been crying. When he spoke to her, he did so not in his normal confident tones but in a quivering whisper.

"I'm so sorry", he had begun. "I should have listened to you, should have listened to myself, but what could I have done? I had to help them, didn't I? I had no choice."

"Daniel," she had said with genuine concern, taking both of his cold yet clammy hands in hers, "slow down, my love."

"I'm sorry, I'm not making sense" he said, shaking his head as though to clear it before continuing. "Sas, the Guard are after Elisabeth. I don't know why, but they are. They want me to help."

Saskia knew her partner well enough to realise there was more, so she waited for him to go on.

"I've seen the Guard for who they really are tonight. Seen things I never wanted to see. Oh, my eyes are open now, Sas. Why didn't I listen?" he exclaimed with frustration as his wife gently stroked his arm, calming him and bidding him continue.

"The Swede, the terrorist. We caught him. I caught him, and gave him to them, and they took him inside their bloody building and," he said, but he couldn't continue.

Still she held him, cradling him now as his body shook with emotion, using her sleeve to dry her man's cheek.

Daniel took a deep breath, and then another, sniffing and drying his eyes. In a more stable, controlled voice, he continued speaking. "Sas, they know that I knew Elisabeth at University. I know how they work now, and they'll try to get to her through me. They'll try to get to me through you and Lexi. We can't let that happen. I'm so sorry I didn't listen to you, believe me I am."

She understood what he was saying only too well; they were all at risk now. This is what she had feared, this was why you stayed away from the Guard, why you didn't get too close to their filthy web. Her maternal instincts took over as she began to think practically; where could she take Lexi to be away from all this? Before she had chance to air her thoughts, Daniel began speaking again.

"I've been to see Isa. She'll look after you and Lex. You'll be safe at the country house."

Saskia thought on this for a moment, and despite her own misgivings about Daniel's past with this woman, she could see his logic. The Senator was one of the very few people in the city that the Civil Guard could not touch. She was, quite literally, above the law, protected from their grasp by the authority of her position. Isabella's house was probably the safest place in all of London for them now.

"Okay. We'll go. When?"

"The transport will be here in two hours."

thirty eight

Diodes covered the ceiling and walls of the cell, regularly spaced and brightly lit to banish any hint of shadow from the room, no matter where the prisoner stood or lay. Many days had passed since Joao Batista could stand on his own legs without the guards hauling him upright from the armpits. He lay huddled in the corner, his naked skin a travesty of itself. He wore the dark earthy shades it displayed after weeks of beating like a coloured coat; the deep weeping incisions cut by Pickering's knife like mis-positioned pockets.

His body was nearly destroyed, but hiding deep within was his mind; lost and confused and struggling to cling on through the incessant pain, but flickeringly sane still. He knew that this was real. He knew the pain was not a dream, that each vicious stroke brought him a step closer to the end. He remembered his life; remembered what it had felt like to run his fingers in the sticky sap of a freshly harvested cork tree on his family's old plantation; remembered the sweet scent that rose above the dusty soils and danced upon the breeze; remembered his father's hand on the saw, and his mother's on the wheel; remembered the fierce look of perseverance on his beloved sister's face as she tried to carry the bark to the trailer, but could not reach its bed.

He did not know how, but he knew she was gone. He, alone, remained in this forsaken place.

It would not be long now, and what looked like a grimace when displayed on his grossly distorted features was actually a smile. He knew what was coming, in days or even hours if he let them continue. It was time to take control.

He hauled himself onto his hands and knees, and crawled into the centre of the cube-walled cell, his open wounds painting their bloody lines across the stark white floor. With difficulty he managed to arrange himself so that he sat cross-legged, facing the wall that he knew was a one-way window; white with points of light from his side, but clear from the viewers outside. He would face them as he did this, even if they would not face him.

His left foot had been crushed by a Guard's hammer-stamping boot, days before; holding the swollen mess in his hands, he found the loosened nail on his crushed toe. It did not hurt him to pull the remnants free of his skin; nothing could hurt him anymore. It was hard and sharp at the edges, as he had hoped. Their scalpel-cuts had been meant to scare him but keep him alive, he had realised soon after the sessions had begun; his cut would be different. Slowly, deliberately, he began to slice the nail against his wrist.

Minutes later the reddened floor was expanding, a velvety wave reaching for distant shores. The guards did not realise what was happening until it was too late; by the time they had entered the cell and applied pressure to the artery, Joao Batista was dead.

One of them would have to tell the Commissioner; the custody-sergeant, as the most senior guardsman present, knew it was his duty.

He could hear the shouting the instant the elevator doors opened, and it was still going by the time he reached the outer doors to Davis' command post. The Commissioner sounded furious, and was bellowing at one of the Lieutenants who stood to attention, taking the full broadside of his leader's fury.

"What do you mean, vanished?", he roared. "One woman in a plantation forest should not be that difficult to find."

"Sir."

"Well? Come on."

"As I said, sir. The trail just goes dead. The trackers have lost her, sir."

"And what do you want?" Davis continued, wheeling round to face the newly entered corporal.

The junior guard swallowed. "The prisoner, sir" he began, struggling to get his words out.

"Speak up for fuck's sake."

"The prisoner Batista, sir. He's dead."

Davis' eyes widened. Their prisoner, the one they had captured from Soon, the one whose relative had killed seven of his men and destroyed one of his lifters, dead? This Batista was their main lead.

"Pickering?", Davis shouted, his voice losing none of its fury. "You said he wouldn't die."

"Shouldn't have done," replied his assistant curiously. Pickering turned to the sergeant asking, "How did it happen?"

This was it, the guard realised. They would blame him for the death; as custody-sergeant, he was responsible. "The prisoner managed to sever his own artery sir. We believe he used his own nails."

Davis shook his head in disgust. Another bloody failure amongst his men; he could not allow this to keep happening.

"Sergeant, you are guilty of dereliction of duty," he said coolly. "Get him out of here; stick him in Windsor," he continued, but now speaking to the guards on the office doors.

The sergeant looked horrified; he would not last long in the prison, not as a guardsman. Davis may as well have shot him on the spot; that would have been better. As he was dragged away forcibly, pleading with Davis to have mercy, the atmosphere in the Commissioner's office noticeably tightened. Everyone knew that their leader didn't tolerate failure, but the senior staff hadn't seen him this worked up since their days in the military. Every man present realised what this meant; they were on a war-footing now, and failure would be dealt with as it was on the battlefield: swiftly, decisively, and brutally if needed.

They would all have to be at their best; and yet, despite the risk to themselves, they relished the challenge. They lived for it.

"Gentlemen," Davis said firmly, his tone only hinting at his earlier anger, "We have the Swede and we need to find this woman, I want options."

thirty nine

The entire chamber was in uproar as the various groups of Councillors argued angrily, shouting their accusations around the circular room as each faction sought to blame each other. The government information channels had showed the pictures of the exploding lifter just as Pickering had suggested, and the so-called invasion had dominated all the screens ever since. The city was simmering as every citizen awoke to a state of paranoid threat that they had not experienced for years, not since the walls were built and the last battles decisively won. The army had cancelled all leave and doubled the units on border patrol, the Civil Guard were on their highest level of alert, and even the municipal police were making a concerted show of strength on the streets.

They hadn't consulted Haldane before releasing the cover story; instead Davis had taken the initiative, and was waiting to see how their leader would respond. If he didn't rise to the task, well; then they would go on without him.

The Mayor had initially been furious when he was told of the deception, but had realised quickly enough the path his subordinate had chosen. He had a choice: to crush Davis and risk bringing down the entire Civil Guard that he had spent so long packing with his people, or he could lead them from the front. He despised the man for forcing him to act before he was ready, but the outcome would no doubt be the same if they made their move now or in a week, or a month, or six month's time. Haldane did at least realise the genius of the hoax invasion, understanding the effect this would have on the fractious and divided Council. It would paralyse them, tie them up in bitter dispute at the only time when their swift action would still be able to stop him assuming total control. As he made his way down towards the Council chambers he knew it was working; he could hear their anger-fuelled shouts from two floors above.

"Please, Councillors, some quiet," pleaded the amplified voice of the Speaker above the politicians' din.

Slowly, as his remonstrations continued, the Council members began to settle down as they prepared for the session proper to begin. Once there was silence, or as near to it as they were likely to get even with aid of the dampening sound-fields, the Speaker opened proceedings with the required formalities.

"Councillors, I bid you welcome to this emergency session of the Chamber. We have been called to respond to the egregious desecration of our border, and the despicable and deadly attack on our troops. First we shall hear from the Executive Branch of government. Lord Mayor Haldane."

Haldane bowed slightly to the assembled ranks of the political classes, and took up his position in the centre of the floor.

"Members of the Council, you have seen what I have seen. It is incumbent upon us, as leaders of this great city, to judge the facts as we see them, and to act accordingly. We must not overreact to the slightest provocation, but we must also take heed of the warning signs as they occur. This attack, as worrying as it may seem to our people, and to myself, should not be exaggerated out of proportion. A small force managed to penetrate our borders, but was intercepted by several units of the Civil Guard who had been in receipt of certain intelligence relating to a specific threat. A small force I say, not more than twenty strong, and posing very little threat to the people of London at large. I will not exaggerate the importance of this desperate band, but I will say this: if this is indeed a warning sign of renewed aggression on our borders, we will indeed take heed. Thank you," finished Haldane, stepping back and waiting for the members of the Council to begin.

"Councillor Mabstone", called the Speaker, and an elderly male with short white hair stood up on the second row. The sound fields in the Chamber automatically recognised his voice and amplified it to the room at large.

"My Lord Mayor, I should like to know how our border was breached, and what we are doing to prevent it happening again."

Haldane grinned inwardly; they would do this for him, he knew. "The section of border in question was having its security systems upgraded at the time of the attack. We thus cannot rule out the possibility that the invaders knew this to be the case, and therefore that they may have received inside help."

A collective gasp went around the Chamber; the politicians could sense a conspiracy like a pack of wolves could sniff out their prey.

"As regards prevention," continued Haldane, "we are doubling the number of units on active border patrol, and the Civil Guard will be conducting an investigation into the Regiment responsible for this lapse."

Ordinarily, such an investigation would be the exclusive preserve of the Army itself, but Haldane knew that the Council would not challenge his authority given the situation.

"Councillor Hewlett", the Speaker called, and this time a forceful looking woman in the bloom of middle-age rose near the front.

"My Lord Mayor, are you seriously suggesting that there may be elements inside the city responsible for this attack?"

Haldane could not have planted the questions better himself. "All I can say at this stage is it cannot be ruled out," he replied, adding, "we have all been aware of the rise in dissident activity in recent times. The security forces have long been of the opinion that these groups have been directed from beyond our borders, by outsiders with an agenda of their own. Yesterday's events would seem to confirm those suspicions." Haldane knew they did nothing of the sort, but he also knew how this would be reported on the screens, and how they would edit his comments. His hypothetical statements would likely be presented to the people as fact.

As the questions kept coming, one after the other demanding action from the executive branch, one after the other subtly shifting the balance of power in his favour, Haldane began to relax. Perhaps Davis had been right to make the move this early, he thought to himself. It was certainly playing out well in the Chamber so far, although he knew that the questions would get tougher as the Speaker called on Councillors from the factions less closely aligned to his own coalition. It was one of these later ones that caught him off guard.

"Councillor Epstein", called the Speaker, and Yves rose to his feet. Epstein, as one of the most experienced members of the Council, was widely respected, particularly on matters of security.

"My Lord Mayor", he began, "have you spoken to Mr Soon since these dreadful events took place?"

"The Pioneers continue to advise the Mayor's office of a rising threat beyond our borders", replied Haldane, hoping to brush the question aside.

"My Lord Mayor," said Yves again, despite the rules of the Chamber preventing follow-up questions from the same councillor. The Speaker made to rise and cut off the veteran Councillor, but then thought better of it and allowed him to continue. "My Lord Mayor", Yves continued, "if you had spoken to Mr Soon since this footage was filmed, you would know he is of the opinion that it has been misrepresented. That the pictures we have seen are not of an invasion force at all. That the explosion that has been splashed across all the screens in this city was an accident, a tragic misfortune but not, I repeat not, the work of outside forces. Where are these alleged invaders? Why can we not see them in the pictures from lifter? Why is there apparently no footage whatsoever of these people? Where are they, my Lord Mayor?"

Haldane had been expecting someone to ask these questions, but he had not thought they would do so with such accusatory ferocity. The background noise in the Chamber was starting to overload the sound-fields, and he could hear the anger and surprise in parts of the Chamber. Epstein was, his tone implied, accusing him of faking the pictures himself. That would not do, he realised. This man would have to be dealt with.

"Councillor, I can assure you that these pictures are accurate. I can assure you that it was no accident that led to the deaths of ten of the city's defenders and the total annihilation of one of our lifters. I can assure you that we will be asking Mr Soon some very tough questions indeed, like why he had no warning of this invasion. It is, after all, his job to gain intelligence about exactly this type of threat. We will also ask why he seeks to deny what is so obviously clear to everyone who watches the screens, although I think we can work out why for ourselves, can we not?"

Yves started to speak in his reply, but the sound fields had been adjusted to mask his voice, and the Speaker turned to the next question. Epstein, furious, stormed out of the chamber, and was swiftly followed by some plain-clothed operatives of the civil guard. Fortunately, he managed to control his anger in time to realise he was being followed, and managed to lose them in the warren of tunnels beneath the Cone. He had openly challenged the Mayor, and it had made him a marked man. Is this is what it had come to? he asked himself, as he started to plan his escape.

Back inside, Haldane had taken strength from this verbal encounter, and had decided to flush out the opposition. He brushed away the more critical questioning that followed Epstein's attack with increasing disdain, each time making a note of which Councillors were daring to challenge him on the Chamber floor, each time promising himself that they would regret their bravery. By the end of the session, the lines were firmly drawn, and he estimated that he had support of around a third of the Council, with at least a third accusing him of abusing the power of the executive and questioning the actions of the Civil Guard, and the remainder seemingly sitting on the fence. He would have to alter the balance somehow, and he had a plan.

forty

Elisabeth woke with a start. She felt comfortable wrapped in the soft cotton sheets, but something did not make sense. Where was she? She opened her eyes and saw that she lay in a small, featureless room. There was a jug of water and an empty glass sitting on a small table to the side of the bed, and beyond her feet a closed door; no windows, nothing at all on the plain white walls. She did not know this place, and did not know how she came to be here. Where had she been, she asked herself, and started to remember. The tunnel; safety at last but on and on it went and she had to rest. Then how did she come to be here? What was this place? Had she been captured? If she tried the door would she find it locked?

Using the pillows for support she sat up in the bed and poured herself a drink; her mouth was completely dry and it took a few glasses to quench her thirst. The white nightgown she was wearing felt light and comfortable, if unfamiliar. Her pack – where was it? She scanned the room hurriedly but couldn't see it. That did not bode well, she thought to herself; maybe this was a prison-cell. She wondered if she was being observed. It was impossible to tell without the right equipment; if there were any cameras, they would be too small for her to see. "Not that it matters," she thought, "I'm not likely to get up to anything in here on my own"; and as she let out a small laugh at herself, the door opened.

"I am glad you can smile," said the woman as she entered. Tall and beautiful, carrying the confidence that such a combination

258

engenders, the woman seemed to radiate energy in the colourless walls. "My name is Constanza. Yours is Elisabeth, I believe?"

Elisabeth nodded, pulling her knees up into her chest under the sheets and holding them there in locked arms.

"You are safe here, and welcome," continued the woman, reaching out and placing her hand warmly on the other's arm. "You have many questions."

Elisabeth nodded again, her mind racing.

"I will answer them if I can", she said, her body language encouraging Elisabeth to speak.

"Why are you here?" she asked eventually.

Constanza smiled. "A good question. I am here to make you welcome. I am here to answer your questions. I am here to help you mourn."

Elisabeth's eyes widened at the last of these and she flinched involuntarily, shaking off the woman's friendly hold.

"Yes, mourn," Constanza repeated, watching as her lower lip began to contort and her eyes glisten.

"She is dead then," Elisabeth stated. It was not a question. She had not allowed herself the futile hope that somehow her friend would survive the fireball; she had seen it with her own eyes.

"Yes, the woman you knew as Batista is dead. She was dear to us too. We share your sadness, and your pain."

Elisabeth buried her head in the now damp sheets as the memory of the dark night overwhelmed her. As her body convulsed with grief she was comforted by Constanza who had climbed into the bed beside her, holding her as she cried. They lay together in the comforting sheets until Elisabeth's muffled sobs were replaced with the rhythmic breathing of sleep. Constanza slipped out gently and let her be.

It was many hours later that Elisabeth woke again, but this time she remembered all too well. She was filled with sadness, shaking her head as she relived the sacrifice her friend had made so that she could escape. She felt sure that she must be wherever it was Batista had been leading them to; but even so, she would be on her guard until she found out more about this place, beginning with what lay beyond the door.

Edging herself carefully to the side of the bed, she stood up gingerly. Her legs were stiff, the tendons tight and twingeing after the brutal yomp from the city. Walking was possible, but not without pain. At least she was still able to feel the pain, she thought. The door opened onto a larger room, again windowless but this time furnished with a table and chairs. Constanza was sitting on one of them reading a very old book, but looked up when Elisabeth entered.

"You must be hungry by now?"

"Yes," Elisabeth replied weakly. She didn't know how long she had been asleep, but she the felt light-headedness that came with not eating.

"Please, have a seat. I will bring you some food."

As Constanza left, Elisabeth leaned against the chair for balance whilst scanning the room for any sign of her pack. With a sudden flush of relief she saw it leaning against one of the walls, its contents spread out by an old-fashioned radiator. What was this place, she wondered again, sitting down to take the strain off her weary frame. She felt sure she would find out soon enough.

The food that Constanza brought was just what she needed: hearty, warm and full of goodness. She hardly paused for breath as she devoured the stew, using the hunk of bread to wipe up every last piece of sauce from the sturdy bowl. As she wiped her mouth clean with the table napkin, Constanza pulled up a chair beside her.

"How do you feel now?" she asked.

"Full", replied Elisabeth, allowing herself a small smile.

"Good. Let me answer some of the questions you must be thinking of, while you let that feast go down. I'll start with the obvious ones. We found you inside the tunnel under the forest, and we brought you here. Your pursuers followed your trail as far as the rocky wall, but they did not find the entrance. We knew that Batista was leading you here; we hoped that you would both make it. There was nothing you could have done to save her, nor anything we could have done to stop it happening. This is how it must be."

Elisabeth was listening intently as the woman beside her answered her questions almost as soon as they occurred; it was uncanny, as though she were reading Elisabeth's mind as those deep brown eyes stared into her own.

"This place is a Sanctuary. You are welcome here, and you are certainly not a prisoner. You have slept for the best part of two days. When you have regained your strength, I will show you around. No, we are not beneath the forest anymore; in one sense we are close, in another, we are far away from that place. It is complicated, but in time you may come to understand. Yes, you will meet the shepherd; he is expecting you."

"Thank you," said Elisabeth simply; there was no need to ask anything more, for now. "Thank you for saving me."

"You are welcome here," replied Constanza, before rising gracefully and helping Elisabeth to her feet again. She led her through another set of doors into a bathroom, simply fitted and complete with freshly laundered voluminous towels. "Please, take your time. When you feel ready for your tour, I will come and find you."

Elisabeth soaked in the soothing bathwater until the tips of her fingers began to wrinkle like an old woman's. She found herself pondering them, being reminded of her lost friend, and she found the tears returning again. Batista had been so much to her: a mentor to the orphaned schoolteacher, an elder sister to the woman she had become. Always so kind, so willing to suffer so that others may live a better life; even to the end. Especially at the end.

Enough, she told herself; whimpering would not honour her memory. Batista had died to give Elisabeth a chance to reach this place; she must find out why. Still sitting in the now-dirtied water, she removed the plug to let it drain away, leaving her dripping naked in the empty tub. She let the taps run again, diverting the water into the showerhead, standing to let it rinse her finally clean.

When she had dried herself, she returned to the other room to find some clothes neatly folded where she had been sitting before. She put them on: a pair of thick white trousers with soft fleece lining that comforted her freshly-scrubbed skin, and a long-sleeved top of the same fabric that clung tightly to her figure. There was a pair of slippers on the floor so she put these on as well, at which point Constanza re-entered the room.

"Do you feel renewed?" she asked.

"Yes, thank you."

"Then let us proceed".

The Sanctuary was nothing like Elisabeth had imagined. She had suspected they were underground from the lack of windows in the few rooms she had seen, and in this much she was correct; but not in the way she expected. They walked along a broad corridor lined with the doors to living quarters like the one in which she had slept and eaten, before emerging into a high ceilinged rotunda. Its roof was bare rock, roughly hewn and reminiscent of the roof at the entrance to the tunnel in the forest. The walls, however, were smooth, plastered and finished in the colours of the earth, encircling the open cavern for three quarters of its circumference. Tall windows made up the last part of the wall, looking out onto the land below. Elisabeth gasped as she saw them, and the view beyond. She found herself drawn towards it, accelerating on her still painful legs towards the glass.

The view was incredible. This section of the circular room emerged from a wall of rock into which the rest of the complex must have been excavated, hanging like an eagle's nest hundreds of metres above the valley floor below. The cliff face was vertical, and horizontally slightly concave so that she could see it stretching away on either side of her, and looking up she saw it must rise at least another five hundred metres above them. She had thought they were still beneath the forest-plantation somewhere, either just inside or slightly outside the border. This didn't make sense; this cavern was set into the side of a mountain with a vertical face a thousand metres high. There was no such mountain near the London city-state, no mountains of note anywhere near; at least none she had ever heard of.

She looked back at Constanza who had followed her over to the windows, her face imploring an explanation. Elisabeth pointed outside, at the air and the wooded valley far below.

"That is not London."

"No."

"Where are we?"

"We are here, in the Sanctuary. As to where the Sanctuary is, it is where you find it."

"I'm sorry?"

"You entered the tunnel, and now you are here, is this not true?"

"Yes but where is here?" Elisabeth asked, for the first time starting to feel some frustration. Constanza could sense her discomfort, and took Elisabeth's hand between both of her own.

"I know it seems difficult, but you will come to understand. Let us just say for now that we are far from London, hidden away in some distant mountains. But if we wanted to return there, it would not seem so far."

Elisabeth's mind was struggling to accept the words, but she found herself mesmerised by the calm beauty of the woman at her side. She was accepting the explanation, not because it made sense – to her rational mind it didn't – but because deep inside she trusted this woman. The two of them stood together, hand in hand, looking out at the rolling alpine forests and the peaks in the distance, Elisabeth lost in the vastness of the landscape. She could see great frozen waterfalls leaping from the snow-covered upper slopes, their icy cascades sparkling in the sunlight; lower down, she could trace the course of the streams by the folds in the landscape, following them as they disappeared into the forests only to burst out from the trees again, babbling boisterously as they carved their path down through the ancient rockfall; here and there she could see clearings in the rolling forest where avalanches must have carved their outwardly funnelling paths in winters gone by, the stunted remains testament to their awesome power. There – there – above the canopy, a bird of prey hovering stationery, eyes fixed below; then the swooping dive. Slowly, as she watched, her ears as well began to pick out the different sounds of the world in front of her; the workmanlike clacking of the woodpecker, the occasional high pitched bark of the fox. Behind it all, the ever present white noise of the water seeking its way back to the sea; how that must roar come the springtime, she thought to herself; it would be here soon enough. Could she smell the land from here, she wondered, behind the glass. Was that dry, slightly sweet aroma coming from the cavern behind her or the world below?

"Tell me what you see," came a deep, sonorous voice from behind them.

Elisabeth did not turn around, but continued to watch the alpine scene as she answered the unknown voice.

"I see mountains and forest," she replied.

"Tell me about them."

Still facing away, Elisabeth answered. "It is beautiful, and yet it looks so random and unmanaged; I have never seen such a view with my own eyes"

"What does it say to you?"

She felt her brow furrow as she pondered the question. What did it mean? Should she be hearing the land speak to her? She could hear the birds singing and the thermals rustling their way up the slopes, but did not know what answer to give.

"I don't know," she replied simply.

"Listen to it," he instructed, his tone gentle yet firmly commanding.

"I can hear the birds. And the wind, and the water."

"Go on."

"I can see the trees and the rocks and the streams."

"And?"

"And I don't know what I'm supposed to say," she said with exasperation. She moved to turn around but Constanza, still holding her hands, caught her in time and directed her gaze back out of the windows.

Elisabeth took a deep breath, pausing to gather her thoughts. Was this some kind of test, she wondered? The man behind her must be the Shepherd, of that she was now sure. What, then, was this landscape supposed to be telling her – what did he want her to say? Something about his voice had stirred an almost childish instinct to please, and she found herself concentrating, trying hard to find the solution like the keen girl in the classroom she had once been. She tried again, hoping it would come to her.

"Up there I can see the mountains, covered in snow. Below, I can see the trees, but they are not arranged like the forests at home. There are no straight lines, no grids, no firebreaks. It all looks so inefficient, but it must have a purpose. It could be like the Estuary,"

Yes, she thought to herself: that would make sense. The Estuary looks disorganised but actually it's managed - they harness the natural processes for flood defence. Maybe this jumbled plantation works on some similar principle.

"Is it similar to the Estuary?" she asked. "I can't see the pattern but that is for some other reason?"

"What reason?"

"I don't know. What is the forest used for?" she asked.

"That depends on your perspective", came the reply. "To the boar, it is a home and a foraging ground. To the eagle, a roost and somewhere to hunt. To the trees, it simply is."

"But to us? What do its rangers use the lumber for?"

"The rangers? I have told you, for they are the boar and the eagle, the badger and the deer."

"You mean this forest is natural?" Elisabeth asked, surprised.

"And what does it say to you?" he asked again.

Elisabeth took her time in answering. She had never seen anything like this before. They had small parks in London, but they were managed just as much as the crops and the plantations. There were patches of wild growth for sure, like the gully she had fled in with Batista, but they were all still designed-in – they all had a purpose, whether it be to clean the water, or hold the soil in place, or store the floodwaters. The closest thing to a truly wild woodland she had ever encountered was the arboretum at Isabella's, but that was tiny compared to this. What riches these people must have if they could afford to leave such vast swathes of territory unutilised. Where was this place, she found herself wondering again? She must answer this shepherd-man's questions, and yet still felt unsure of how. If the land and forest below her had no purpose for the people who lived here, then what could it say to her?

Then she found the answer, as it could be no more or no less than this.

"That it is alive."

She felt a slight pull on her arm as Constanza turned her gently away from the viewing windows and towards the man behind them. Elisabeth found herself tightening and standing taller as she saw the man. It wasn't that he was beautiful, although clearly he was attractive, well-built with long blondish curls falling both sides of a broad forehead; it was his very presence that affected her. Elisabeth could feel him having the same effect on Constanza, who returned her glance with a shy smile. He beamed radiantly at both of them, raising his arms in a gesture of friendship as he said, "Welcome to our sanctuary."

"You have had a long and difficult journey."

"I have," replied Elisabeth, holding her head inclined upward towards his gaze.

"We will honour the sacrifice made that you might reach us. We will honour their family."

Elisabeth looked at him questioningly, and he continued, "they are both gone now, Maria and her brother Joao. He died, so we have heard, within minutes of her own end; a welcome release perhaps from his incarceration." He grimaced as he mentioned the evil perpetrated by the Civil Guard, and Elisabeth found herself welling up once more.

"We will honour their bravery this evening. Until then, I leave you in Constanza's care."

The man and her companion both bowed their heads towards each other, slightly but deliberately; and then he left them at the windows, disappearing through one of the many doors leading off the rotunda.

"His name is Bastien," Constanza said before she could ask, "and he is the Shepherd that Batista bid you find."

"He is your leader?"

Constanza smiled oddly, as though she had been asked a question that made little sense. "Perhaps he could be thought of in that way; certainly, if it helps you to do so."

Elisabeth was confused by the answer, but let it lie as her companion led her by the hand back inside the cavern and away from the glorious landscape beyond the windows.

They spent the afternoon exploring together, for the morning had long been over whilst Elisabeth slept. Constanza took her through the tunnels, showing her the complex room by room. The rotunda was their meeting place, she explained, where they could relax and socialise; but it was also somewhere they could all assemble, when they needed to talk. The living quarters led off this hall, their dimensions all fairly similar but the decor different, reflecting the diversity of the sanctuary's residents. There were around fifty of them living here she explained, although at any one time half that number would be back in the world. At the end of the corridor was their study area, where three walls were lined with old paper-printed books which they could read at the few desks and armchairs set between them. As she let her finger run along the spines stacked tightly on the shelves, Elisabeth realised what was missing from this place: there were no screens, anywhere. Not in the room she had slept in, or where she had eaten, or any of the living quarters; or even on any of these desks – they just had small spot lamps by which to read the printed pages. She had never been in a building that didn't have at least a few screens spread about the place; even the homes in her neighbourhood, with all its deprivation, would have one in their living room, if only for communication. Surprisingly, to herself at least, she wasn't sure how this made her feel. Sure, she felt liberated from their incessant presence, free from the electronic chains of the virtual prison the city had become; but at the same time she felt isolated, cut off from the community's umbilical, alone and disconnected outside its walls. So be it, she told herself, if independence was the cost of freedom.

They went to the canteen next, with its circular tables and cheerful-looking chef who stopped his work to greet them as they passed through. The stores followed, and then the growing rooms, rows of vegetables lit from above; apparently fibre optic pipes delivered sunlight from vast reflectors set into the mountain-top hundreds of metres above them. Down a level, she found herself being led through the exercise area, a larger chamber containing a pool and a row of treadmills, beyond which was a secure-looking metalled door. Constanza turned the wheel which released the thick iron bolts, and slowly pulled it open. Behind was another large chamber, but this one with a distinctly militaristic feel. Elisabeth was surprised by this, though she wasn't sure why; perhaps it was because of the peaceful scene she had been watching minutes before from the upper windows.

"This is the armoury," Constanza told her, asking, "are you familiar with any of these weapons?"

"No, not really. Batista – she showed me how to use one of those," she replied, pointing at one of the rifles set in a long rack on the wall, "but I haven't fired one for a couple of years."

"You look as though these guns worry you."

"They do." Elisabeth replied truthfully. Weapons made her uncomfortable.

"It is not the rifle that you should fear, but the person holding it."

"So I have been told," Elisabeth replied, remembering Batista uttering the very same words in the barge's cabin, "but I worry that the rifle changes the person."

Constanza kissed her cheek lightly, saying, "You are right." Then she took down one of the rifles from the rack, placing it on the table in front of Elisabeth and starting to load an empty cartridge with bullets. "With these weapons a person can create such horror, and yet be deadened to its meaning. And yet, should we stand idly by whilst others would destroy us? How do we fight for freedom if we do not stand up to those who would deny us?"

"I have always thought that peaceful protest could, in time, lead to change," Elisabeth said, looking away from the gun.

"No you have not. You have always hoped it could, but you have always known that it was an unlikely dream."

There was some truth to this, Elisabeth could admit. As much as she argued with Batista, with herself even about the principle of non-violence, she could see that they were not having any impact. The Council's propaganda machine was contorting their message and hiding the truth; and their attack dogs in the Civil Guard were hunting them down and destroying them. Of the six who stood on the Dam because of an idea, who tried to help the people of the city see the truth, who remained?

John Gates was dead. Olof had disappeared; in all likelihood he could was dead too. She had never known the other three and wondered where they were now. On the run? In hiding, like her, or blown into a thousand pieces like Maria Batista. She had never known the woman's full name, she realised; that the shepherd did elevated him in her eyes.

"It has come to this, then," she said to Constanza, half-asking, half-telling.

"That is for you to decide. For me, it has," the woman replied, cocking the rifle and handing it to Elisabeth. She took it without hesitation.

"The range is this way," Constanza told her, not commenting on the fire she saw anew in Elisabeth's eyes. "You must practice."

Despite wearing protectors, Elisabeth's ears were still ringing slightly when they returned to the upper level. The canteen was packed with people eating dinner, which surprised Elisabeth; the complex had seemed almost empty during their afternoon tour.

"Where have they all come from?" she asked.

"They have been on a training mission, in the forest," replied Constanza.

"Training? What for?"

"This is not simply a place to hide from those who would abuse us. This is where we gather the strength to strike them back. Would you, Elisabeth? Would you fight those who have hounded you from your home, and killed your friends? Those who would oppress anyone who stands in their way?"

Fresh from the armoury, with the smell of cordite still lingering on her hands, Elisabeth pondered the question. She was willing to defend herself, of that much she was decided. Was she willing to attack?

Constanza could see her hesitation, and understood where it came from. Elisabeth still clung to the dream that ideas could be countered by other ideas, that those who held power would listen; in another time, perhaps, but not in their world. Constanza had felt the same way for many years, but she would not be blinded by her own naivety any longer. They would have to stand up to those who would usurp their freedom. They would have to take it back.

As the two women walked through the room, Elisabeth spotted a face she recognised. Approaching the man, she asked, "Kanton – is it you?"

"Elisabeth", he exclaimed, clapping both his powerful arms around her, his expression genuinely pleased to see her standing in front of him. "I was told you had arrived, and it is wonderful to find you here. I only wish that our friend could be here too."

"As do I", Elisabeth replied, having to suppress the sudden feeling of guilt about Batista's sacrifice.

"She was a brave woman. But that we may be so, in her memory," he continued solemnly, before his eyes lit up again as he was filled with emotion at seeing Elisabeth again. "It really is good to see you. Come, eat with us".

The two women filled their plates from the big bowls the chef had laid out, and then joined Kanton at one of the round tables. Elisabeth had not seen him since the morning of the Dam, when he led the group who created the diversion which had allowed them to slip through security. He recounted how he had been arrested by the Civil Guard for public disobedience and sedition, and hauled back to the cells in Little Smith Street; how they had soon lost interest in him when Elisabeth's group had let off the smoke canisters and scrawled the message on the bridge. The Guard had sent the other protestors to the Windsor Prison for indefinite incarceration, which was an unusually harsh reaction to a peaceful protest, and a clear sign of their growing abuse of the rule of law that was supposed to exist in London.

Kanton himself, however, had been released. He had guessed immediately that they were tracking him, trying to see if he led them to the rest of the organisation; but he had been too clever for his pursuers. He had managed to remove the implanted tracking devices with the help of a sympathetic surgeon in the backstreets of Old Chelsea, and then boarded a wherry going downriver to Chatham. He was almost recaptured at the docks, which were crawling with Guardsmen; looking for the Swede, he found out later. Happily, though, he had managed to stow away aboard a viking trawler, and make good his escape.

"And the rest of your group?" asked Elisabeth hopefully.

"Are still in Windsor", he said with meaning.

"Have you heard anything about the others on the Dam? I didn't know their names, only Batista."

"Nor did I, at the time. Everything is different now though, as you will find out soon enough. Olof – the Swede – we think has been captured by the Guard. We should find out soon, one way or another. Gates, as you no doubt saw on the screens, didn't make it", he said, the regret clear in his voice. "Of the other three up there with you, we managed to find Salveson and Winder before the Guard. They are both here, you'll meet them tonight. Escobar – he was the last - drowned during his escape from the Dam. Seems the Guard were getting too close to his hideout in the marshes, so he attempted to swim the Estuary."

Elisabeth was drinking this in like a parched desert nomad, thirsty for news of the cell. She had not known the others in the group – they were anonymous to each other, for their own safety as much as anything. Yet she felt linked to these five people, their fates intertwined by the actions they had taken to wake up the people of their city to what it was becoming. Then it was Elisabeth's turn to tell her own story, as her new companions listened rapt with attention.

How she and Batista had made it out of the marshes and as far as Chatham; how she had attempted to hide in her own life, by going on as normal; how Batista had gone missing and then re-appeared, and the two of them had fled together towards the border. How she made it to the tunnel, but then had fallen asleep.

"The tunnel?" asked Kanton. "I do not know that one."

"There are various ways to sanctuary", Constanza replied. "Each of us takes their own chosen path."

"I came through a waterfall in the Nordic fjords," Kanton told Elisabeth. "It was strange. I had been on my own for a couple of days after hopping off the trawler in Stavanger, and was making my way inland towards the mountains on some skis I had liberated from an outhouse. As I skied along the shore-line, I had an overwhelming desire to climb one of the steep streams that cascaded down the fjord walls. It was hard going, and I nearly turned back – why was I trying to climb out of the valley when the trail led along the shore-line, after all? But I trusted my intuition, and a couple for hundred metres up I found a plunge-pool below a magnificent waterfall. I decided to wash whilst I had the opportunity, and it was then that I discovered the cave, and the passageway."

Elisabeth could feel her confusion returning. How long had she been unconscious? Had she somehow been carried across the seas in her sleep? She felt Constanza taking her hand in hers, leaning in and whispering to her.

"Do not try to understand for now. It will make sense in time." She found reassurance not in the words, but in the soothing touch of the other woman.

forty one

"It's simple. We have to move now," Davis said gruffly.

Haldane's face betrayed his indecision, but he knew his old comrade was right. He had made too many enemies on the Council not to act. If he hesitated, it would give them time to organise against him, to impeach him for abuse of power or gain support for a new election. He would not surrender the city to that gaggle of braying cowards, the sycophants and the appeasers. He knew that he had made mistakes, knew that they should have acted earlier to improve the squalid conditions in the projects and curb the divisive power of the Corporation, but he told himself it was not all his fault. Was it too late now?

He had been elected a decade before on exactly that promise, that he would champion the rights of the commoners just as he had fought for them in the wars. It had not been an empty commitment at the time: he had meant those words as he hammered them home on platform after platform. He united the disadvantaged and the dispossessed and the refugees all struggling to make a home in the city-state, and through them he beat the Corporation's candidate for the first time in years. Yet somewhere along the way he had lost sight of the very people who had brought him to power. He could not lie to himself about this – he knew they were no better off under his administration, knew he had done nothing to redistribute wealth from the industrialists in their fortified towers. If anything, the rich and powerful had become richer and more powerful under his rule.

Where had it gone so wrong? When had they become interested only in power for power's sake, and not for what it could achieve? He had always known that some of the men in his cadre were driven by this addictive lust and not by more altruistic motives, but he had always hoped he was in the latter camp.

Perhaps it had been the institutions of government that had turned his eye; perhaps the Council and even the office of Lord Mayor had become so intertwined with the interests of the Corporation that it was unavoidable. Yes, Haldane told himself: that was it – an institutional bias that he had been unable to shake off. If only he could free himself from the influence of the Council, he could serve the interests of the people he had for so long forgotten. The Council was the enemy of the people, and he and his men were their protectors. It was a convenient lie.

Davis could see the features on his superior's face begin the settle into an expression of resolute determination. It was an arrangement that he recognised well; they were in business.

forty two

Elisabeth had settled into the routine of the Sanctuary with surprising ease, although she had not yet ventured into the forest below on any of the daily training exercises. Instead, she slept on in the bed she now shared with Constanza when her new friend rose in the morning, grateful for the extra rest after the traumas of the previous few weeks. The two women had become very close in their short time together, and Elisabeth was experiencing feelings she had not known for many years; emotions that she had long thought locked away.

The two lovers had talked for hours on end, telling each other about their lives and what had brought them to the sanctuary. Constanza told her the story of how she had been born in the wildlands south of the Continental mountains, an orphan like her, travelling in a wagon convoy with her mother's people as they tried to survive in the shadow of the wars. How they were kept moving by the search for food and shelter, how they found safety in numbers from the scavenger gangs, how they lost people in every attack. When she was in her seventh year, the convoy was struck by one of the plagues that had swept across the lands like a rolling wave, smashing and subsuming everything in its path. Not many survived, and too few to protect themselves. It was then that Constanza had been rescued by a man who took her to a place she had never imagined. It was untouchable, hidden from the wildness and inaccessible to those who did not know its secret. It was a haven for those who were lucky enough to find it, or were fortunate enough to be found. It was there, in this library, that she found peace; there that she was educated and raised; there that she found purpose. When she became a woman, she vowed to serve the organisation and became what they called a reader.

It was then that she moved to the mountain stronghold in Zermatt, and Elisabeth marvelled at the tales of this foreign city and its incredible buildings and towers and peoples from around the known world. She knew of the city of course, and had seen the pictures on the screens, but Constanza's stories brought the place to life, made her want to see it with her own eyes, made her want to walk the snow-locked passages in the winter or sit in one of the sunken roof-square cafes when the storms had passed. It all sounded so different to the London she had always known; and so much more enlightened.

And yet, Elisabeth found herself questioning her own struggle. She agitated for change in London because the government was failing the very people it was supposed to protect; she protested because these calls for change were stifled and suppressed, and those who made them beaten and imprisoned. And yet she could not help thinking that even the people in her own neighbourhood, as poor as it was, were better off than if they had been born to Constanza's world. Her people were malnourished, but they did not starve. They were powerless, but they were protected from marauders beyond the walls by those with power. They were more prone to disease than the well-looked after children of the Corporation, but they still had clinics – overcrowded, underfunded, and the cynics might suggest only there to prevent epidemics that may in turn threaten the wealthy – but clinics nonetheless. Was she guilty of ungratefulness, she wondered? Were the conditions for her people in London at least better than for those left in the wildlands to fend for themselves? Was this not why the refugees still continued to arrive, year after year?

"No", Constanza told her. "That is not the way I perceive it. I will fight for the freedom of people where ever that freedom is curtailed. That is as plain to see in London, as it was in my childhood. I would not romanticise the wildlands. We were not free on the wagons: not free of hunger, or thirst, or cold, or fear. But nor are your people free to live with dignity and respect."

"But it was so much worse for you" replied Elisabeth.

"For me," replied Constanza, "London is worse. Injustice is absolute, but it is also relative. In the wildlands, everyone was hungry. That helps to explain, although it does not excuse. In London, only some are denied the food that would feed them, the clothes that would keep them warm, whilst others sate their greed and gluttony. That I cannot condone."

Elisabeth ran her finger along the depression in the sheets where her lover had lain a few hours earlier, a smile finding its way onto her face like a long-gone traveller returning to his half-forgotten home. She pulled a stray hair from the pillow, and held it up to the light, wondering if it had come from Connie's head or her own; she couldn't tell, and it didn't matter. She had, for this moment, and in this place, found a happiness that filled her consciousness and gave her the strength to go on.

Later, when she had risen and washed and sat by the windows in the rotunda looking out at the forest, she was joined by Bastien. She had not seen him since that first morning in this same spot, and found herself affected by his presence once again as her cheeks flushed.

"What is it you look for?" he asked.

"I don't know,"

"I hope you can find it", he replied, and then they both sat in silence for some time, watching the forest beneath them.

"Bastien," she began.

"Yes, Elisabeth"

"What are they training for?"

"You have not asked Constanza?" he asked, sounding a touch surprised.

"Not yet."

"I understand. You feel ready to know, but you worry about how you will react. This is to be expected."

"Please, could you tell me?"

"Yes, I can. I believe they intend to occupy the Barrier, and hold it for ransom"

Elisabeth need not have been concerned about her reaction, for it was not disapproval that lit up her features, but disbelief. Occupy the dam? Occupy as in capture? When she thought about the trouble they had to go to just to let off some smoke and deliver a message.

"You think it audacious?" Bastien asked.

"I'm not sure. I would have said it was impossible", Elisabeth replied thoughtfully, "until I came here. But occupy the Dam? What for? You said a ransom?"

"I believe Kanton will ask for the release of political prisoners, and also present a list of demands to the Council relating to improving conditions in certain areas of the city. You will have to ask him for the details; it is his plan."

"I thought you were in charge?" Elisabeth asked, surprised.

"Not in charge, no; but I will do what I can, when it is time."

"There will be security. Soldiers probably", Elisabeth mused.

"I believe there are plans in hand to deal with such problems," replied Bastien.

"We'll all be killed."

"We?" he repeated, with a knowing glint in his eye.

forty three

Daniel took the weapon out of its leather holster and placed it on the table in front of him. When he had returned to Little Smith Street the morning after they had interrogated the Swede, he had reported to the quartermaster and requested a handgun. They had called up to Lieutenant Sparrow for confirmation, who had gladly obliged, taking this as evidence that Daniel had decided where his allegiance lay. For the first few days he did all he could to help them assemble a background profile on Elisabeth, knowing that he wouldn't need to tell them anything they couldn't find out themselves; as long as he told them first, they would trust him. Almost immediately he had slipped into the same role he had held on the hunt for the Swede, the independent expert doing all he could to help the Guard with their enquiries. Within days, though, they had exhausted even his knowledge of her past, and with nothing to go on they had almost given up the search.

Pickering continued to try and prise information out of the Swede, but even his ghoulish tactics were getting nowhere; he had decided that the man genuinely had nothing to tell them, and so let him die a solitary death on his butcher's floor, washing away the stains of the man's life with an industrial hose.

Strangely enough, for all his anger during the manhunts, Davis seemed curiously unconcerned by this lack of progress. Some other investigation seemed to be occupying his time now, and the Commissioner's office was packed with the senior staff at all hours, although what they were discussing no-one outside of the upper ranks seemed to have any idea, Sparrow included. With the hunt for Elisabeth winding down, and the officers otherwise engaged, Daniel found himself with nothing to do for the first time in weeks. He sat in the canteen, cleaning his handgun the way that Walker had shown him to, and then caught a lift down to the basement range to practice his marksmanship. If they realised he wasn't needed anymore, they might send him back to the Authority, and remove his access rights. He wanted nothing more than to escape this building and everything it now signified, but Isabella had asked him to stay and find out what he could, and that was what he was going to do.

His determination came partly from a desire to make amends for his role in the capture of the Swede; no matter what he told himself about terrorists, he could not condone what these men had done to their prisoner. If he could play some small role in helping expose a plot within the ranks of the Guard, and in doing so help protect the city, he hoped it might ease his burden of guilt. At least his family were safe now that he had assisted the guard with the search for Elisabeth. He hoped that his continued presence in Little Smith Street on a different mission would not put them in danger again, but he knew that they were as safe as he could make them within Isabella's home.

forty four

"The city might be about to fall", Helio told his master. "Haldane is ready. The Chamois cannot stop him, on her own."

"So it may, and yet there is more to come" replied the Librarian.

"You speak of Bastien?"

"I do."

"Do you know his intentions?"

"I have an idea; that is all."

"What is his role in all of this?"

"He is the fire that brings flowers to the scorched forest floor. He is the flood that nurtures the grassland to rise in its wake."

"You would have me stop him?"

"You must face him, Helio. The choice must be theirs to make. You will know where, and when. For now, return to the Chamois; help her if you can."

forty five

"Lexi, come away from the window," she shouted in an unusually harsh tone. Her daughter was bright enough to realise the urgency in the command and ran back, wrapping her small arms around Saskia's waist and burying her head the folds of her mother's dress.

The three women stood together in an upstairs bedroom, watching the column of troops march up the main driveway six abreast, its tail out of sight around the distant corner and in the trees.

"What is happening?" Saskia asked the other woman.

"That is something I would very much like to know", replied Isabella. She tried to activate the screen on the bedroom wall by flicking her fingers, but nothing happened, nor when she tried again. She walked over and tried the manual control panel, but it was dead.

"Not a coincidence, I am sure", said Isabella out loud. She flicked a dial on her antique watch which was itself a well disguised wrist terminal, but it did not respond. Opening the door to the landing, she found that screen was also useless. So, they were being jammed somehow.

"Mister Johns", Isabella called, raising her voice but not shouting. A few moments later he appeared at the head of the stairs, carrying a couple of projection pistols and with two high-powered rifles slung over his back.

"Ah, well done Mister Johns," she continued, taking one of the pistols and a rifle for herself. "Please could you take our guests to the bunker?"

"Yes maam" he replied.

"And the rest of the staff."

"In position."

"Has my husband returned from the city yet?"

"No maam."

Maybe he would be better off away from the house, she thought, surprising herself with her concern. She returned to the window, carefully looking around the curtain at the soldiers below. The column had come to a halt fifty metres from the front door, and what looked like a deputation of three men was approaching on their own. Isabella hurried down the stairs and into the front reception room. There was a spy hole concealed behind one of the pictures, looking out onto the front driveway and set behind reinforced walls; it had been thought more prudent to place it here than behind the front door itself, for obvious reasons. They were nearly at the steps now, and she could make out one of the figures as the Colonel from the Intelligence Section with whom she had recently met. She didn't recognise the third man, but between them it was unmistakably

General Lucas, commander of the Sixth Regiment and titular head of the Army itself.

She couldn't speak to them from in here, and yet she must know why they had come. Holding the maple cane loosely in both hands, she considered her next move carefully. She would open the door.

"General Lucas"

"Senator Hardwicke. I believe you know Colonel Fairweather," he said, indicating the man on his left. She nodded. "And this is Colonel Steynson, my chief of staff."

"Gentlemen, please, come inside," she said, and beckoned them into the reception room. She did not have to check to know that Mister Johns would be monitoring their every move from behind a glass screen disguised as a mirror. "Tell me, to what do I owe this pleasure?"

"It has started," replied Lucas, as the Colonel she knew nodded. "Haldane is making his move as we speak. Elements of the Second have joined forces with the Civil Guard and are securing key points inside the city. Unsupportive council members are being rounded up and held under house arrest, or worse. We suspect that both your colleagues, Senators Skillane and Lewis, have been murdered. This is a coup d'etat, make no mistake about it."

"And what role would you play in this drama, General Lucas?" asked Isabella, head held high, her face a picture of calm.

"The Sixth remains at the command of the Council and the Senators," replied the General, "which right now means you."

It was starting to make sense, thought Isabella. Lucas had seen this coming, and had moved his regiment to their Chiltern barracks so that they would be close to her estate. The barracks were not particularly well-suited as they were more of a training encampment than a permanent base. Her house, by contrast, was well positioned on the high ground, well fortified, and well provisioned. It would be much easier to defend, if events unfurled that way. The fact that it was also the home of their new de facto commander was a fortunate coincidence. This was the threat to the city that Lucas' spies had been warning about for all these months; no wonder he would not divulge his sources to Davis – half of them were probably inside the Civil Guard.

"If you would permit, Senator, I would like to the Regiment to take up defensive positions around this building."

"Do what you must, General. Let me show you the bunker."

forty six

She wanted one last look at the forest where she had found happiness; one last glimpse through the sanctuary's cliff-windows to the tapestry of life below. The hanger woods with their secret paths and elusive inhabitants where she had walked hand in hand with Constanza, just the two of them together in the early evening light. The pools where they had bathed together, and the glades where they had helped each other to dry. The training always came earlier, exhausting as it was, leaving them drenched in their own sweat with bruises all over their bodies; but it was the evenings that would remain with her always.

She could see Constanza approaching from her reflection in the windowpane, and turned to face her as the other woman used a sleeve to dry Elisabeth's wet eyes. It was the last time either of them would see this view; neither had said it, but both instinctively knew it to be true. Whatever happened on the Dam wall, they would not be able to return here.

The rotunda had been filled with their equipment, vast piles of military cases holding weapons, ammunition and explosives as well as food and water, medical supplies and shelter. Each of them knew the details of the operation intimately, had rehearsed their own role and those of the people close to them in case the worst occurred. Soon they would depart, leaving the safety of their mountain home for a small wood on the Isle of Sheppey from where they would launch their mission. Looking around the room, she could see she was not the only one of the group to be feeling the emotion generated by their departure; she had not been alone in finding peace in this place.

When everybody was finally ready, Bastien walked to the centre of the room and stood there, resting on his shepherd's crook. Elisabeth had never understood how she had come to the sanctuary, nor even where they were, and she still had no idea about how they would return – that was the one part of the plan that no-one discussed; it seemed to just start on the Isle of Sheppey, as though getting back into the city-state would prove no problem at all.

It would not.

Bastien asked, "Are you all ready?", and everyone in the room murmured that they were.

He then continued, "And you do this freely?", and looked to each of them in turn.

As his eyes met with individuals around the room, they each replied "Yes", one after the other, until just Elisabeth was left.

She swallowed. "Yes".

"Then let us begin."

He held his staff firmly in outstretched arms, and watched as the curved end began to emit a bright light that spread like the points of a star until it filled the entire rock-walled chamber. And then, as everything turned white, they were gone.

It took Elisabeth a few moments before she could see clearly again, and before the light came the dampness. It was raining hard, she realised, as she felt the droplets massaging her head through the cap she was wearing and that had started to drip from its rim. As her sight returned she realised that they were all here, equipment as well, in the same circular formation as they had stood in the mountain rotunda; and yet now they found themselves surrounded by trees. These were not like the dignified firs she had come to love beneath the sanctuary though, standing proudly erect and steadfast in their eclectic gatherings amongst the rocks. Instead, these trees were stunted and whorled, their darkened boughs sheltering them from the worst of the storm that she could hear raging above.

Constanza was still holding her arm gently, as she had been in the sanctuary before the light, and now gave it a gentle squeeze.

"I don't understand what just happened," Elisabeth whispered in her ear, "but I accept that it has."

Constanza pulled her closer, and kissed her lightly in the nape of her neck, smiling as she did so.

"Let's get ready to move out", called Kanton to the assembled crew of outlaws.

The trek through the woods did not take long at all, or at least it seemed that way to both women in their state of nervous anticipation. The group split into smaller teams before they left the shelter of the trees, each with its own task to complete which together should secure the dam. Elisabeth and Constanza were paired with Salveson and a woman called Caitlyn, and had to make their way on foot towards a service access tunnel set into the base of the southern end of the dam. Other teams were unpacking the blackened dinghies with their silent motors that would transport them through the night towards the middle and northern ends of the colossal structure, and then the attack would begin simultaneously when everybody was in place. That meant a long wait for Elisabeth's team, hiding in the waterlogged undergrowth near their designated entry point; a long time wondering whether the access codes that they had somehow managed to discover would actually work.

Since her conversation with Bastien, Elisabeth had come to understand the plan in all its detail; she had to admit, it was brilliant. If they were successful in capturing the barrier in the first place, they only needed to hold the strategic points for it to work – a handful of dam gates and the control centre would be enough. The idea was that they would close the barrier, and rig the gates with explosives. They would then make their demands. At this time of year with the western reservoirs, deep though they were, nearing peak capacity, it would not take long for the river water to begin to back up. Especially if it rained.

The longer that Haldane delayed, the higher the floodwaters would rise inside the barrier, as it would truly be acting like a dam, turning central London into a massive lake as the river water would have nowhere to run. This would hit the lowest lying areas hardest, and there was no escaping that these were also the poorest and most deprived, the eastern projects and old Chelsea and the southern slums; but given that the water would be rising slowly, over a matter of days, there would be time to evacuate the residents into safer areas. It would force the government and the Corporation to remember the people; they would have no choice, as they would have to make room for them in their comfortable towers and flood-protected lands.

If on the other hand Haldane's forces tried to recapture the barrier by force, they would blow the explosives. Without a working barrier, the city would be exposed to the next storm surge or spring tide; and would still have to evacuate the same areas. Either way, they would not be able to ignore the oppressed for any longer.

As they sat huddled, hidden from the surveillance cameras under cam-netting and watching their target, Elisabeth hoped that the plan would work; and that she would live to walk in another forest with Constanza, when this was all done.

When the time came to begin the assault, they were ready. The four of them made their way towards the door set into the base of the dam as it crossed the Isle of Sheppey, and entered the codes into the security locks. For a moment nothing happened, but then with a short buzzing noise the door opened outward, allowing them access. Inside was another door, this one heavy-duty and watertight and opened by a wheel set into its front. Salveson pulled it open, and let them through before turning the wheel closed from the inside and locking them in. When the waters started to rise on the inside of the dam, as they would if the plan worked, they would need that watertight seal to hold or this corridor would become flooded.

The four of them made their way along a short corridor which ended in a service shaft; they would have to climb from here up an iron ladder, twenty metres high, to reach the main access tunnel that ran through the centre of the dam walls towards the gate engines. Salveson took the lead, climbing hand over hand as his three companions sheltered out of sight. When he reached the top, still unchallenged, he motioned for the rest to join him. Elisabeth went next, slinging her rifle over her shoulder and checking that her pistol was safely in its holster before making the ascent.

When they had all reached the top, they began to make their way north through the tunnel. It was wide enough to allow a truck to drive through the inside of the dam if they needed to replace any of the heavy machinery on the gate engines, but punctuated by massive water-tight lock doors every two hundred metres that were, in the normal operation of the barrier, kept firmly closed. Into each of these was set a smaller access door, and it was these that they let themselves through, one by one.

Their target was gate room ten, two kilometres north of where they had entered the dam wall, and Elisabeth was starting to think they would reach it unchallenged when the alarms started to ring. The tunnel lighting changed immediately, from a normal ambient effect to a deep red, and she could feel the tension rising inside her body. It was a feeling she recognised from her previous operations with Batista, a natural response to danger that she could harness and control and, as she felt her pulse begin to rise, she actively concentrated on controlling her breathing.

Each access door they opened now they did so expecting to meet opposition on the other side, but each time they were greeted with the sight of an empty tunnel identical to the one they already occupied, with another door two hundred metres further north. It did not take them long to cover the ground and finally they were opening what they calculated to be the last door before the gate house itself. They knew there would be a security checkpoint on the other side, but did not know how many guards and engineers they would find behind the door, so just as planned they took no chances. When each of them had pulled breathing apparatus out of their packs, Caitlyn prepared the gas canister, and hurled it through the door as Salveson first opened and then slammed it closed again. They would wait for the gas to take its effect before they entered.

Constanza was counting the seconds, and signalled for them to go after a minute had elapsed. The area on the other side of the door was still thick with the smoke they had unleashed, but as it began to dissipate they could see that there had only been a couple of soldiers stationed in the control post, both of whom were now unconscious. As Caitlyn and Salveson went to deal with them, cuffing them to railings set into the wall, Elisabeth and Constanza entered the gate house itself. It looked like there was only the duty crew inside, five engineers all soundly asleep, knocked out by the canister's fumes. The four of them locked these men with the soldiers, and then set about securing the gate house from attack, soldering closed most of the access doors and mounting the explosive payload they had carried with them. As she handed the last of the inert material to Salveson who would then prime it with a detonator, Elisabeth could not help but wonder how such a small device could unleash such enormous power.

If Elisabeth's capture of gate house ten had gone surprisingly smoothly and according to plan, the same could not be said of the rest of the operation. As they finally broke communication silence to establish links with Kanton's control team who had now captured the Administration offices, high on the dam wall towards the northern end, the fate of the rest of the mission became clear. The alarms had been triggered by a fire fight in the tunnels close to gate house two that had left the whole attack team dead; the battle for gate house four had been equally bloody but with reinforcements directed in by Kanton, they had now secured both of those targets. The southern end had been much quieter; adjacent to their position in the tenth gate were teams in the ninth and eighth who had, like them, encountered relatively little resistance.

Within an hour, the position was much clearer. The southernmost gate, known as the Swale, had been disabled and could no longer be opened; it made no sense to try and hold it from attack, isolated as it was south of Sheppey, but they could not allow it to be opened if the plan was to succeed. The team that had accomplished it had now joined Kanton in the command post. Gates eight, nine and ten were still operational but each was controlled by one of their teams, as was the case with gates one to three. The engines that controlled gates four through to seven were currently being vandalised to such an extent that they would not be operable without at least a month's reconstruction, which essentially meant they were locked shut on any meaningful timescale.

Elisabeth could hardly believe they had done it, but they had captured the barrier. She found herself grinning at Constanza, but did not find her smile returned with the same enthusiasm.

"Holding it, that will be the difficult part", she said.

forty seven

There was no traffic running once again on the four lanes of the Dam wall; the road had been closed when the alarms were activated, and now the outlaws were keeping it empty. Above the darkened seas, a lone figure stood in the driving rain, the tails of his longcoat flapping in the violent gusts. He closed his fingers, one by one, around the crook that he always carried, waiting for something.

Behind him, a flash of light, and another figure appeared.

Without turning, the first man spoke.

"Helio. It has been some time."

"And yet, perhaps, not so long", replied the newcomer, walking around so that he could see Bastien's face, his long hair bedraggled in the salted winds but the eyes sparkling still.

"Much has changed, my old friend,"

"You have taken a different path, Shepherd. Why have you abandoned us?"

"There comes a time when order is not enough for salvation, Helio. When chaos is the only true path."

"Many lives will be lost. That is not our way."

"If lives are lost by inaction, is this not the same?"

"I will not allow it."

"It is not your choice to make, Helio. You know this to be true."

Helio did not reply, but turned and walked into the darkness of the storm.

forty eight

Davis was laughing, a careless, empty, usurious sound. They were in the crisis room deep inside the Cone, and watching the terrorist leader catalogue his demands on an open screen broadcast.

"I fail to understand what is funny about this, Commissioner," shouted Haldane. "My assistants inform me you released this man from custody after the first attack on the barrier."

"Bloody perfect, that's what it is" replied Davis in his usual gruff monotone. "Terrorist invaders", he said, and started laughing again.

At the Commissioner's side, Pickering stepped forward. "Mayor Haldane, this vindicates our actions. There is no way the Dam's security could have been compromised without internal assistance, and that assistance had to come from high within the security apparatus. There is a conspiracy sir."

"A conspiracy" repeated Haldane.

"At the highest levels," continued Pickering.

Haldane knew what the man was saying; knew he was right. So long as they played this right, these terrorists would justify their coup. If they could draw a link between the terrorists and the parts of the Council they had arrested, use the association to justify their actions in the minds of the people, this could be exactly what they needed. The coup would succeed with or without public support – the civil guard would see to that; but it would be much less bloody if they could convince the city that they were in the right.

"Davis," commanded Haldane, "I want to know who on the council has been directing these people. Understand?"

Davis nodded, still laughing to himself before being consumed by a coughing fit.

"Now," continued Haldane, "I want options. How do we kill these vermin without them blowing up the bloody barrier? Where is General Lucas?"

"Sir, I am sorry to report that Lucas appears to be with his regiment in the Chilterns, and that they have taken up a defensive position around Senator Hardwicke's estate," said a man in the uniform of the Second Regiment.

"Really? Rash move, Lucas", replied Haldane. "So be it; General Mainse, that makes you acting head of the army."

"Sir."

"Any idea where Soon has disappeared to?"

"We believe he is also with the Senator sir, although we cannot confirm it."

"Never can with Soon," Haldane murmured to himself. "Do we perceive Lucas as an immediate threat?"

"No sir," replied Mainse. "Most of the army is on border patrol, and the attack on the barrier has made the officers more interested in preventing an invasion than worrying about internal politics. As for the Sixth, it looks like they are playing a waiting game, sir."

"Who said anything about an invasion? Davis, do you have any intelligence about this?"

"Sir," interrupted Mainse, before Davis had a chance to speak, "we circulated the invasion story to keep the men at their posts; it isn't real."

"Good idea. Well done. Now, the Dam. How do we get it back?"

For once, none of the soldiers, guardsmen or bureaucrats stepped forward to speak, for they could all see the problem. The terrorists had been more than explicit in their broadcast; if the city sent in troops, they would blow the dam. Without the dam, London would be defenceless against the next abnormal tide or storm surge.

Mainse decided to try his luck, and spoke again. "How long would it take to repair the gates if they did detonate the bombs?"

"You must be mad," spluttered the head of the municipal police.

"Not necessarily," interjected Pickering, seeing where the soldier was leading them. "If we knew we could repair them before the next spring tide, we could go ahead with a military solution."

"When is the next big tide due?" asked the General to one of his men.

"Sorry sir: one week's time."

A collective frown flashed across the faces around the room. They all knew they couldn't risk it; an undefended spring tide could easily spell disaster for the lower lying areas if driven on by bad weather, and the omens in that department were not good either. They would lose the city just when they finally had it in their grasp.

"Could we negotiate?" asked one of Haldane's advisors.

"What for?" he replied. "We cannot give into them. The people of London would throw us out; not even the civil guard would be able to keep order." Haldane could see Davis muttering at the suggestion of his force's emasculation, so continued. "It's true; we can overthrow the Council because the people see it for what it has become – on obstacle in the way of progress. But they will never accept us as their leaders if we are beaten by a rag-tag bunch of terrorists with a bomb. You know this, Davis, so don't bloody pretend otherwise," he finished angrily.

"We may as well open the channels of negotiation, if only to find out as much as we can about their strengths," suggested Pickering.

"Agreed," snapped Haldane, attempting to regain his composure.

Contacting the terrorists was surprisingly easy; they put in a call to the head of the Barrier Authority over the crisis room's screen, and found it being answered by a flushed looking Val Banerjee, sitting behind her desk wearing handcuffs. Standing to her side, holding a pistol to her head, was Kanton.

"You know who I am?" asked Haldane to the man in the screen picture.

Kanton nodded. "You understand the situation?" he replied.

"We do. We have your demands. We are," he paused, looking for an appropriate word, "considering them."

"Take your time," replied Kanton confidently. "You will find that time is on our side."

"Maybe," replied Haldane, taking an instant dislike to this man who would dare mock his authority. Swallowing, he continued with the course they had agreed before the call. "We need to know that you will keep to your word."

"Trust me", said Kanton simply.

"I would like to," replied Haldane, "but I need something to base that trust on. Free the hostages, and we can speak again."

"That is acceptable," replied Kanton, and flicked off the screen.

In the crisis room on level seventeen-deep, the silence was broken by Mainse.

"That was easy," he said, confused.

Taking hostages had never been part of the plan, but Kanton had explained to the team that they had no choice if they wanted to take the Authority administration complex, and the control room, with the minimum of casualties. They had always intended to release these people as soon as possible. The dam itself would be their hostage; they didn't have enough people to guard them in any case. Within a few hours a river patrol craft was docking at the base of the Dam near the northernmost gate pile and loading the terrified office-workers and engineers, and the few captured security staff and soldiers aboard. Kanton's band held the boat in the sights of their rifles and rocket-launchers all the while, until it was safely out of range again.

Sitting in the cabin, Val Banerjee was rocking forward and back, humming to herself as she played with the stitching on the hem of her jacket. Pennells had not returned to work since that whole business with the Civil Guard, and his replacement Sarah Jones had not arrived at the office this morning. She knew she must face the Mayor's wrath on her own. When the boat docked at Westminster, she did not even notice the soldiers sent to escort her to the crisis room, but walked to the Cone's lift bank of her own accord as they followed discretely behind. She said her name in a hesitant whisper, and asked for level seventeen-deep.

She was met by some senior looking guardsmen who took her into a small room to debrief her. She told them everything she knew. How many terrorists she had seen, helped identify the sort of weaponry they were using from screen pictures they showed her. She confirmed that she had seen the bombs, and the gate engines that they had broken. She explained to the men what they already knew, that if the gates were not opened the water would begin to build on the inside and the barrier would start to act like a dam; that the water level would endanger the low lying districts in a matter of days if it kept raining like it had been for the past few days. When the men had finished, they led her to the main room, where she was asked the same questions again by Haldane and Davis and the rest of the senior staff.

"It really is a nightmare," she said again. "With the gates closed this rain is going to flood the city; we need to get them open soon."

General Mainse was getting frustrated, and interrupted her. "So we should just bomb the barrier ourselves and get it over with, correct?"

"No, that would be worse," she said, horrified. "If the barrier isn't closed in a week's time when the spring tides hit, the city will be flooded for sure."

"Yes but the difference is that the terrorists would be dead."

"Thank you, General," Haldane said, "we all know where you stand."

"Sir."

"Is there anything else you can tell us?" Davis now asked her, the aggression apparent in his voice.

"No, I don't think so," she stammered.

"Good. I'm sick of the sight of you. Twice this has happened on your watch. There won't be third time," he said, almost spitting the words at her. Before anyone had time to react, Davis had pulled a pistol from his side holster and pointed it straight at Val Banerjee. He pulled the trigger, and she slumped to the floor, dead.

"What the hell?" roared Haldane.

Davis turned to him, still holding the pistol and eyeballing his leader defiantly.

Haldane returned the stare, but broke away first. "Get that body out of here", he shouted at the nearest junior officer, "and somebody find Daniel Mason. We need somebody in here who knows that bloody barrier."

forty nine

The ancient city had risen to its share of challenges over the years; it had needed to, to survive. This time was no different.

The stand-off between Kanton's fighters and the massed ranks of soldiers and guardsmen continued, as the military leaders dared not attack the barrier until the spring tides had passed; but still, the rain came.

The river began to swell, gorging itself in every direction, growing bloated as it started the slow march back upriver. First to succumb were the marshes of the northern banks and the Medway, as the river absorbed them without even a struggle, overcoming their labyrinthine defences and smothering them with a liquid carpet of uniformity. Olof's last hide-out, gulped away. The reed bed where Elisabeth and Batista had waited out that first day, subsumed under the waters. Next came the upriver terraces and their fixed cargoes of rice-plants, swallowed whole and soon forgotten. The abandoned districts were soon reinhabited by their aquatic tenants, swimming through the doorways of Sand's End and Wandsworth, of Rotherhithe and the Isle of Dogs. And still the rain came.

Stepney and Stratford were soon being evacuated, their penniless communities being moved en masse towards higher ground, finding shelter in the empty barracks of the soldiers on border patrol, in the public schools, in the prisons, but there was soon no room left. Still, the rain came.

Blackheath and Hackney, Plaistow and Forest Gate, all full of people who now became refugees as the river claimed their lands as well. Nowhere for the municipal police and the soldiers to take them, unless the Corporation officials opened the gates to their communes, to their protected towers and their comfortable homes. Still, the rain came.

Old Chelsea next to succumb, its crumbling defences no match for the flood as the lake continued to spread, little by little, hour by hour. Too many people with nowhere to go; too many people shivering and hungry; desperation, their worst enemy, swelling amongst the newly homeless with nothing left to lose. Haldane sensing it, feeling the threat, giving the order; Haldane granting emergency powers to the municipal police, not the Guard, to open the doors to the communes; Haldane feeling something of the man he once hoped to become. Still, the rain came.

How some of the tower-people opened the doors of their own accord. How their numbers grew, as the city awoke to its own humanity. How towels were offered, and rugs were found. How meals simmered and baked as hot drinks were shared. How the people came to know themselves, for this brief time, in this watery place. And yet, outside, across the land and lake, still the rain came.

It took a week for the blue skies to re-appear and the sun to shine on the shrunken, floating city. Haldane stood in the glass-walled circular office of the Lord Mayor atop the Cone building, transfixed

317

by the reflection of the towers in the water-filled streets. The tension in the crisis room was unbearable. Despite his best efforts to direct the civilian evacuation programme, still the hyena were not content. The guardsmen and the soldiers he had assembled around him seemed more interested in crushing their enemies than in preventing civilian casualties from the flood. He, Haldane, had done what he could to get the people to safety.

Now he would have to let the pack loose.

fifty

The soldiers of the Sixth had prepared for an invasion of Senator Hardwicke's estate, but they had not expected it to be like this. The grounds were full of hastily erected tents and shelters as the refugees poured westward towards the hills, and Isabella welcomed them with open arms. The soldiers were running the canteens, requisitioning food from the agribusiness fields on the lower slopes and reminding the security staff of why they shouldn't tangle with the might of the army in the process. The house had become the nerve centre of a massive mobile community, with some of the upper rooms converted into a hospital wing, and the lower floors occupied by Lucas' men. Isabella herself was walking in the Arboretum, taking the time to stop and talk to the children she found playing amongst the yew trees and climbing on their aged branches. It was here also that she found Helio, sitting on a waist height branch and leaning on his ubiquitous dog's head cane.

"Chamois, it is good to see you,"

She smiled, and arranged herself next to him on their living seat.

"I see you carry your cane," he said, motioning to her marble-topped maple branch.

"Everywhere I go. I feel somehow powerless without it."

"Only true in part, but let us save that for another day. What will you do?"

"I don't know. The city is still in grave danger, if not from the water then from the military who seem intent on making Haldane their dictator. In all the panic, the destruction of the Council has been swept aside."

"The waters will ebb one day, just as they flow," replied Helio.

"But what will be left when they do? Tell me, how do I stop a group of terrorists destroying the city, only to save it for a power-hungry cabal of immoral war-lords?"

"The two are not unrelated, you will find. The answers lie in the barrier."

"I cannot approach; they will detonate the bombs if anyone comes close," said Isabella sadly. She had spent hours trying to think of a way around the problem, but had not come up with anything.

"I think that rather depends on who it is, and how they get there. Walk with me, and I will teach you a thing or two about our Assistant's canes."

fifty one

The strike force assembled on the lifter pads; three hundred men split between thirty lifters, a motley assortment of soldiers from the Second and veterans now with the Civil Guard, these were very much Haldane's own. All of them knew that once the terrorists were killed and the waters retreated that London would be left a very different place; all knew that their loyalty to the Mayor would secure their position in the new order. Daniel boarded his designated lifter and sat on the bench, checking his equipment one last time. He could still scarcely believe what he had been sucked into, but here he sat next to Lieutenant Sparrow and his recent colleagues from the River Patrol.

"Local knowledge", Sparrow had laughed, clapping him on the shoulder outside the briefing room; "invaluable."

From the upper windows of the Barrier Authority offices, set into the wall itself, Kanton was waiting to see the fleet of lifters emerge from the city. Where once there had been marshland and sedge, gullies and culverts and creeks, there was now simply a vast lake stretching westward and into the city itself. Holding position in the still inner waters, five hundred metres from the base of the wall, were a line of Naval craft that had been moored at Tilsbury when they had moved on the dam. Outside the barrier, where the water levels were just as high, were three times as many ships, those that had been on patrol when they closed the gates, and the requisitioned trawlers, all blocking their retreat by sea. There was no way for them to escape, not that he could see.

The tides were rising that morning to their seasonal peak, and Kanton noticed how for the first time since they arrived, the levels on either side of the barrier seemed equal. Soon though, the tides would begin to turn, and the North Sea would retreat from their walls like a beaten siege-army, regrouping for another time. No such retreat would be possible for his team.

Bastien had come at daybreak, appearing out of the sea-mist that shrouded the upper walls in the early-morning light.

"They will come today," he had told Kanton. "You know I cannot help you leave this place. There is something else I must do."

"That was our choice," he had replied, "and we made it freely."

Kanton sighed to himself. It did not have to be this way; their demands were not so unreasonable. The prisoners in the jails were there under no process of law he had ever studied, and the rights they demanded for the people were no less than any responsible government should have granted them without a moment's hesitation. This could have ended peacefully; should have ended peacefully if the Council still had any powers left. This was the work of Haldane and his cronies; he promised himself that if he survived this day, he would not rest until they were brought to account.

He then reluctantly set into motion the plan they had all agreed in case it came to this. He assembled two mobile detonators, and tuned each of them to the frequencies for each individual bomb. If either of these triggers fired, every explosive they had planted across the barrier would explode simultaneously. He would hold one, and Salveson in the southernmost gate house the other. If either of them died in the fight, the other could still destroy the barrier.

He made his way from the offices into the depths of the inner wall, visiting each of the teams, telling them that the attack might come today, wishing them luck. They had always agreed that if anyone wanted to try and escape they should do so, but none of the outlaws thought they had a chance against the troops stationed at either shore or the marine blockade. They would stay together. Elisabeth and Constanza lay together in the store-room they had bedded down in for the past week, holding each other tightly, whispering promises that they hoped they could keep. They would have to rise soon, take their positions in the tunnels, ready to fight.

On the stretch of empty road that crossed the barrier above the tenth gate, a sharp light blinked in and out of existence, and two figures walked nonchalantly towards the service staircase; before they reached it, a second light appeared behind them.

"Helio," called the voice. "and the Chamois, I believe."

Isabella turned to see the speaker, and immediately felt the power of his presence; he made her feel both weak and strong at the same time, made her frightened and yet eager to please this stranger who had appeared from nothing behind them.

"Who is he?" she asked Helio quietly.

Helio replied so that the stranger could hear his words.

"He is Bastien. Some called him the shepherd. He too once sat with us in the Library. But he left, and chose a different path."

"My way is not so different, Helio."

"Then why do you shroud yourself in secrecy, hide your designs from those who would help you?"

"Would you help me, Helio?" he asked, seeming to ponder the question himself a little. "Maybe, but perhaps not."

"I would stop you here, old man", replied Helio, raising his dog's head cane with one arm and shielding Isabella with the other. To her, he said, "Run, Chamois. Do what you must do."

Bastien started to laugh, gently. "There is no need to protect her, Helio. You and I want the same thing. We want them to have a choice. I will not interfere. But neither will you," and with these last words he raised the shepherd's crook and in a burst of light both men were gone.

Isabella stood, alone in the sunlight, shaken and stunned by what she had seen. She sat for a while, breathing deeply, trying to settle her mind. It made no sense, but everything involved with the Library seemed to break the normal rules of the world. There would be time to learn all of this, Helio had told her, but not now. Instead he had talked about a choice that must be made, as had this Bastien. What did it mean? Where had they gone? Would she see him again?

There was no time for this now, she told herself. Helio and Bastien were not here, and she was. The city was in danger, and she had to act. Before all of this had started she would have wished for a few hours in the white room to control her thoughts, but she didn't need it anymore. Looking into the distance, she found she could think with serene clarity.

To the east, the sun was rising on its low early-spring trajectory, and the gulls, impatient after a week of silence, had begun to call. Soon though, she could hear another noise growing steadily behind her, and she knew without looking what it was: the troops had arrived.

It did not take long for their ear-pieces to start singing a deadly song. The troops that landed near the Authority offices were the first to strike, and all of Kanton's unit were killed within minutes, their leader included. This left just Salveson with a trigger, and Elisabeth could see from the expression on his face it was not a responsibility he wanted.

The northern gate houses were the next to engage Haldane's forces, but here the advantage was on their side; the vast water-tight doors were also fairly bulletproof, and the soldiers were under orders not to use heavy explosives so as to not damage the barrier machinery to too great an extent.

One by one, though, the screams and the silence were testament to their fallen comrades, and soon it was clear to all of them that the entire team in the northern half of the dam had been either captured or more likely killed.

"What's that banging sound?" asked Caitlyn from her firing point inside the gate house upper door.

"Sounds like its coming from the underground," Constanza whispered back, meaning the tunnel that ran under the gate itself, through the superstructure to the next gate house.

"I'm going down," said Caitlyn, "Connie, can you cover this door?"

"No problem", she replied, climbing up the small ladder to the upper door, leaving Elisabeth and Salveson on the gate house ground floor, both taking cover behind part of the engine housing. Salveson was sweating heavily, Elisabeth noticed, and he kept glancing at the detonator clipped to his webbing, repeatedly checking it was securely fastened.

Caitlyn climbed down the lower ladders to the steel door that led to the narrow under-gate tunnel, and listened for the sound they had heard from above. It came again, three equally spaced taps and then three short ones. She recognised it as their emergency signal and opened the door. Inside the tunnel were the teams who had been occupying the eighth and ninth gatehouses.

"We decided to take our chances getting out through the main service tunnel", they explained, and Caitlyn pointed them to the ladders back towards the main floor.

"Sanctuary", she called up as they climbed, letting the others know it was safe.

"Come with us; we don't stand a chance if we stay here," said one of the men.

Elisabeth looked at Constanza who nodded back. Twelve of them in all, heading into the main service tunnel that had led them to this place a week before. They opened the first of the small doors and saw with relief that the space behind it was empty; climbing through one by one they made their way to the next door two hundred metres south, hoping their luck would hold until they could find an exit.

A little further south, in the same tunnel, Lieutenant Sparrow's detachment of guardsmen were making their way forward towards the gate houses. Daniel was at the rear, trying to think of a way out, hoping he would not have to use the rifle he held in his sweaty hands.

"Clear," came the call, and they all flew through the next small door, fanning out on the floor to provide cover for the stragglers. If they met someone coming the other way, he realised, it would be carnage. As he passed the door to an emergency exit, a stairway leading to the road on top of the dam-wall, he decided to come back this way if the soldiers started firing.

As they went through the next door, they did. The guardsmen burst into the tunnel to find Elisabeth's group doing the same through the door at the other end of the section. The gunfire was deafening in the enclosed concrete corridor, and the fight was deadly. Three of the men from gate house eight were cut down immediately, their bodies knocked lifeless to the unforgiving floor.

"Back, go back!" screamed Salveson, running towards the inset door. He had almost reached it when he took a round in the hip, crashing to the floor in agony. Elisabeth was almost through but saw him fall and ran back.

"Take the detonator," he spluttered, struggling to pull it free from his webbing straps.

"Come on, I'll help you," she said, pushing away his hand and trying to help him to his feet. They began limping together the last few metres, when he took another round in his torso. This one was fatal, stopping his heart. Elisabeth felt him fall, and could see in his eyes that the man was gone. She pulled the detonator switch from his tunic and dived for the safety of the door.

Five of them had made it through, and were sheltering behind the main structure of the larger watertight section door. Elisabeth lay next to Constanza, holding her sweat-soaked face in both hands.

"Where?" she asked.

"Just the leg. I'm alright." Constanza replied, as she pulled a bandage out of her pack and set about compressing her own wound.

"Get her out of here," said the man who was firing back at the soldiers through the small doorway. Elisabeth recognised him as Winder, one of the six who had been with her on the first fateful mission to the barrier. "Go! We'll cover you here."

Elisabeth turned and helped Constanza to her feet, and the two of them made their north, through the doors and back towards the gate house.

As they reached the next section she shouted back to the three left covering the doorway to join them. They did not respond, and she realised with horror that all three were dead. Only two of them left, and she was holding the detonator. If she pressed it, they would all die.

Daniel had made his way back to the stairwell the minute the firing had started, and in the midst of all the shooting no-one had thought to try and stop him. He let himself through the exit door, and then used his rifle to shoot out the control panel, effectively sealing it closed behind him. He ran up the stairs, flight by flight until he reached the door to the roadway. He sat inside it, listening for any signs of gunfire on the other side, but he could hear none. Carefully, he eased it open, looking outside across the deserted carriageway. It was empty, he decided, as he made his way onto the tarmac that steamed gently as it dried in the sunlight.

From up here he could see the vast lake that had grown on the inside of the barrier, and the massive tide that rivalled it on the outside of the walls. He could see the warships, stolidly sitting in their designated lines, all their guns ready, waiting for the terrorists to try and escape. The air above the northern gates, kilometres further north, was buzzing with lifters; they would make their way down here soon enough, once the troops had secured the gate-houses.

Then he spotted a lone figure leaning over the side rails, a short walk away. A woman, and something familiar in the way that she stood. He made his way along the carriageway to meet her, calling out as he walked.

"Daniel," she said, turning.

"Bella?" he asked. It didn't make sense. "What are you doing here?"

"We must find Elisabeth."

Something in her voice told him not to question her.

"Where?" he asked.

"Close," she replied.

In gate house ten, Constanza was holding the blow-torch ready as Elisabeth pulled the door closed, the bullets shattering into the other side of the wall but not breaching it. They sealed it, as they had the other doors when they arrived apart from their escape routes: underground to gate house nine, or to the top of the barrier through the upper doors.

"Which one?" asked Elisabeth.

"I'd like to see the sea, I think." replied Constanza. She didn't need to finish the sentence; they were both thinking the same thing. "How about you?"

"Yes. The sea sounds better."

They made their way to the ladders, Elisabeth helping as Constanza struggled to climb with her wounded leg. Through the upper door and onto a stairwell, step by step, arm in arm, they climbed their way to the top, Elisabeth still holding the trigger in her left hand, waiting until they could see the waters below.

As they reached the top, she heard the voice.

"Elisabeth."

Isabella and Daniel, her oldest friends, standing in the brilliant blue light. Waiting to meet her. The three of them together, finally, after all these years. Was she dead already, she wondered?

She couldn't be. Constanza, very real, holding her arm and in pain. Constanza, the woman she loved as she never knew love could be. Constanza, sitting now, resting the battered limb, watching as the three old friends moved towards each other, all eyes wide. What did it all mean?

"Elisabeth. What will you do?" asked Isabella, looking at the detonator still held firmly in her hand.

Elisabeth looked herself, holding this strange device up to the light and turning it over. Could she really destroy all of this with a touch of her hand?

"Beth, put it down," pleaded Daniel, but she merely smiled at him quizzically.

"Have you come to save the city, Daniel?" she asked. "Like father, like son?"

"You don't have to do this, Beth," he replied. "It worked. The evacuation worked. The Corporation and the communes opened their doors. The people heard. You don't need to destroy the barrier."

"People forget," she replied. "When the waters retreat, what happens then?"

"They won't forget," Daniel argued, "Not this time. You have changed things, don't you see?"

"They will forget," Elisabeth replied gently. "You know they will."

"Beth, don't do this," he said again, frustrated tears starting to mingle with the dirtied sweat.

"It hasn't worked, Daniel, don't you see? Not what we have done, but the barrier itself. It hasn't worked. It was supposed to free the people, free them from fear. Free them from floods and hunger, from the chaos of the wildlands. Free them so they might live their lives. It hasn't worked, can't you see?"

"What do you mean?" he asked in a whisper.

"The barrier was supposed to free the people, yet it enslaves them. It is the prison wall that locks them up with no hope of release. It is the foundation from which the whole exploiting city draws its strength. You know what this place has become. You used to understand Danny. Can't you see it now?"

Daniel fell to his knees, holding his head in both hands, whispering to Elisabeth, to himself, "don't do this, Beth, don't do it. Don't destroy the city, please."

She moved over to him, kneeling too and putting one hand to his face.

"Danny, can't you understand? There is no other way."

As he continued to rock forward and back, he looked at Elisabeth, eye to eye, his own tears now streaming.

The two of them, kneeling in silence, rocking in the breeze.

"Yes," he finally whispered.

"Elisabeth, wait," said Isabella, speaking once again, her voice calm and soothing.

"Bella, I must do this."

"That is your choice," Isabella replied, "but first let us stand together, the four of us".

And they stood, watching as the first pair of swallows arrived above them, darting and flitting in the crystalline skies.

Epilogue

It was a garden, of sorts.

"Where are we?" asked the man.

"It does not matter," she replied, continuing her slow circuit around the snow-covered walls, listening to the sound of the snow crunching under her feet.

He walked with her, watching her expression for any hint of her thoughts, but finding none.

"I found Epstein before he died", he said, and saw her flinch, just for a moment. "I know you were close. I'm sorry."

"We were. Tell me, what happened?"

"He nearly escaped, but Haldane's men found him in the end. Arrested him, took him to Smith Street. When I found out, I did what I could, but he was nearly gone when I reached him."

"Thank you for trying," she said after a time, meaning it.

"Haldane released them all, in the end," the man continued. "Killed Davis himself, for trying to interfere."

"Where will you go now, Mr Soon", she asked.

"I'll find somewhere, I'm sure."

"Yes, no doubt," she smiled.

They reached the fountain, its boisterous display caught in a frozen instant, hanging in the air.

"Epstein gave me a message, before he died," Soon said quietly.

Isabella raised her eyebrows; he had not mentioned this before.

"He said to tell you, and only you, that the Bouqetin still lives."

She looked directly at the spymaster, unable to disguise her shock.

"He said to look for him amongst the vikings."

THE END.

Printed in Great Britain
by Amazon